EX-PAT

A Novel by Christopher Watts

ISBN: 1503173186
ISBN 13: 9781503173187

1

OCTOBER

We're sitting in the garden of the Kleftiko Music Bar and Happy Snak Café. Most people just call it the Klef. It's a nothing little bar in a fading resort called Pilafkos. Thirty years ago Pilafkos didn't even exist. It was built on land owned by farmers and shepherds who gladly sold up for a slice of the new tourist pie. Some farmers and shepherds got very rich indeed. Some never really got the hang of the whole 1980s' thing at all.

Not so many tourists come to Pilafkos these days. Even less come to the Klef. The bar is too far from the beach and shopping arcades to be convenient. Nikos the owner blames the lack of passing trade on the surrounding hotel compounds. He says their all-inclusive meal deals and evening entertainment shows have killed his business. Whatever. Personally I attribute his lack of passing trade to the fact that Nikos himself is a swingeing, screeching screwball who couldn't run a fucking bar if his mother's life depended on it. Which it does. After eleven years it's now looking pretty certain that she'll never get a new hip. Or even an eye test. She doesn't complain. She dotes on Nikos. She will dote on Nikos until the day she dies. Such is Greece.

It's a beautiful afternoon. Sometimes in August it can be too hot to breathe but towards the end of the season the white heat always turns to the deepest blue. In two weeks Pilafkos will close down for the winter. Bars, shops, restaurants and hotels will all shut for six months. The beach apartments will be boarded up. The rental cars will be mothballed. The glass-bottomed tourist boats will head for dry dock. Nothing will stir. Only the bakery at the top of the hill will stay open. As far as we know Pilafkos has only two permanent residents. One is this weird little guy with bandy legs who looks like he ran away from the circus just to look after all the stray cats in a deserted holiday resort on a Greek island. The other is Nikos who lives in the family apartment over the Klef.

In a few days Nikos would normally close the bar and retire upstairs to watch American pornography and English football. Every year he spends a fortune buying tat and memorabilia on-line to hang behind the bar. He thinks it makes the tourists feel at home. No one really knows what else Nikos actually does for six months of the year. Many bar owners travel to India or Thailand or even Northern Europe for a break, but Nikos never ventures far. Every year he travels to the mainland for some industry convention. Last year he returned with a stack of flat-screen TVs and an automated sound system. The year before it was an air hockey table and a vibrating armchair. The year before that it was a giant plastic elephant for the kids to climb. The elephant still stands outside the Klef as some huge, tawdry monument to moronic graffiti. This infuriates Nikos but he won't pay to get the elephant repainted. He was recently telling me that he was going to install a CCTV system instead to catch the culprits who return every season to add new tags and slogans in the middle of the night. Tagging the elephant has turned into a popular Pilafkos sport.

"Why don't you just charge them to write on the elephant?"

Nikos looked mortified. "Who am I, my friend? I am not a fucking pirate! Let them write. I will shoot them."

This winter, however, everything is going to be different for all of us.

It is undeniably another quiet afternoon at the Klef. My wife and I are sitting at a table in the garden watching Nikos behind the bar. No one is saying very much. There is no traffic. There is no passing trade. Nikos looks furious. I suppose this is understandable. He's probably not used to being handcuffed to his own bar wearing a waistcoat made out of shitty Greek explosives. To be honest I have no idea whether they are shitty explosives or not, but I bought them from a night fisherman who spends his days drinking Ouzo in the sun so I'm not holding my breath. For all I know they might do little more than knock an ice cube off a cocktail or they might obliterate Pilafkos altogether. I'm not an expert on these things. I only really strapped them around Nikos to make a point.

We sip our beers in silence. Kat has that look on her face that suggests I might have gone too far.

"Handcuffs?" she says eventually. "Where the fuck did you get the handcuffs from?"

"The fisherman," I reply.

"Why would a pissed-up fisherman own a pair of handcuffs, for Christ's sake?"

It's a fair point.

"He told me he uses them to hit the fish over the head when they land in his nets."

"And you believed him?"

"This is Greece, Kat, so yes ... I believed him. How else would you stun a fish?"

She arches an eyebrow. "A rock? A stone? An oar? I don't know. Jesus, Cal, I wouldn't use handcuffs to even *restrain* a fucking fish! And why didn't you tell me you were going to handcuff Nikos to his own bar and then blow him up?"

"I didn't think you'd be very interested."

We argue like children. We have always argued like children. The very first time I met Kat we argued like two small kids about Debbie

Harry, or something, and then made out in the shower. I only argue with people I actually like.

The sun is beginning to go down behind the yellow elephant outside. Shadows grow longer by the minute. Daylight is turning to gold. We both reach for our sunglasses at the same time. Kat always looks so cool wearing her shades. Like some motorcycle gypsy assassin or something. I just look like the guy from the bakery. Even with our shades on, however, the sun is still bright enough to make us squint. I guess it won't be long now. They'll come out of the sun while it's low and still alive. They'll always come out of the sun. It's classic, entry-level combat cover.

I guess I always knew I'd eventually get caught. To believe I could escape undetected and see out my days wandering the beach wearing a crumpled white linen suit and sneakers would undoubtedly be a massive vanity. There are, after all, fourteen bodies buried up in the mountains. Six, eight, ten… I can't quite remember. I just know it was very important at the time to have an even tally. That's why I stopped. I'm not an addict or anything. Addicts can't stop. It's just that I have always been unsettled by odd numbers. I like my numbers to be complete. Odd numbers just look unfinished. I was born in 1963 and just look at how that year panned out for mankind.

It's a whole different world up there in the mountains. The villages never sold out. There are no water parks or cocktail bars, no bungee cranes or rental cars. Crazy old folk live in crumbling white cottages with lame dogs and shotguns. Toothless old men drive toothless old machinery to the markets and festivals. You can buy enough honey and fruit to last a week for the price of a beer in Pilafkos. The mountain villages are both devout and godless. Ornate shrines for the dead decorate the roadside. Candles in these shrines are constantly kept alive by old women wearing the black of the bereaved. There are bandit laws for bandit souls and these are seldom broken. At night it is so black that you can drive by starlight. Log fires burn in every taverna. Faded photographs hang from every wall. It's a dark and enchanting neverland for the foolish and fearless alike. Only a fool would choose to live in the mountains. Only the fearless survive. A part of me always wanted to rent a cabin up there for the winter. Just to see what would happen.

"For fuck's sake, Nikos *malaka*," I snap.

Nikos is clearly wrestling with an obvious dilemma. On the one hand he is chained to his own bar and is in imminent danger of exploding all over the place. On the other hand it looks as if Olympiakos are going to stuff his beloved Liverpool F.C. for some sort of championship. This would be a miracle indeed. I realise he's torn between the TV screen above the bar and doubts concerning his own mortality but I wish he would just stop rattling the handcuffs. It's futile and inconsiderate. I consider switching off the game just to save all our sanities but I admit I'm a little intrigued.

Kat lights another cigarette and exhales like a movie star.

"Do you think the police will be here soon?" she says.

"Maybe. The bakery shuts at five. They're probably here now."

In fact I know the police are already here because I can see them. It would appear that every policeman on the island is here. And the army. The police are standing in groups around their Citroen squad cars parked across the one main road leading out of the resort. Eventually the road beyond the Klef starts to disintegrate and soon disappears altogether. Beyond the rows of shabby, half-built holiday villas there is nothing except scorched shrub land and jagged granite rocks. Effectively the police have blocked off Pilafkos by parking badly.

The army arrived a while ago in a couple of old German trucks. I saw them up at the top of Bakery Hill. The trucks crawled down into town and now there are soldiers hiding behind the bushes which surround the Klef. They are perfectly still and silent. This alone suggests that they are not conscripts. The kids on National Service would all be posting siege videos to the internet by now. These guys are shapeless and patient. They are simply waiting for the order to shoot. I'm not particularly worried because I am not armed. It's unlikely that even the Greek army would open fire on a defenceless man and his wife sitting in a bar. This is not West London.

I can see two marksmen on the roof of the apartment block over the road. They are staring down the scopes of their rifles which are permanently trained on our table. Both marksmen are wearing full combat kit. It must be really uncomfortable up there.

I finish the last of my beer and gather up my cigarettes and wallet.

"Right then," I say in a voice which I hope sounds both confident and defiant. "We should probably leave now."

As I push back my chair and stand up, three totally unexpected things happen almost simultaneously. They happen so fast that my brain barely has time to register anything before it is too late. The first thing to happen is that Liverpool score a goal. This in itself is not entirely unexpected but it came from out of nowhere nonetheless. Nikos cannot contain himself. He hurls himself towards the TV screen cheering with shock and delight. As a result a fairly hefty explosion rocks the Klef. The blast is loud enough to make Kat and I instinctively duck for cover and knocks the air from our lungs. Shattered glass rains down everywhere as thick white smoke billows across the bar. We can hear the explosion rolling around Pilafkos. As the noise and smoke begin to clear we straighten up and survey the damage. Remarkably the TV screen is undamaged. Liverpool are still celebrating. Nikos is nowhere to be seen. He has simply disappeared. The only trace and clue he leaves behind is an arm. It is still hand-cuffed to the bar. At least Nikos died happy.

The third and probably most unexpected thing to happen is that some damn fool then shoots Kat in the head. She drops like a brick at my feet.

2

DOG

Everyone warned us that the winters on Kolasios could be grim. Everyone warned us about the storms and the power cuts, the floods and the paranoia. Everyone warned us about the isolation and the inertia, the drinking and the bickering. To be honest we didn't pay too much attention. We didn't care. Absolutely no one, however, warned us about the squabbling ex-pat tribes who all told us that the winters on Kolasios could be grim.

Every Greek island has its own little huddle of immigrants and Kolasios was no exception. We met them all during our very first winter. We met the bottle-blonde divorcees spouting self-help nonsense like lunatic royalty. We met the angry old wives and their unemployable husbands propping up the local bars with their venom and pomp. We met the idle artists, hopeless mechanics, deluded poets and fanciful romantics. We met the retired copper shambling through another winter in his stinking shell-suit and obnoxious world view. He died a couple of years ago. Gassed himself alone in his little caravan on the beach.

We met the faded Welsh DJ with his stack of classic rock CDs and a ham radio set in his shed so that he could broadcast live every Saturday night to absolutely no one. We met the craggy old Ted who was always just one more beer away from jetting out to Brazil to jam on stage with Carlos Santana.

"Next week, son," he'd say. "Looking good. Pretty sure Eric will let me out of the contract. If not I'll chop his balls off. Ha!"

"Right."

Sod it, I thought. I had to ask.

"Eric who?"

"Clapton! Old Slowhand himself! Wants me to play bass on his next album."

"Right."

We met the brash and the brazen, the damaged and the downright dangerous. Harry Haz was a nasty piece of work until some Greek boy kicked his head in one Tuesday night. Haz reckoned he'd enjoyed an illustrious career at Bristol City F.C. until injury forced his early retirement. The internet, however, appeared to disagree. He told us his uncle owned a string of strip clubs in Birmingham and that he'd done time in jail. He'd joined other rioting inmates on the prison rooftop. The police sent them up fried chicken and wine gums. After three days the authorities managed to lure the offenders down. Apparently all of them except Haz were shot at dawn or something. Haz managed to escape to Kolasios. He can't go back. He's a fugitive.

"He's a fuckwit!" Kat hissed when Haz was out of earshot.

After his altercation with the Greek boy half his age, however, Haz went back to Birmingham. He now works for a car rental company near the NEC. Another total Haz-Been.

So the cash-strapped and brain-dead lurched through the villages seeking beer and a bar tab. A true Brit can never be parted from his pint for long. We listened to them all as their tales became so tall that Kat and I soon began to spin out with abject awe and disbelief. We listened in silence for a while as some self-styled, fifty-something urban artist with a lank ponytail told us that he had once turned down the chance to work alongside Banksy because he didn't believe that great street art should be anonymous.

"But Banksy isn't anonymous," Kat said. "His name is Banksy."

The guy peered down from his lofty perch at the bar and tipped his beer to his face.

"Yeah, right, but Banksy isn't his real name. That's my point. That is my fucking point."

"What is Banksy's real name then?" asked Kat.

"I don't know. He's shifty like that. You can't trust shifty people."

"But he's famous for being Banksy."

The artist snorted his beer up into his head and helped himself to my cigarettes.

"Famous for being shifty. Shifty Banksy. That's what we used to call him back in Bristol. He was nothing back then. A little turnip with a hoodie. Doodling on concrete. That's all. Doodling and noodling on concrete. That's not art. That's vandalism. Should have chopped the little prick's arms off when I had the chance."

"Right," said Kat.

"Banksy slags," said the artist under his breath as we walked away.

Generally we were welcomed to Kolasios with open mouths. We were novelty new blood to be sought out and collected up into specimen jars by the winter locals. We didn't look the same and we didn't sound the same. To be honest we probably looked like we'd just crashed a space rocket into a haystack. We were soon bundled up into bars and prodded with beers by ex-pats fighting like mother-bugs for tit-bits of information.

We arrived on Kolasios towards the end of the summer season. Pretty soon the island began to close down around us and after a while it was as if the modern world had ceased to exist altogether. We had chosen to move from London to a tiny picturesque village on the east coast of the island called Kavindos. From a distance it was a beautiful postcard. Essentially Kavindos was a pretty little jumble of white-washed houses nestling at the foot of a ruined Acropolis which had gazed down on the village for more than three thousand years. It had once been a major merchant port at the heart of the ancient

Greek civilisation. Over the centuries, however, Kavindos' influence as a political power base had shifted north towards Kolasios Town itself. The little village on the east coast was now no more than a working museum and a protected archaeological site.

We'd rented a house at the top of the village for one year. From our roof terrace we could watch the full moon rise red behind the Acropolis and spend hours just staring at the glittering blue sea beyond. Electrical storms would often light up the village at night as the torrential winter rains lashed the little houses and narrow cobbled streets. It was breath-taking and elemental. It was certainly a far cry from the farty drizzle we had gladly left behind on the other side of Europe.

Kavindos' modern reputation as an idyllic retreat had been cemented in the 1960s and '70s by the flamboyant, hippy rock stars and artists who would all pass through and party before moving on to die in bathtubs. Rose-tinted tales of hedonistic nights spent dancing on tables were rife. Twinkly-eyed bar owners would tell you about the nights spent drinking tequila with Marianne Faithful or waking up next to bits of Heart, or shooting rabbits with Lynnrd Skynnrd. Allegedly Lynnrd Skynnrd loved the village so much that they rented a huge mansion just a few kilometres along the coast. Quite why a redneck, hillbilly boogie-band would want to rent a big house on a remote Greek island and live in it together like the fucking Partridge Family or something was never really adequately explained. Especially since quite a few tie-dyed barflies loudly insisted that they were drinking with the band years after half of them had actually died in a plane crash. But the Greeks love a legend and *Free Bird* is still Kavindos' unofficial anthem to this day. Which, as Kat and I both agreed, was highly unfortunate. Legend has it that Pink Floyd also came through Kavindos a couple of times but no one really noticed.

Kavindos as an ancient heritage village was a very pretty place to live. We paid a year's rent up front to an enormous property pirate called Hercules. Hercules promptly disappeared to the mainland for the winter and left us to our island life. Sometimes we both swore we could hear his laughter on the wind. The storms would knock out the power for days on end. The nearest shop was a twenty minute walk down a treacherous track that even the goats feared to tread. As a result Kat and I found ourselves gravitating towards the neighbouring village of Elythia.

It was a scrappy, pot-holed village about six kilometres from Kavindos. Elythia wasn't pretty but at least it was open during the endless winter months. Unlike Kavindos you could actually drive into Elythia and park pretty much anywhere you wanted. Local fishermen and farmers sold stuff from cranky old pick-up trucks in the main square. It had a pharmacy and a butcher and a baker and way too many bars for the local population. The self-important Greek puff-elders drank coffee and played backgammon in one. Shrieking local teenagers sat on scooters outside another. The ex-pats had their own where they organised darts tournaments and quizzes. The village priest strode from bar to bar accepting shots of neat whiskey. Papa Dimitris never paid. It was unethical to charge Papa Dimitris for neat whiskey. It was unethical for anyone to charge any priest for absolutely anything.

We spent our first Christmas in Elythia. The faded Welsh DJ had invited us to his house for a Boxing Day buffet.

"Bring a bottle or three," Mervyn had chirped. He was a fat little man with a strange mid-Atlantic valley voice. "All our friends will be there. They're good people. Our kind of people."

We were sceptical but there wasn't much else to do. Kavindos was shut. It was raining. So we found Mervyn's house at the bottom of a muddy path just outside the village and parked in a puddle. It was another in a long line of identical flat-packed white boxes scattered across the island which the builders had failed to finish. We had little sympathy. If you were stupid enough to hand over your life savings to a man in a bar who told you he could build you a house then you got exactly the unstable, unlicensed bomb-site that you deserved. You can buy practically anything in a Greek bar. You can buy car insurance, chainsaws, oranges ... even animals. But you would never buy a fucking house. Especially from a man who wore white wooden clogs and styled his hair like Marc Bolan's grandmother.

The garden was full of old car batteries and junk that the builders had left behind. They had walked off the job two years ago when the property developer ran out of money. Mervyn had threatened to sue. The property developer threatened to counter-sue Mervyn for defamation of character. Such is Greece. The house remained unfinished.

Mervyn had married Moira back in Wales when he was still drinking heavily as a club DJ. Moira's pink thongs fluttered on the washing line as we picked our way through the debris on the front lawn. Moira was the wrong side of forty to really pull off the whole ditzy, blonde lush thing but we found her holding court in the little kitchen with a glass of champagne nonetheless.

"Cal! Kat!" she gushed. "Look everyone! It's the new people! It's Cal from London and his wife Kat!"

Everyone in the kitchen and the living room beyond turned to inspect the new arrivals. Kat and I stared blankly back at the strange array of golfing jumpers, party hats and elasticated denim slacks gathered around us.

"Hi," I managed to mumble.

"Dear god!" Kat said under her breath.

We handed over our bottles and cans to someone as Moira descended on us with a tray of cheap fish sticks and celery.

"Cal! Kat! It's Welsh crab! Try some! Champagne, darlings?"

I felt Kat bristle.

"Katerina," she said. "My name is Katerina."

Moira looked flustered.

"Right, sorry," she said. "It's just that, well, Merv always calls you Kat, and ..."

"No," Kat interrupted. "My name is Katerina. It's a German name. On account of the fact that I'm from Germany. The only person who is allowed to call me Kat is my husband Cal. He's English. His real name is actually Callum but he doesn't mind being called Cal. In fact he prefers it for some silly reason."

There was a pause.

"But my name is Katerina. Thank you."

She smiled sweetly and we left Moira in the kitchen looking baffled. The living room was stuffy and airless. People stood around grazing from paper plates. The furniture was too big to negotiate so we shared one wooden chair near the alcohol cabinet and helped ourselves. A huge flat-screen television dominated one corner. It was tuned to the BBC. The sound of Victorian carols filled the fug. It wasn't long before Mervyn appeared.

"Not my sort of thing," he said, nodding towards the television. "More of a rock fan myself. Zeppelin, Floyd, Skynnrd, Heart … still got them all on vinyl. Vinyl and cassette. You just can't beat analogue really for all that sort of thing."

"Don't they melt in the sun out here?" asked Kat.

"Yes, they do," said Mervyn. "But then I switch over to CDs, Kat."

"Katerina."

"Sorry?"

"My name is Katerina. I'm German."

"Right," said Mervyn. "Sorry."

He sipped his tonic water awkwardly. Mervyn had vowed to remain teetotal until his house was finished. Quite how sobriety was going to speed up the process was a mystery.

"Have you met Flippitty yet?" he said eventually.

Flippitty, it turned out, was the ugliest dog in the world. She was enormous and bloated from giving birth to something like a thousand puppies. Her belly sagged to the floor like a balloon. Her eyes were piglet-pink. She seemed to do very little except lie comatose on the carpet in a pool of her own drool. Every now and then Flippitty would heave herself upright and waddle outside to slobber from a yellow water bowl on the patio outside the kitchen.

"Fucking yuk!" said Kat every time the animal farted past.

We probably drank more that afternoon than we'd intended. When Moira suddenly stood up in the middle of the room and announced loudly that everyone was going to watch her entire back-catalogue of *Dr Who* DVDs we figured it was time to make a move. It took us about an hour to get out of the house. Despite the fact that most people had ignored us all afternoon, it suddenly seemed as if they were loathe to let us go. Everybody leapt to offer us advice about Greece. They tried to cajole us into pub quizzes and curry nights. Moira even made us a little parcel of chicken wings and fish sticks wrapped in tin foil to take home. Mervyn was the last to shake our hands.

"Don't forget, Cal," he said, "these are good people. If you and Katerina need anything at all then you know where we are. Don't ask the Greeks for anything. They're all crooked. Rob you blind without breaking a sweat. Believe me, Cal, they'll rob you blind they will."

"Right," I slurred and followed Kat back to the car. She was leaning against the bonnet trying to flick a light for her cigarette. It was a cold night. The sky was deep-sea black and starless. I dropped the car keys.

"Fuck!" Kat snapped. "My bag!"

I heard her run back towards the house over the gravel patch that was Mervyn's lawn. Eventually I found the keys and waited for Kat whilst trying to clear the mist from the windscreen. It was hopeless. After a while Kat came back. She was out of breath and laughing.

"Drive!" she said.

So we drove back to Kavindos in stunned silence. We sat around our little halogen heater with a glass of wine. We went to bed. I dreamt of old-school bank robbers with sawn-off shooters and Ford

Granadas. Proper scum. Most of them were called Micky Two Lips or something. Davey Both Feet. Larry the Lung. Kenny the Kidney.

Later the following day we heard that Flippitty was dead. Moira phoned me in tears as we sat in yet another bar nursing the hair of the dog. I stared at my beer on the table. The hair of the dead dog now. Apparently somebody had poisoned Flippitty by topping up her water bowl with battery acid. Moira wanted to know if we had seen anything. Apparently someone said they had seen a couple of Greek kids hanging around. Maybe Kat saw something? I said I would ask her. I hung up. To be honest I couldn't really muster up much sympathy.

I told Kat what had happened. She shrugged.

"That's not much of a shame," she said.

"True," I replied. "But the point is that at some time after you went back for your bag and before the end of Moira's DVD marathon someone poisoned Flippitty. With battery acid."

We rolled cigarettes in silence.

"Kat?"

"What?" she snapped.

I searched her face as she hunted through her pockets for a lighter.

"Nothing," I said. "It doesn't matter."

3

FLIGHT

Some people thought we were brave. Some people probably thought we were pretty stupid. Some people didn't even realise we had left the country. After four months a friend phoned out of the blue wanting to download some software from the internet on to our computer.

"We're in Greece," I told him.

"Great," he said. "What am I supposed to do now?"

"Download it on to your own computer?"

"Can't. Tried that. Thing has totally crashed and burnt. Blue screen of death and all that. When are you coming back?"

"Never," I said. "We've moved here permanently."

There was a pause.

"Really? That's ridiculous. Oh, hang on, I could always try Midge. Ok, gotta go, bye."

"Bye."

We didn't feel particularly brave as we sat eating oysters and drinking champagne at some hotel hosting a convention in Rheims. We motored south through France at a leisurely pace in our trusty Transit van. Our original plan to stop at modest motorway lodges soon fell by the wayside in favour of the most expensive hotels we could find. Kat and I had never been meek enough to really budget that well. After Grenoble we crossed over the Alps into Italy. The industrial north was grim and toxic so we pressed on south down the east coast and partied one night in Brindisi with a bunch of cute young Goths at a rock bar in town. They couldn't believe that we were leaving London for a new life in Greece.

"London is the future," one of them said from behind her black and perfectly feathered fringe.

"The Clash are so cool," said another. They all nodded in agreement.

London will always be the future if you come from somewhere like Brindisi. So will Berlin or LA or New York or Paris or Barcelona. Those cities and many more were all put on this planet just to attract the beautiful hopes and ambitions of kids old enough to dream of the bright lights and the buzz-saws of the cityscape. After 27 years, however, Kat and I had already seen the future. The future was harsh.

"London is maybe your future," we told the young Goths. They all giggled. We stayed out drinking cheap beer and toasting Simenon and Strummer.

Late the following afternoon we hopped on a ferry to the Greek mainland. We booked a cabin with a bath and spent most of the night drinking in the bar with truck drivers and acrobats. The boat docked at Patras around midday leaving us just three hours to get to Piraeus for another overnight ferry heading south to the larger Greek islands. We made it with minutes to spare. Kat and I stood on the observation deck and watched the mainland gradually slip away beneath the bluest sky we had ever seen. After maybe an hour we were truly in the middle of nowhere. We stood in silence watching the deep green waters slide past us below. We had come a long way together just to get this far.

"Cal?" said Kat after a while. I had to lean closer to hear her voice above the wind.

"Do you really think we're going to make it?"

I squeezed her hand.

"Sure. Why not?"

Back then we had great hopes for our big adventure. We were both forty four. Like everybody else we had been scrabbling for pennies whilst racing to stand still. Kat and I had spent the last three years living and working together in an old factory space in the East End. It had once been owned by a brewery. We rented it from a soulful old woodworker who was sad to see us go. But the council was driving the artists and hustlers out of the borough to make way for the Olympics. Commercial rates had been randomly hiked to the stratosphere. Now only the property developers and corporate sponsors could afford to live in the city's poorest areas. Kat and I had been strictly freelance. We had always been freelance. We had a string of wiped-out bank accounts to prove it. We had been music writers and models, photographers and chefs, designers and van drivers … freelance-anything just to live and survive in a city that had undoubtedly changed since we had both arrived in the early '80s.

London should never have been about sushi bars in Shoreditch or coffee clubs in Clapham. It should never have been about Oyster travel cards and cycle lanes, multiplex cinemas and megastores. London should have been better than all that. London had been about the angels and moths waiting in the rain for a night bus on Charing Cross Road. It had been about racing down the escalators to catch the last tube train home. It had been about skinny kids in Soho bars and bagels from Brick Lane. London had been about subversive art in Dalston and elegant spooks in Whitehall. It had been about flagging down illegal mini cabs on the Old Kent Road and watching the morning mist rolling up the Thames towards the Greenwich peninsular. It had been about looking over your shoulder all the time just to see your shadow. It had been about the noise of the markets and the hustle in the pubs. So much hustle just to make a point that no one could ever remember. It had been about us.

London had changed and everybody let it happen. We were all to blame. It had become an angry surveillance city. Gangs watched other gangs. Communities watched other communities. The frail watched the young. The sharks watched the blood trail. The police watched everybody and everybody did no more than watch an endless, idiot parade of micro-celebrity on TV. How the fuck did that happen? Where the fuck had we all been looking? Within ten years we had sacrificed our freedom to exist for a pair of branded shoes and a mobile phone. Sale of the century.

My father died the year before we left London. He left enough money in his will for us to pay a year's rent in Greece whilst we tried to establish a business. Kat and I got married. My mother wore a hat and gloves. My sister looked amazed. We held the civil ceremony in an old historic house in the East End. I wore an off-the-peg suit with brothel creepers from Camden. Kat wore vintage lace from Whitechapel. After the ceremony we bought fish and meat from the Turkish shop on Morning Lane and lit a huge barbecue in London Fields. The party carried on all night back at our little factory and for most of the following day at Pub On The Park. We were happy to be married.

One month later we were more than happy to be gone. Submarines submerging.

We had to wait for the commercial rigs to disembark before we could move. I had always fancied being a trucker driving around Europe with a three-legged dog and a one-eyed hooker for company. The king of my own little cabin. Apparently Greek truck drivers get cheap drinks on all the ferries and so half of them were probably drunk by the time our Blue Star docked at Kolasios commercial port on Monday morning. It was barely nine o'clock yet already the spires of the medieval Old Town were shimmering in the heat haze.

It had taken almost exactly a week to drive across Europe. It is possible to make the journey much quicker but Kat and I are easily side-tracked. It was another hour's drive along the east coast to Kavindos. We had arranged to meet Hercules at the hotel he owned at the top of the village. He wasn't so much pleased to see us as the envelope stuffed with cash we handed over in exchange for our house keys. They were tied together with tatty blue string.

Hercules was a legendary figure. Despite looking like a punch-drunk beach bum he was a wealthy man. He had first come to Kavindos in 1971 having joined the police force. Apparently he secured such an idyllic posting because he was the only policeman on the island who knew how to operate a cassette recorder. He bought his first bar for a pittance at the age of 28. He quit the force and bought another. Then another. Now he owned a chain of bars, a hotel, restaurants, clubs and property. He rode around the village on a battered Harley Davidson looking benevolent and bemused. It was all an act. Hercules was as sharp as a tack. We had, after all, just given him eight thousand pounds.

He bought us a cold beer at the hotel pool bar and scrawled out a contract which probably wouldn't stand up in any court of law other than a witch trial. We didn't care. It was a beautiful morning. We had a house. We had beer. Later we went for a swim in the dazzling blue sea and collapsed happy and laughing under the stars. We spent a few days unpacking the van and getting our bearings around the village. It was easy to get lost in the narrow cobbled streets which all seemed to lead to a bar. Eventually we figured we should really start preparing ourselves for the battle that is Greek bureaucracy.

Greece operates an expert system of organised chaos which has taken centuries to perfect. It is the envy of the western world. The phone company would not connect our land line socket until it had been re-wired. The electricians could not re-wire the socket until the phone company had supplied the correct cable. The phone company would not supply the electricians with the cable without proper authorisation from the landlord. Hercules was nowhere to be found. This went on for maybe a million years. Eventually we took our contract from Hercules to the phone company who then gave us the cable. We gave the cable to the electricians. The electricians could still not re-wire the socket because the socket itself belonged to the phone company. So we handed the cable back to the phone company who then re-wired the socket. We breathed a sigh of relief. We had a new land line. We had won. And then the power went down for forty eight hours.

Every now and then the system worked in our favour. I was awarded life-time Greek registration by the Kavindos authorities simply because they had run out of temporary ones. We traded in our van for a little VW Polo. She had seen better years and plenty of kilometres but we liked the wooden cross hanging from the rear view mirror. Rather than negotiate down on the asking price the dealer offered to handle all the paperwork on our behalf. We were wary but in fact this offer, as we were later told by anyone who had ever re-registered a second-hand vehicle, was worth a ton of gold. People had gone to re-register a vehicle up in town and never been seen again.

Our primary goal was to get through that first winter with our sanity intact. After six long months we emerged into the spring sunshine for the Easter festivals feeling battered, rattled and exhausted. We had spent far more money than planned and earned practically nothing. But at least we had survived. We felt delirious and elated. We had started a small graphics business from home designing artwork and web sites for the hotels and rental villas. Gradually we began to make some headway.

At the end of our first summer we moved out of Kavindos to an even smaller village about ten kilometres north. Haraklos was barely more than a pretty fishing bay and a promenade with a few bars, restaurants and holiday apartments. We rented a little house on the main beach road. It was weather-proof and relatively modern. There was constant hot water and electricity. Even the phone company transferred our number without blinking. We had a little walled garden full of lemon, peach and orange trees. A vivid pink bougainvillea tree shielded the house from passers-by on one side. Fields of nothing stretched out behind the house on the other. Hercules' house in Kavindos had been extortionately over-priced and unhealthy. I don't think old Hercules himself bore us any malice. In fact he was probably amazed we had survived the winter and this was undoubtedly the reason why he had asked for a year's rent up front. If we'd quit and gone back he would still have been rich. The concept of refunding money is not one that has been completely embraced by Greece. We learnt a lot from Hercules. We still see him riding around the villages and he always smiles.

We acquired two dogs. Our grasp of the impossible Greek language began to improve. Kat enrolled in classes. She said it was only polite. The locals were delighted. The ex-pats didn't have a clue what she was talking about. Friends from London would often fly over although not so much anymore. I guess we were a cheap holiday. We could show them the sights and cook them meals and in return they would sit in the sun and get in the way. We quickly learnt that sharing a few beers with someone in the pub for an evening in London was one thing but playing nursemaid and chaperone for two weeks on a Greek island was entirely another. We began to lose interest in their big city gossip and stupid schemes. Some people were probably disappointed that we had become so simple. It just didn't seem to matter anymore. We were glad to see most of them leave the island. Some people we kept in touch with via the internet and they always wished us well. Some people lost touch. Some people forgot to keep in touch and some people simply disappeared.

4

ISABELLA MAY

We picked Isabella May up at stupid o'clock in the morning. Her flight had been delayed. Kolasios was not a big island but it still merited an airport nonetheless. In the winter there were only four flights to the mainland a week. In the summer, however, the charter flights and budget airlines flew in and out practically non-stop. It was still dark. Even at this hour the arrivals hall was chaotic.

I was not looking forward to the next two weeks. Kat was not Isabella's biggest fan. In fact she couldn't stand the woman. Isabella called herself an adult actress but this was stretching reality. In fact she'd made something of a name for herself on the London spanking scene. She had that rosy, pink-cheeked thing going on that retired headmasters seemed to go for. She worked for a couple of creepy guys in Dulwich who organised spanking parties and photo shoots. She'd made a bunch of cheap flicks for her own website playing disobedient schoolgirls, insolent ballerinas and bratty maids who all end up getting their arses soundly slapped. At the age of 27 Isabella May was a scream queen. A mutton for punishment.

Kat and I had watched one of Isabella's movies together a while ago. It was some ridiculous Victorian epic involving several nubile servants frolicking around an old country mansion and bending over a lot. We lost the plot after a few minutes.

"Do you think she can act?" I asked Kat, as Isabella was being birched by the lady of the manor on screen. Kat snorted.

"She acts like a little bunny rabbit," she said. "I don't get it. She just stands around pouting and sulking and then someone smacks her bottom for a bit. What's that all about?"

"It's a spanking movie, Kat. That's what they do in spanking movies."

"Why?"

"It's England."

"Oh," said Kat and shrugged. "Do you think it hurts?"

"Probably," I replied. "No pain, no gain and all that. Her arse is pretty red."

"Her arse is pretty fat."

I was not looking forward to the next two weeks at all.

We'd first met Isabella when she'd been trying to get some sort of jazz band off the ground. Isabella, however, could not sing. Not even jazz. Drunken sailors can sing jazz. Smack-addled hooligans can sing jazz. Despotic bishops can sing jazz. But Isabella May could absolutely not sing jazz at all. So the band had folded after just two rehearsals and we all breathed a sigh of relief. Isabella went back to the Smack Shack in Dulwich.

"I need an agent, babes," she had grandly announced to us one afternoon. "I'm fed up with everybody slapping my fucking arse all day. Where's my fucking motivation in that, babes? My arse is splintering! Look!"

She stood up in the middle of the pub and hiked her dress to her waist. The old guys at the bar nearly choked. The landlord tutted loudly. Isabella pulled her dress down and carried on.

"I'm sick of it all, babes. I'm an actress. A fucking actress! Somehow I don't see many people slapping Julia fucking Roberts' arse!"

"You could always try sucking cock for a change," Kat said, far too sweetly.

"Nah! You need tits for porn and I ain't got tits. Look!"

She stood up again. The landlord frowned. We both leapt to our feet and forced her back into her chair.

"Don't flash your tits all over the pub, Iz," I hissed.

"Why not?" she retorted loudly. "No one's gonna notice anyway!"

Isabella May never got an agent. She did, however, eventually move out of the spanking scene and into the fetish clubs and rubber balls. It was a natural transition for someone who craved as much attention as Isabella. Personally I thought Iz was over-compensating for something. When all was said and spanked she was just a middle class kid from the Home Counties.

"Can I spank her properly when she gets here?" said Kat as we waited in the arrivals hall. "Can I spank her head with a shovel?"

"No," I said. "Be nice to her."

"Spanks for nothing!" Kat muttered.

Despite the fact that it was the middle of the night Isabella May swanned through passport non-control wearing shades and the tiniest ra-ra skirt the island had ever seen. She made a big deal about bending over to drag two huge suitcases from the baggage carousel. The entire airport could not fail to notice her satin green knickers and pink polka-dot bra. I had to smile. Iz always knew how to make an entrance.

"Fuck me, babes," she yelled as she burst into the hall. "Fucking flight from hell! Cheap divvy airline couldn't fly in a straight line if you gave 'em all cocaine and a doughnut! You alright Cal? Katerina?"

"Fine," said Kat stiffly and leant forward to kiss her on both cheeks. "Nice outfit."

"Innit," Isabella said. "Robbed it off a four year old in Croydon! Not really. Where's the party then, babes?"

The sky was turning pink and gold by the time we got back to Haraklos. We sat out in our little garden drinking tea and Metaxa.

Isabella regaled us loudly with tales of her new-found fetish fame. Personally I don't think anyone has ever looked good wearing black leather since the Ramones and Iggy Pop back in 1977. Most people just looked like stupid sticks of liquorice.

Isabella was shorter than I remembered. She'd cut her hair since quitting the Smack Shack. She said she was fed up with the whole pigtailed, schoolgirl thing. A shock of spikey white icicles now framed her angular face and green eyes. She had a butterfly tattoo on one ankle. She was loud and brash and bitchy but Isabella was never dull. She quickly made an impact in Haraklos. Isabella was an exotic distraction for the locals. She spent the first few afternoons toasting on the beach in a tiny orange bikini. Haraklos was too remote to be particularly popular as a tourist destination and even in the height of summer the beach was never that busy. In the early evening Kat and I would stroll down to the sea front and meet Isabella for drinks in Billy's Bar. During the winter Billy's was a kind of home-from-home for the ex-pats who drove over from the neighbouring villages for cheap beers, pub quizzes and the Premiership on satellite TV. In the summer, however, you could sit outside in the shade for hours just watching the sea lap at your feet as white wooden fishing boats pottered in and out of the bay.

Billy himself was a gentle Greek giant. He welcomed everybody with a smile and a handshake. He took a shine to Isabella and made sure the locals left her alone. Isabella commandeered a table for us in the middle of the bar. The little huddle of ex-pats sniggered and tittered in one corner at such a riot of loud peroxide, day-glo accessories and skinny-fit chic. Terry the Squaddie was perhaps the most unsubtle.

He was a short, balding little man with a violent temper. He'd been in the Forces for a while and battled the bad guys for Thatcher or something. Now he was just another short-order cook tossing omelettes and burgers on a Greek island. For weeks Terry had been pestering me to ghost-write his autobiography. To be honest I wasn't about to tell him that no one in the whole wide world gave a flying fuck any more about squaddies. Every soldier thinks he has a story to tell. The only interesting soldiers never say anything. Terry would constantly allude to dark, covert missions behind enemy lines in grey man's land.

"I've seen stuff, Cal," he slurred as I waited at the bar for our drinks. "Bad stuff. Stuff a man shouldn't have to see."

"Where?"

"Can't tell you, chap. Official Secrets Act and all that. But I've seen it and there's a book in there somewhere. People should know the truth."

"It's not really much of a book, Terry," I ventured. "Squaddie Sees Stuff Somewhere? Actually, it's more of a pamphlet."

Terry looked momentarily alarmed.

"Are you calling me a fucking pamphlet?"

I sighed.

"A pamphlet is a small book, Terry. A very small book."

"Right," said Terry after a long pause. "Can I ask you something, Cal?"

He put his arm around my shoulder like we were best friends. He seemed to have forgotten about the book.

"Can I have a go with the blonde?"

He waved his bottle of beer in Isabella's vague direction. "She's as fit as fuck."

I looked over at Isabella and Kat as they sat making awkward small talk.

"You'd probably have to ask her yourself, Terry," I said. "But I wouldn't recommend it."

"Right," he mumbled. "Lesbian? Got it. Enough said, chap."

His girlfriend came to the rescue. Grace was enormous. She was only 23 or something but a crap fried diet and too much beer had turned her into an airship.

"Come on, Tel," she mooed. "You're in the way."

Thanks for that, I thought, as I watched her waddle away holding Andy McNab up by his elbow. Thanks for that you bleating, fat heifer.

Isabella thought the whole thing was hilarious.

"Me?" she shrieked. "Screw a squaddie? Sod that, babes! Last time I fucked a squaddie he sat up all night crying. Proper mental! They all want to do it up the arse cos they secretly fancy their mates but they won't admit it and then they want you to dress up like a Hong Kong hooker or something. They're not right in the head, babes!"

After a couple of hours Kat feigned a headache and made her excuses.

"I can't stand much more of this," she hissed at me on the way out.

Isabella and I stayed out drinking beer and shooting pool until the early hours. Billy kept bringing us lethal shots of tequila. It seemed rude to refuse. Tequila always made me think that I was going to explode. Tequila also made Isabella and I think that snogging each other in the toilets would be a good idea. It wasn't a good idea. It was a stupid thing to do but it's not like we even got to first base or anything. When we realised that we couldn't focus on the pool cues any more we sat at the bar and watched old music videos on VH1.

Eventually we made it back to the house and poured ourselves another couple of shots. Isabella leant her head on my shoulder as we sat in the garden staring at the stars in the sky. I stroked her hair.

"It's beautiful here, babes," she said softly. "Really beautiful."

I left her asleep in the red canvas hammock that we'd strung up between two fruit trees. In the morning Kat had invented a client who needed her urgent attention for the next few days.

"Which client?" I asked.

"Our very popular and famous client called Peace and Fucking Quiet! See you later."

So for the next few days Kat took the car out during the day and left Isabella and I knocking around Haraklos. Isabella would sit on the beach whilst I worked on the computer at home. She would come back just as the day began to cool for a shower and something to eat. Kat would return around seven. She told me she drove over to the west coast just to watch the surf. She would have coffee in a little remote taverna and then drive home. Sometimes she would join Iz and me for a beer in Billy's. Sometimes she would just stay in the house and watch TV or read a book. Personally I thought Kat was being a little ridiculous. She said she resented the intrusion.

"She doesn't buy food, she doesn't cook, she never buys a drink and she never stops talking. I can't hear myself scream when she's around. Why don't these people book into a hotel and give us back our lives? I feel like we're being held to ransom by an orange bikini and a cheap tattoo!"

Kat resented Isabella because we got on well together. Iz was a good drinking partner. She was attractive and funny and shameless. Kat and I had spent so long watching our words and trying not to offend anyone on the island that I found Isabella a breath of fresh air. The bars on Kolasios have eyes and ears. Isabella was just another visitor and so she didn't count. Isabella wouldn't be around to pick up the pieces.

One morning after another long night in Billy's I awoke around noon. The house was empty as usual. I felt rough. I made coffee and watched a little news on TV. The dogs were quiet. They could smell a hangover and knew better than to hustle me for a cuddle. I showered and drank some juice but my head still felt like shit. After a while I decided Iz and I needed a beer.

I scanned the beach but Iz was nowhere to be seen. She was hard to miss. It was a warm afternoon. The sea was calm and listless. The promenade was quiet. It was too hot to be out in the sun. I sat at a table in the shade outside Billy's and ordered a beer from the Lithuanian waitress. I saw Terry and Grace sitting at the bar inside. They were already pissed. I asked them whether they'd seen Iz.

"Not today, chap," said Terry. "I normally keep an eye out for her but I haven't seen a sign."

I bet you keep an eye out, I thought. I bet you all keep an eye out. As well as take bets on when she was going to take her top off.

I phoned her mobile but there was no answer. So I picked up an old copy of Q magazine and sat outside on my own reading an article about Faith No More, a shotgun, some groupies and bars of soap. Isabella could look after herself.

It was only when Kat arrived that I began to worry.

"Where's Isabella?" she asked.

"I don't know. I haven't seen her all afternoon. I've been here since about 3 and no one's seen her. Is she at home?"

"Nope. I've just come from home. She's not there. And neither are her suitcases."

Kat sat down and ordered a white wine. Billy brought me another beer without asking. We sat in silence for a while.

"Do you think she's gone?" Kat said.

It seemed unlikely. She hadn't mentioned anything about going anywhere. I think Iz knew that Kat didn't like her but she was thick-skinned enough not to take offence. I tried her mobile again. I tried phoning the house but no one picked up. As it began to get dark we phoned the airline but Isabella hadn't checked in. We stayed up most of that night hoping Iz had just gone bush for a while and that she'd return with a bottle of something and a brainstorm. The following morning we checked the emails and all the social net-working sites. Nothing. We thought about calling the police. As Kat pointed out, however, the fact that Isabella had taken two large suit-cases with her seemed to negate anything suspicious. There were no sign of a struggle. We found her spare keys on the kitchen counter. Isabella had simply disappeared. After a few days we figured that no news was probably good news. If by some miracle the police on the island ever found out anything then I was sure that we would be the first to know.

We never heard another word from Isabella May. It was a shame. I guess I kind of missed her. Isabella May was always a good laugh. The house was quiet. Haraklos was quiet. Kat and I were alone again as the rhythms returned.

5

HOTEL

So I got to thinking about dead children. Not the unfortunate stillborn or the aborted but rather the tubby, squealing little pancakes splashing about in the pool at the Aphrodite Grand Palace hotel. I was sitting at the pool bar waiting for Giorgos. He would be late for our business meeting. He was always late. He reckoned he was a busy man and that the hotel required his undivided attention at all times. The Grand Palace could not function without his presence. His guests were his friends and he could not let even one of them down. Blah-blah-blah...

Giorgos was an idle, arrogant emperor. He thought he owned the goddamn island when in fact he simply owned a huge, shitty, beige-brick hotel which looked like it had been built in a week and decorated by a five year old with a box of crayons. Who in their right mind would paint giant bumble bees and flowers all over the exterior of something which called itself a luxury family resort? A madman would think twice.

The pool bar was busy. I helped myself to a coffee and sat in the shade as far away from the sun-wrinkled and the beer-drenched as possible. Fuck this place, I thought. Really. Fuck this place to hell.

Hotels like the Aphrodite Grand Palace were slowly killing Kolasios. They were starving the island. They were freezing the cash-flow which the island so desperately needed. The all-inclusive packages meant that the lazy, the boorish and the ignorant had no need to ever take one step outside their hotel compounds. They could wallow in the familiar and the crass for two weeks until it was time to pack up and head back home. Everything at these hotels was pre-paid in advance and laid out on a grimy plate. Visitors sold out the right to any quality of anything as soon as they accepted those stupid hotel wrist bands. The wrist bands were worn like trophies. They kept people docile and thankful and loyal like little rattles for a baby. They kept people captive.

I watched them queue up at the pool bar like retarded bovine simpletons. They were always so fucking grateful for plastic cups of coloured sugar water and a microwaved burger. The alcohol was the cheapest and nastiest the hotels could find. Then it was watered down. Then it was watered down again and slopped out into frosted mugs by frantic bar staff who were so tired they could barely raise a smile. The fat monkeys couldn't get enough. They would order 10 mugs at a time and return to their family sun loungers like triumphant bull elephants in swimming trunks. They would neck those 10 mugs and then heave themselves back into the queue for more. This went on all day, every day, for six months.

The smell of chlorine hung heavy around the pool. Hotels like the Grand Palace needed gallons of the stuff every day just to dilute the clouds of piss and sweat and sun lotion dripping off the bloated human bodies floating aimlessly in the water. Sometimes the filter systems would break down and within hours the pools would look like acrid swamps. The water would be hastily skimmed. No one seemed to care. Especially the mosquitoes.

So, as I said, I got to thinking about dead children. I mean, just imagine for one horrific second, that a child got a leg or an arm stuck in one of the skimmers and drowned? Even if the gormless parents even noticed, there was not much they could do. There were no cameras to record the accident. No lifeguards to dive to the rescue. No clocks. All inclusive hotels work on Las Vegas time. If people don't know what time it actually is then they will never be in a rush to get anywhere else. Parents wouldn't even be able to tell for how long their child had been missing. It would all be over before the buffet had gone cold.

There were no cameras. There were no fucking cameras anywhere on the island. Kolasios was invisible.

I rolled another cigarette and phoned Giorgos. The tips of my fingers were yellow with nicotine. They were pretty disgusting. I should clean them with lemon juice when I got home.

"One minute, my friend, one minute," said Giorgos. He sounded like he'd just woken up. "*Siga siga.*"

Everything in Greece is *Siga* fucking *siga*. Roughly translated it meant that someone might do something for you when they'd finished talking about doing something for someone else. This was a waste of time. Giorgos didn't really want Kat and I to upgrade his website or photograph his refurbished canteen. Giorgos just liked playing Charlie Big Potato. He would keep me waiting until sunset and then buy me a cheap beer at the pool bar and argue about our fees. He was just another greedy Greek bandit from the mainland with an ugly hotel built illegally on family land with crooked finance. I shouldn't even be here. I shouldn't even care.

I groaned out loud as the hotel animation team water-boarded into the pool area.

Animation teams were put on god's great earth to inflict some kind of permanent, sugar-coated brain damage. Like the watered-down alcohol and unlimited sausage rolls at the bar they were just another weapon of mass holiday distraction. In the afternoons it was always water aerobics. In the evenings it was an Abba tribute show. They slept for maybe three hours a night before the Childrens' Club started up in the morning. As a result they all had that same look in their eyes like the Chinese gymnasts forced to rehearse their routines in the dark and at gun point. It was a kind of desperate, shrieking mania that never seemed to unnerve the obese and the moronic around the pool. The animation teams were greeted like old friends and superstars with applause and laughter. They led the eager volunteers like uncomplaining little kids to the water and made them dance in the shallow end like gurning retards to a soundtrack of disco nursery rhymes. The up-beats were incessant. It was a barrage of mind-numbing, bubble gum nonsense. The up-beats could tip a sane man over the edge.

The upbeats could make a sane man throw an industrial toaster into the pool. Dance, splash and chirp your way out of that, you fucking incinerated disgrace!

There was a big cheer from the pool. It was all over for the time being. I called Giorgos again but his phone was switched off. Two of the animation team sat down uninvited at my table and gulped from plastic water bottles.

"Oh my god, oh my god, oh my god!" said one in that kind of breathless, high-pitched, over-enunciated squeal that young camp boys use when they want to be noticed.

"Did you see Charlene? Oh! My! God! She missed her cue! She so totally missed it! She was dancing like Gary Barlow!"

He took another swig from his water bottle.

"I'm going to have to talk to her, Rox. She knows that back step in *Nellie the Elephant* is really, really, really, like, super important! Look! There's Russell! Mwah!"

He air-kissed the girl from the team at our table and sashayed over to an identikit image of himself waving back from the bar. That must be confusing, I thought, as they hugged each other. That must be really confusing on so many levels.

The girl at the table leaned over.

"Sorry," she said, "but could I steal a roll-up? I'm supposed to have given up but some days, well, it's really difficult."

I rolled her a cigarette and handed it over.

"Thanks. Don't tell. Smoking's bad for our public image. But it doesn't really matter coz we're all mingers!"

She threw back her head and laughed. She was quite cute.

"You're welcome, Rox," I said.

Eighteen? Nineteen? No more than twenty at the very most. Despite the stupid shorts and high visibility team bib she would probably look good naked.

"How do know my name?" she asked.

"Your friend just announced it to the hotel and the rest of the world," I replied. "The loud one? The one who's got to have a word with Charlene about *Nellie the Elephant*?"

"Yeah, right," she sniffed. "Aldo can talk. Aldo dances like a right clogger himself but he's going out with our boss so we're kind of stuck with him! Don't tell!"

"I won't."

I would really like to have sex with you, Rox, and then smash your fucking head in with an iron. Don't tell.

"Well, I gotta go," she said. "I think we're all playing Techno Chicken Fight in the Pirate Pool in a minute."

"Right," I said.

She paused and looked at me for a second.

"I don't suppose..."

"No, Rox, thanks all the same."

"Right. I don't blame you. Cheers for the smoke. I'll see you around maybe?"

I nodded.

"See you around."

Thanks, Rox. I'll maybe see you around. Maybe we'll all see each other around someday. Before the end of the season. That would be nice.

My mobile phone rang. I ignored it. It was Giorgos. *Signomi*, my friend, but I really can't be bothered with you any more. Instead I gathered up my cigarettes and laptop and walked out of the pool bar. On the way back through the hotel to the car park I stopped at reception. There was a young English guy behind the desk looking happy and efficient in his rinky-dinky uniform. He smiled as I approached.

"Sir?"

Don't call me fucking sir! Neither of us is in the army or at boarding school. I hate being called sir. I despise restaurant staff who call me sir and place napkins in my lap and ask me to test a mouthful of wine. Deference is an ugly human trait.

"Hi, I said. "Look, I really don't want to speak out of turn or anything but I'm pretty sure I just saw one of the animation team lift a room key from a guest at the pool bar."

The geeky kid's face fell. He looked around to make sure I hadn't been overheard.

"Are you sure, sir?"

"Pretty sure, yes. As I said, I don't want to cause any problems for the young man in question and maybe there was a totally innocent explanation. I just thought it looked rather suspicious from where I was sitting and that the best thing I could do was to inform someone in authority. Maybe you could go and have a word with the young man in question? His name is Ardo or Aldo or Allo or something like that. He's quite, well, extravagant, if you know what I mean."

"Aldo, sir? That would be totally unexpected."

I peered at his name tag.

"Look, Brian, I'm just reporting what I saw. I'd hate to cause any trouble or anything. Maybe you could just wind back through the security tapes or something? Double check the whole thing before deciding whether or not to take any action?"

"I can't do that, sir," Brian said nervously. "We don't have any security cameras at the Grand Palace. Not many hotels feel the need. Kolasios is one of the safest islands in Europe."

"Right," I said. "Ok, well, I just wanted to let someone know. I'm sure you'll look into it, Brian. Bye."

I helped myself to a boiled sweet from the jar on the reception desk and walked outside into the sun. Instead of driving back to Haraklos I headed north up the coast to the airport. I liked the airport. It was full of movement. That afternoon I sat in the mezzanine coffee bar for a while. It wasn't particularly busy but the arrivals board clacked constantly with updates and information nonetheless. Occasionally a rasping tannoy announcement in Greek would shatter the comforting hum of conversation. Nervous flyers fiddled with their boarding passes as they waited for the gate calls. A huddle of charter transfer reps sat at a table in the corner waiting for more arrivals from the North of England. They had kicked off their shoes whilst they scribbled on clip boards and compared schedules. Repping was a thankless dog's life. A couple of armed police in combat uniform strolled past. They stopped to chat with the cleaning crew. They laughed.

After a while the overhead lighting, the drone of the air conditioning and all the other niggling electrical pulses which keep an airport in business began to grate. I left the coffee bar and walked slowly around the terminal. It was really just a long, pre-fabricated shed. I paused to roll a cigarette. The airport was the only place on the island where you weren't allowed to smoke. I stepped outside to light up. A cloud of diesel fumes and aviation fuel filled my lungs. It felt good.

I walked back to the car park. I was humming a song I couldn't remember as I dodged the coaches and taxis. It's funny how you can hum a song that you've never knowingly heard. Where did they come from? Outer space? Jukebox satellites? I paid my ticket and smiled at the girl in the kiosk.

"*Yassas*," she said and handed back my change.

I drove home happy. Kat was out at Greek classes by the time I got back to Haraklos. So I sat in the garden with the dogs and a bottle of beer.

There really were no security cameras on Kolasios, I thought. Not even at the airport. Kat and I had left a city obsessed with surveillance technology and a nation who pretty soon would be nothing more than tiny dots of biometric data. They say no one can walk through London's Square Mile without being constantly caught on a camera every step of the way. There were cameras in buses and taxis. There were cameras at supermarket tills. There were cameras in the parks and malls and schools and subways.

I took a sip from the bottle and lit another cigarette.

There were no eyes in the sky over Kolasios. There was nothing. No satellites, no rocket ships, no ray guns and no laser beams. She was unmapped and submerged deep out of sight as the busy world sped through space searching for fortune and fury. The skies above Kolasios were empty and blue. There was just a hole through which all the gods had escaped long ago. No bombs would ever drop on Kolasios. No armies would invade. In time she would be forgotten. We would all be forgotten. So it didn't really matter.

I smiled. It was a miracle.

6

KITTYHAWK

Y ou could drive around the whole island in about seven hours. I liked driving. Driving was a re-assuring freedom. Kolasios could be a spectacular backdrop if you avoided the road works just south of the shit-pit that was Skataki with its foam parties and idiot bars. Christ alone knew just when those road works would be finished. It had been years. That particular stretch of road was positively dangerous. So it was best to dodge the East coast altogether from Kolasios Town down past Skataki and the crappy, peeling tourist resorts along the way.

South of Kavindos the roads were wide and relatively quiet. As you reached the bottom of the island and started heading back up the West coast the scenery changed completely. The scorched dust and dry air gave way to lush farmland and fierce winds. Relentless waves pounded the deserted beaches for mile after mile. You could taste the sea salt and smell the wild herbs in the air. After centuries of storms and vicious winds the trees along the coast road grew at an angle. Their branches pointed inland towards the white wind turbines which stood tall and elegant against the horizon.

After a while the road led you away from the coast and towards the mountains. The air became fresher and cooler. You seldom saw another vehicle except for maybe an old sedan with no windscreen being driven erratically by an even older farmer oblivious to the breeze. The roads wound through sleepy villages and dark pine forests. Occasionally I would stop in a bar somewhere for a beer or a thick local coffee. Everybody would nod and smile. We had no common language.

Several crumbling villas and municipal buildings were scattered across the mountain landscape. Unlike the many picturesque monasteries and pretty chapels, those ruins were not included on any tourist map. Most were hidden from view. They had been built during the Italian occupation and had deliberately been left to overgrow and collapse. You could feel the ghosts of the dead in the old torture asylums and sanatoriums. Cruel winds whipped through those shattered structures. Leaves and dirt now blew along corridors that must have once been ornately tiled by proud craftsmen. They were sombre, uninviting, dank places still scarred by bullet holes and fingernails. Recently the Greek government had been trying to sell the dilapidated buildings to foreign investors. They were unanimously regarded by islanders and investors alike as cold property and cold property, for whatever reason, should never be sold. Instead they were left empty as unofficial memorials to the tormented souls who many believed still paced the shameful cells and chambers.

In the winter the mountains were frequently obscured by low cloud. Roads and villages alike were shrouded in a damp, ethereal mist. It was a treacherous environment. Rivers of thick mud ran down the hills sweeping trees and rubble into the middle of the road. The dark granite rocks loomed a little too close for comfort as you negotiated the winding, pot-holed tarmac. Headlights were useless. Headlights just cut a path into the grey cloud without revealing anything of the world beyond. The mist played tricks on your eyes. Ghostly shadows flashed past the windscreen. Men in black rags hung from sign posts. Witch-finder generals would race up behind you on terrified horses only to disappear into the driving rain.

I spent a lot of time driving across the mountains. In the summer you could park and look down on the rolling green valleys to the shimmering sea beyond. It was a long way from the bustle of the East Coast. It was a long way from anywhere. Up there in the mountains you could believe anything. You could believe all the island myths and folklore. You could believe the dark war secrets and sacred village tales. After a while you could even start to believe the rumours which surrounded the Kittyhawk Club.

The Kittyhawk was not an easy bar to find. There were no signs, no mention in any guide books and no internet presence whatsoever. Most people didn't even know the place existed. Someone once told me that all you had to do was drive up into the mountains and follow the sound of gunfire. Others spoke of rabid bike gangs and snarling dogs, armed guards and crystal meth. The only real truth was that Tommy and Gina were not about to walk down from the mountains and hand out a fucking map. If you couldn't find the Kittyhawk Club then you probably wouldn't be welcome anyway.

I found the Kittyhawk late one afternoon completely by accident. It was on fire.

I had been driving home across the mountains when a goat stepped out into the road. Goats are a common hazard on any Greek island. They're not as stupid as sheep but they can be stubborn. This particular goat strolled out of the undergrowth without a care in the world. It was huge. I slammed on the brakes and closed my eyes. The goat didn't flinch. It just stood about three feet from the car and glared at me with grape-ball eyes. Then it lay down. I tried to inch around the animal but it stood up and walked across the road to block my manoeuvre. Then it lay down again. This happened maybe five times. I sighed. The goat kind of grunted. So I switched off the engine, rolled down the window and lit a cigarette. I was in no rush. The goat ignored me.

It was then that I smelt smoke. It wasn't wood smoke. It was sharp and acrid and smelt like burning plastic. There was a small, narrow track just up ahead. A black haze was drifting down the track from the hills above. Wood smoke was white and often just a sign that farmers were burning the branches from harvested fruit trees. Black smoke was a rare sight. It was spring and the countryside was already dry enough to feed a fire that could rapidly spread out of control. It was the island's worst nightmare. So I turned on the engine and nudged the goat out of the road. It ambled out of the way looking spiteful.

I turned off the tarmac and headed cautiously up the rough track into the smoke. After about thirty metres the track levelled out. Two old trees and a white wooden gatepost stood guard over a large gravelled clearing. The Kittyhawk Club stood on its own in the middle of this clearing surrounded by several small out-houses and a forest. It looked more like a farm than a bar. The black smoke was spiralling into the sky from behind the main building. I parked next to an old Russian URL motorcycle. I could hear shouting. As I walked around the building I could also hear laughter.

The source of the fire was something that looked like half a small helicopter. A tall guy with white hair turned and waved as I approached.

"Hi," he said nonchalantly, as if I'd just dropped by for a hot dog.

"Goddamn chopper caught fire, man! Goddamn fucking chopper caught fire!"

"Right," I replied, edging around the flames and smoke billowing from the helicopter's charred cockpit. I lit a cigarette. There didn't seem much else to do.

I noticed a young girl sitting on the wooden steps which presumably led to the back door of the bar. She was barefoot and smiling. Her arms were tattooed and she wore little more than a white satin negligee. A purple feather attached to her dark hair fluttered elegantly in the breeze. An older woman sat beside the girl wearing black denim jeans tucked into leather motorcycle boots. They took turns swigging from a bottle of vodka. Every time something hissed and popped inside the burning cockpit they raised the bottle and cheered.

The guy with white hair strode over to me and held out his hand.

"Tommy," he said. "Name's Tommy Kittyhawk. This is my bar. You wanna stand around here watching this heap of shit or you wanna go inside and have a beer? Don't worry about the chopper. Thing'll piss itself out after a while. Cheap Italian crap anyway."

The two women cheered again as the perspex cockpit windows exploded in the heat. Tommy nodded towards the older woman.

"That's my wife, Gina," he said. "She started the goddamn fire!"

Tommy told me the story of the helicopter over several bottles of cold German beer at the bar. Gina and the girl with the feather, whom I only ever knew as Honey, played pool. There were no other customers. Apparently the helicopter had been shot down by mountain resistance fighters during the war. Despite losing its tail fin, rotor blades and landing skids it had crash-landed relatively intact. It had sat rusting for decades exactly where it was burning that afternoon. It had never been moved. It was purely ornamental. Tommy considered it to be lucky in some way.

"Nothing more beautiful than a war machine with no teeth," he said with a grin and popped another beer.

Tommy said that one day he had met the son of the man who shot down the helicopter. He drove this man up to the Kittyhawk Club and proudly showed him what was left of the bullet-ridden chopper. The man promptly unzipped his pants and pissed all over the machine before shaking Tommy by the hand and walking back to his village.

Apparently Tommy, Gina and Honey had been up all last night drinking together and pumping coins into the old Wurlitzer jukebox which stood at one end of the bar. At some point Gina had decided that the helicopter should be lit up at night for all the world to see. So that afternoon they had been trying to spot-weld a huge arc light onto the main rotor mast. The mast was badly rusted and had crumbled under the weight of the arc light. The heavy light had fallen through the roof of the cockpit and knocked over the acetylene tank which was still attached to the red-hot welding torch. There had been an explosion.

"No shit!" said Gina from the pool table.

All four of us raised our bottles to the remains of Tommy's lucky helicopter and I was made an honorary member of the Kittyhawk Club.

The Kittyhawk opened unofficially some time in the early 1980s and never really closed. Tommy and Gina never bothered with planning permission, licenses, taxes or permits. The few people who knew about the little bar in the mountains revered its outlaw status. This status was really the only reason why the Kittyhawk tried to keep a low profile and so far the place had successfully survived beneath the Greek state radar. Every few days Tommy would drive to one of the hypermarkets on the East coast to buy alcohol. They ran the power to the bar from an old petrol generator. A few of the locals donated fuel as well as logs for the fireplace and chickens for the oven. Any venture that could survive for so long beyond the reach of the authorities was something to be applauded in the eyes of many Greeks.

Tommy's parents had emigrated from Kolasios to New Jersey just before the outbreak of war. Tommy grew up in Little Falls. He met Gina at college and as teenagers in the late 1960's they fell into the counter-culture together. They began to make art-house porn flicks for fun with an old 16mm film camera Tommy had picked up for a pittance. Gina was a flame-haired free spirit and a willing accomplice. With absolutely no budget for either equipment or crew they made the films wherever they could using natural light and a lot of drugs. The films were only really meant for their own amusement but word began to spread. The unintentional art-house angle attracted patronage. One of Tommy's college lecturers put up some cash which Tommy and Gina used to buy more drugs. The lecturer didn't mind.

He got to hang out on-set and watch the young couple fuck whilst getting stoned. They shot the movie under a railway bridge in super-grainy black and white. They couldn't think of a title for it and so they didn't bother. Instead they took it to New York and punted the show reel around a few grindhouse cinemas and flea pits. An old Jewish guy with thick spectacles and thin hair agreed to screen the film in one of his back-alley theatres. Tommy and Gina were briefly elated. But the old rat insisted the young couple sign a contract giving him sole rights to any future profits. Tommy wouldn't budge. He had decided that pornography was going to make him a rich man. He wasn't about to let anyone cut in on a deal when he and Gina alone were doing all the work.

So they bought an old Chevy and drove across the country selling their movies from the trunk of the car. The money began to stack up as well as the young couple's notoriety. They were heralded as guerrilla artists on the West Coast. They found themselves invited to cocaine parties in LA with radio rock stars and fat-arsed hipsters. Tommy and Gina thought the whole scene was hilarious. They were only taken seriously as artists because they had absolutely no clue how to make movies.

Newspaper articles began to describe the couple as bandit entrepreneurs. Every American loves an underdog. They operated without a distribution network and avoided state laws by asking clients for a donation. The size of the donation was at the client's discretion. In LA and Texas the donations were beyond Tommy and Gina's wildest dreams. In Mexico someone gave them a horse. In Utah someone offered them a church. They picked up a brand new Chevy from a dealer in Detroit. Gina was 18 in 1971 when she married Tommy at a roadside chapel in Reno. They never had kids.

Tommy and Gina continued to make films. They had picked up an extended family of traveling misfits and artists and runaways who all adored the carefree approach and lucrative rewards. The couple would send the reels of film to Canada to be processed and edited by sympathetic contacts. The finished tapes would then be shipped back across the border to the nearest freight depot to wherever Tommy and Gina were staying at the time. It was a sweet system.

The distribution cartels, however, were furious. After five years on the road Tommy still saw no reason to hand over a single percentage of his profits to the Man. The cartels tried to convince the maverick otherwise. Tommy was always polite but he wouldn't budge. The threats began to escalate. One night the Chevy was splashed with acid. Another time someone broke into a freight depot and set fire to several grands' worth of tapes. Things got so heated that Tommy and Gina started driving with a motorcycle gang alongside for protection.

Ultimately Tommy and Gina were defeated not by mobsters but rather by market forces. Pornography was changing and evolving during the 1970s. It was becoming a vast and brazen industry. Bigger budgets were being spent on production values and stars. Pornography was becoming legitimate and respectable. It would never be the same again. Tommy and Gina got out of the race before it was too late. For a while they tried a similar operation in Europe but the miniature border controls and petty bureaucracy sucked the fun out of the business. It was whilst the couple were staying in Spain that Tommy found out he had been left money and some property by a family relative on Kolasios. They immediately packed up their belongings and headed south.

Tommy and Gina fell in love with the island in general and in particular the little patch of land up in the mountains. They decided to stay. They had saved enough money over the years to live comfortably for the foreseeable future. So they renovated the farm house and turned the out-houses into cosy living accommodation. Gradually the bar began to take shape. They named the Kittyhawk after the fighter plane. Pilots would paint sharks' teeth around the engine cowlings in a bid to unnerve their opponents as they flew into battle. Tommy said the sharks' teeth reminded him of the porn business. His old 16mm film camera took pride of place above the bar in a glass case.

Tommy and Gina were notorious and popular figures. Pretty soon their large extended family of followers began to make regular trips to the Kittyhawk. Some stayed for months just vibing in the mountains and laughing about the old days. The place would be full of crazy colour and good humour. There would be bikers and starlets and dancers and madmen all gathered together around the open fire whilst Tommy and Gina presided over events like proud parents.

Over the years a new generation discovered the Kittyhawk. Kids from Russia and Eastern Europe began to hang out at the bar. Tommy was delighted. He had always insisted the Kittyhawk was a stateless nation where kindred spirits could gather together and drink until dawn. The world had changed and the money was now flowing from the East. Tommy always encouraged everybody's ambitious bandit plans with a winning smile and a cold beer. The music on the old Wurlitzer might have changed over the years but the Kittyhawk essentially stayed the same.

Tommy and Gina were happy up there together in the mountains. Tommy was now in his sixties but he looked good for his age. Gina was still a beautiful woman. The authorities never caught up with the Kittyhawk club and Tommy never paid them a cent. The bar remained defiantly unlicensed. Tommy always said he enjoyed the isolation of island life. Personally I think he enjoyed the isolation nearly as much as the fact that he still didn't have to cut anybody else in on a deal.

7

ROX

She was playing pool in Molly's bar. I didn't notice her at first. It was only when Aldo walked past carrying a tray of flaming cocktails that I recognised Rox and the animation team from the Aphrodite Grand Palace. They sat in one corner squealing and gasping and clapping like a bunch of baby seals every time Rox potted a ball. Aldo sat next to his identikit lover wearing a skinny-fit diamante t-shirt. A couple of lardy girls wore blue party wigs and cheap comedy glasses with plastic noses and moustaches. A fat boy with over-gelled hair sported a t-shirt emblazoned with the words 100% MOTHER FUCKER. He was slurring his way through some Abba medley at the top of his voice for no apparent reason whatsoever.

I ordered a beer from the barmaid and sat at the far end of the long bar. Molly's was an Irish theme pub situated slap in the middle of Skataki's Club Street. It was decorated with plastic four-leaved clovers and Guinness towels and pictures of the old Dublin docks which didn't exist anymore because the developers had blown them up to make way for loft apartments and conference hotels. In fact Molly's was about as Irish as olives and pita bread. It was owned by two Greek brothers and staffed exclusively during the season by vacant English blondes who could barely add up without falling down.

Skataki itself was predominantly a British party resort. It had faded in popularity over the years but it was still seen by many as a rite of passage. Last year the only fatality was a lad from Sunderland who had managed to stab himself in the head with a broken bottle. No foul play was ever suspected because he was asleep in his own bed at the time. There should be no laws in the world except the Law of Stupid. Only stupid people go to war. Only stupid people go to the moon. Only stupid people fight with horses. And only stupid people go to Skataki for a cheap summer holiday and end up stabbing themselves in the head.

During the day the place resembled a dilapidated film set or an impoverished zombie town. Around midday the first of the sunburnt and hungover would emerge like beetles from their beds and lurch down to Muff's café, or Bob the Knob's, for a full fry-up and a mug of tea. You could smell the chip fat and stale sweat a block away. Local Greek bar owners would be out in the streets hosing the vomit and broken glass from the night before into the gutter. In the afternoon it was too hot for most Brits to do little more than find a sun bed on the beach and belch their way towards beer o'clock.

As evening fell the holiday reps would round up the blistered gangs of punch-drunk piglets for the organised bar crawls around Skataki. There were always wet t-shirt competitions in the Clit Club, foam parties in the Fook Lounge and karaoke in Benny's Bun. Sometimes the English Jack would sponsor tribute acts and show bands. Every now and then the Fanny Pack would bring over a DJ from Holland that no one had ever heard of, but it was the free shots and football on offer in bars like the Fat Tit and the Armlock Castle which proved more popular.

The night clubs would kick off at around midnight. Clubs like Lingerie and the Pink Power offered pole dancers and bed shows alongside over-priced beers and yesterday's Hard Rock. Larger clubs like Titan, Haze and the Worm Shack played Techno and Trance until dawn. As the sun rose over Skataki the beach resembled a battlefield.

The half-dead and brain-wounded lay groaning and moaning and writhing in the sand. The local police cruised past in their cars keeping half an eye out for genuine distress or disorder. It was a thankless task. The part-time force was sponsored by a large chain of furniture warehouses on the mainland. I knew this was a source of deep embarrassment to Captain Vassilis Tsolakides but ever since central government had run out of money some time ago he had little choice but to advertise quality bedding and shelving units on the side of his three squad cars. Captain Tsolakides himself chose to drive around the island in an unmarked BMW X1. He once told the press that he needed to keep at least some vestige of dignity.

Normally I would avoid Skataki like a plague pit. That night, however, I was restless. I had been looking for a hardware store but it was a saint's day holiday and most of the shops were shut. I had to drive up into the mountains before I found what I was looking for. I had dropped in to see Tommy and Gina at the Kittyhawk. There was an air of exhaustion about the place that evening which was pretty joyless. Tommy told me they had been visited by an Albanian shepherd who had arrived on horseback to dispute ownership of the Kittyhawk. He was a dark and mysterious figure with a handlebar moustache and black leather riding boots. Tommy refuted the shepherd's claims and so ensued a marathon drinking session which lasted three days and nights. Eventually the Albanian shepherd agreed to drop his claims. He saddled up his white steed and thundered out into the forest. Tommy and Gina breathed a sigh of relief. After four hours, however, the shepherd returned with a large goose in a sack. He insisted Tommy take the goose as a token of his honour. Tommy and Gina gingerly unpacked the startled goose and called it Marcus. Unaccustomed to his new surroundings, however, Marcus had done little more than shriek and honk ever since. Tommy said they were all sleep-deprived.

Gina lifted her head off the bar as I walked to the door after a couple of beers. Her eyes were red and swollen.

"Wanna buy a goose?" she said.

I drove down to Skataki for inspiration. Despite Molly's location it was usually pretty quiet. I guess Irish theme pubs – like the IRA - had probably seen better days. It was still relatively early.

There was a loud cheer from the animation team. Rox screamed and slowly laid her pool cue on the table before pretending to bang her head on a corner pocket.

"Fuck! Fuck! Fuck! Fuck!" she said as everyone else squealed with delight.

"Fuck!"

She grabbed a couple of empty glasses and walked over to the bar. She was wearing blue jeans with flip-flops and a yellow Haze club t-shirt.

"Hello, Rox" I said as she passed. It took a split second for the penny to drop. Then her face broke into a wide smile.

"Hello, you," she said. "The hotel let you escape as well?"

"Well, yes, but I had to pay the door staff to let me out after a sixteen hour stand-off. It was a tough call."

She laughed and placed her bottle of beer on the bar. She sat down and pulled a packet of cigarettes from her back pocket.

"I owe you one."

"Thanks." I said and lit up. "Good game?"

She groaned.

"Fucking crap! I'm rubbish at pool. Don't know why I agreed to come really but Aldo's been a bit down in the dumps since the hotel let him go."

I raised an eyebrow.

"They fired him? Why?"

"Oh, we're not really sure but management told us he nicked a room key from one of the guests or something. That's just not like Aldo at all but the hotel couldn't take any chances so they kicked him out anyway. He'll be alright. Russell got him a job on the roller aerobics team up at the water park."

"I'm sorry to hear that," I said. "Let me buy him a drink. Pretend it's from Russell or something."

I waved at the barmaid and ordered some ridiculous cocktail from a list above the bar. I watched her concoct something out of crushed ice, lumps of fruit and oil-slick cordials. Rox and I chatted as we waited.

"We're playing Pool for Pants," she said. "Loser has to take off their pants and hang them on the Hook of Shame."

She pointed to a hat stand near the pool table. Several items of underwear already hung from the pegs.

"What happens if you lose again?"

Rox laughed.

"Bras for the girls and shirts for the boys! Don't know what happens after that. No one's ever got that far. I should've thought about it really coz getting my pants off under my jeans is a major fumble."

"Right," I said.

The barmaid returned with Aldo's cocktail. We stared at each other for a second. I could see doubt in her eyes.

"It's...err..." she muttered inanely. "It's...God, this foreign money is so confusing, innit?"

Not really, I thought. It's just a number. The number is written on the fucking price list just above your head! All you have to do is say some numbers out loud and I'll give you some money. It doesn't matter whether those numbers are in dollars, euros, pounds or yen. It's just a fucking number. It's 5.60. It says 5.60 on the price list. You don't even have to add anything up. Admittedly having to work out the change might be confusing but at the moment all you have to do is say the numbers 5 and 60. It's easy! Just say 5.60!

"It's 4.80," she said.

"Cheers."

I gave her five euros and told her to keep the change. Life was too short.

"Right then," said Rox. "I've gotta go to the loo and get rid of this thong. No peeking!"

The animation team began a slow hand-clap in the corner.

"Rox! Rox! Rox!" they chanted.

"Fuck off!" said Rox loudly.

As the evening wore on Rox spent more time talking to me at the bar. She was drinking quickly. She told me her life story which at the age of 22 was unremarkable. She wanted to work on the cruise ships but thought she might miss her family back home in Basingstoke. Apparently the Aphrodite was ok. The money wasn't great but everyone was friendly. Some of the children could be a pain in the arse. I nodded sympathetically. By the end of the night she was swaying all over the bar. We made a date to meet after the show at the hotel the following night. Rox placed one hand on my arm and winked.

"Pants," she slurred, "are entirely optional."

To be honest Kat had never really embraced the entire concept of tribute shows.

"Why would anyone want to pay to watch people impersonate Abba?" she said, as I packed up my camera equipment.

"Because they're staying at the Aphrodite," I replied. "They don't have a choice. They're a captive audience. And the real Abba doesn't exist anymore."

"I bet they leave out all the Nazi stuff?"

I paused.

"What?"

"Abba were notorious Nazis," Kat said matter-of-factly.

"I doubt it."

"Oh, come on! It's well known! Look at that album cover where they're all dressed in white jumpsuits standing in front of a helicopter. And their biggest song was called *Money Money Money*. If that's not an admission that Sweden and Abba supported the Nazis by secretly flying the gold they stole from the Jews to South America after the war then I don't know what is."

I sighed.

"Simon Wiesenthal tried to ban them in Germany," she continued. "He insisted they were promoting anti-Semitic propaganda. Abba paid him off and bought his silence with a few gold coins and a signed album. It was a tragedy. Shocking."

"Right," I said. "I've really got to go. The Nazi elite are paying me to photograph their show."

I heard Kat humming a song as I put the camera bag in the boot of the car.

"*There was something in the air that night,*
The stars were bright...Adolpho!"

"Very funny, Kat."

She laughed.

"Revisionist!"

I made it to the grandly-titled Aphrodite Amphitheatre in time to catch AbbaTastic's second set. It wasn't so much an amphitheatre as a prefabricated shed on wheels with a mirror ball hanging from the ceiling. Abba themselves seemed to have mutated into four girls wearing short sequined skirts and two boys in drag. They were miming to a medley of familiar hits. I found a seat at the bar and ordered a beer.

For some inexplicable reason AbbaTastic's set included *Bohemian Rhapsody, Last Christmas* and *the Fast Food Song.* Small children ran amok at my feet whilst their parents sat at the tables scattered around the stage and sang along tunelessly. I noticed Rox sporting a straight blonde wig trying desperately to cajole the drunken audience to their feet. I picked up my camera and fired off a few frames just to keep everyone happy. Rox winked at the lens.

The show ended with a shower of confetti. After a few minutes Rox skipped up to the bar and started babbling at me like a hyperventilating cheerleader. I passed her a bottle of water.

"Thanks," she said and drained the bottle. "Needed. That. Phew!"

I smiled and watched her calm down. The heavy stage make-up made her look vaguely alien.

"I've always fancied taking the blonde one from Abba out for a drink," I said. "Jim couldn't fix it when I wrote him a letter. Well, to be honest, I sent him three thousand letters but he ignored them all. Can you believe that? Cost my parents a small fortune. After that I had a plan to kidnap the whole band and keep them in a cupboard. But I was too young to buy tickets for the show. Ridiculous!"

Rox laughed and tapped my shoulder.

"In that case," she said, "you're in for one hell of a night! I'll see you in the car park in fifteen."

She hopped off the bar stool and headed back-stage. I packed up my camera and left some coins on the bar. The barman nodded gratefully. No one ever tipped at all-inclusive hotels.

Rox appeared from the staff entrance still wearing the short, white, sequinned stage outfit.

"Thought I'd stay in character," she giggled. "I'd hate to shatter your fantasies or anything. Do you want me to talk in a Swedish accent?"

I groaned.

"No!"

"Good. I'd just sound like a muppet. Where are we going?"

I passed her a cigarette and turned the key in the ignition.

"I know a place up in the mountains where we can drink all night until we die."

She grinned.

"Excellent! Exactly the right answer. Let's go!"

We headed out of the car park and onto the main drag.

"I have to stop somewhere first," I said. "It won't take long."

We turned inland just south of Skataki and left the lights of the East coast far behind. We drove in silence through the black mountain forests. Rox hadn't said a word for some time. By the time we got to the Kittyhawk club she was in a bad way.

I pulled into the car park and switched off the engine. Marcus squawked like a banshee somewhere close by.

"Don't worry," I said. "That's just Marcus. He's a goose."

I helped Rox out of the car. I had to carry her into the bar. It was as if she'd lost the use of every basic motor system. She moaned as I gently placed her at a table in the corner. Tommy and Gina waved. Honey was barefoot as usual. She came over and smiled.

"Is that one of Abba?"

"Yes," I replied. "It's the drunk one from Abba. She's been partying a little too hard but she'll be ok."

"Ok," said Honey. "If you're sure. I'll get you a beer."

"Thanks, Honey."

I looked around the Kittyhawk and noticed a few familiar faces. The local village priest sat in one corner playing backgammon with a guy wearing a Motorhead t-shirt. A German biker and speed-freak I knew only by the name of Hans was pumping coins into the jukebox. A couple of young kids from town sat at the bar chatting with Tommy.

Honey returned with a bottle of beer. Gina followed clutching a bottle of tequila and sat down beside me.

"Seriously, Cal," she said. "Do you want a fucking goose or not? The stupid bird is driving us all insane."

I laughed.

"Still no, I'm afraid. But I'll have a shot of tequila."

Gina stared intently at Rox as she poured a couple of shots.

"Is that one of Abba?" she said.

"Yes," I said. "The blonde one."

Gina nodded and patted my leg.

"Good for you, Cal. Good for you."

"Thanks, Gina."

She stood up and walked rather unsteadily back to the bar. She said something to Tommy and they both laughed. Tommy looked over and gave me the thumbs-up. I raised my glass and grinned. Rox slumped against my shoulder.

We stayed until dawn. I didn't really know what to do with Rox. Getting her out of the Kittyhawk was going to be difficult because by now I was a little drunk. She was still breathing but her face was ghostly pale. Rox couldn't walk because I'd broken both her feet with a heavy wooden bat. They were black and swollen under the table. In fact Rox couldn't move at all because the splintered tip of a pick axe was still lodged in her spine. It was a problem. A big problem.

Eventually, however, Tommy and Gina disappeared outside to discuss Marcus' fate in private. I quickly drained my glass and hauled Rox upright. I managed to half-drag and half-carry her to the car before anyone noticed. I slammed the door shut, said farewell to Tommy and Gina and drove out into the misty morning. It was going to be another hot day.

After about six kilometres I pulled off the road and buried Rox in a shallow grave. I drove home. I was exhausted.

8

WEDDING

Late one afternoon Kat and I took the dogs out for a run on Magda beach. It was hitting 46 degrees during the day. You could taste the heat in the back of your throat. It was a scorched, funereal kind of heat that baked the earth and melted the tarmac. It was always the same during July and August.

We found Jesus sitting on a rock at the far end of the beach. He was strumming an acoustic guitar whilst his girlfriend curled up at his feet. Jesus wasn't his real name. His real name was Anders and he was a Norwegian boat-bum. He just looked a bit like the Son of God. Jesus was pretty useless. He was tall and tanned and lithe and could play absolutely anything on his guitar so long as it had been written by Neil Young. He was only 25 years old yet claimed no affinity whatsoever with any music written after he was born. Modern pop music, he insisted, was performed by vain-glorious clowns, charlatans and puppets. Modern pop music had no soul.

Young people like Jesus are so fucking lame. He didn't have a cent to his name. He survived on Mikki's unswerving devotion and charity during the long summer months. During the winter he drifted off to the Caribbean and crewed ostentatious motor yachts for the Italian aristocracy in exchange for free food and accommodation.

Essentially Jesus was just another young hippy boy on the island with razored cheekbones and honey-popsicle eyes.

Mikki adored Jesus. She was addicted to his soppy songs, his scrunch-dried straw curls and his rather childish sense of Scandinavian humour. She was a few years older than Jesus. She once told us that she fled the UK seven years ago to dodge impending criminal charges for credit card fraud.

Kat and I liked Mikki. Everyone liked Mikki. She worked hard in one of the nearby boutique hotels. She had to wear a long-sleeved uniform at work to hide the little snake tattoo on one arm. The hotel's pompous Greek management frowned on any member of staff who dared to be individual. Even name-tags were banned. Staff were encouraged to be no more than anonymous faces floating silently along the marbled corridors like perfumed shadows and fragrant ghosts. Management never really grasped the irony in the fact that the hotel's clientele consisted almost entirely of super-rich Russian mobsters who proudly flaunted their intricate mafia tattoos as they sat around the infinity dip-pools and cocktail lounges drinking thick black coffee and petrol-grade vodka.

It seemed that everything in Greece had suddenly become *boutique*. There were boutique clubs, boutique villas, boutique restaurants, boutique hotels...even boutique chapels and beaches. No one really knew what it meant. It was just a word used at random to describe any service aimed at the cash-rich and snobbish rather than the bucket-economy of the all-inclusive drudges. It was a word aimed squarely at the Russians. No one else had any money.

"Hi, bro," said Jesus. "Kat?"

He laid his guitar down on the sand and stroked the top of Mikki's head. We let the dogs lick his face before unclipping their leads. They sprinted across the sand chasing freedom and within seconds had disappeared out of sight. They never went far in this heat. Most of the time I thought they enjoyed the concept of freedom more than freedom itself. Freedom was hard work for a dog.

Sure enough within a few minutes they were back by our side and lay panting heavily in the sand as the sea lapped gently at our feet. Mikki poured water from a bottle into the palm of her hand and let the dogs drink gratefully.

I smiled. The white heat of the day had cooled by a couple of degrees and the sky was golden blue. The faintest pink haze feathered the horizon.

It was a nice day for a white wedding.

The groom and guests arrived in a mini bus. Emblazoned on the side of the mini-bus in fancy purple script was the legend: Boutique Wedding Banquets & Married Treats. The bus was owned and operated by Stefanos the Duke. Stefanos also owned a nearby taverna called the Wild Weston. The bar had been decorated along the lines of an old western frontier saloon complete with wagon wheels and replica firearms. Stefanos himself always dressed like John Wayne. He wore a white Bailey Nervo Stetson, blue Wrangler jeans and a pair of genuine Ferrini cowhide boots. Stefanos the Duke once told me that he considered himself to be a cowboy born by mistake into a country run by Sioux Indians.

The mini-bus parked at the far end of Magda beach. We watched Stefanos jump out of the bus and help the wedding guests down onto the sand. The groom and best man were trussed up like little tin soldiers in waistcoats, 2-button grey suits and tan brogues. The women wore bright summer dresses and feathers in their hats. Everybody huffed in the heat. Nervous laughter drifted across the beach as the party trudged towards a ceremonial arch which stood by the water's edge. The arch had been decorated with white and pink bougainvillea. We recognised one of the local wedding planners waiting at the arch with a clipboard and a poisonous smile.

Weddings in Greece were huge business. The appeal of escaping the grey skies of northern Europe for a package wedding in the sun was easy to understand. The blue skies and sunshine, however, came at a cost and romance was seldom included.

Wedding planners on Kolasios were a jealous, venomous clatter of self-important matriarchs and fraudsters. They guarded their fairy kingdoms with breath-taking arrogance and duplicity. They sat on imaginary thrones in their commercial caves surrounded by white muslin and ivory lace and images of fantasy bridal dream-scapes. They knew that all princess brides have the mental age of six. Brides were chaperoned through consultations like little children with their pushy moms at ballet schools for the retarded. Prices for extra touches such as flowers, musicians, boat trips and champagne were inflated through the stratosphere by the queen bitches of commerce and then handed back to simpering parents with blood-sucking smiles.

The relationship between wedding planners and their favoured service providers could be strained. Strong-arm tactics could sometimes prevail. We knew of one Scottish wedding planner who once threatened to burn down the house of a Greek cake-maker if he provided any more cakes for a rival planner. The Wedding Wars might have been fought on caramel beaches by saccharine assassins but they were violent and cut-throat nonetheless.

Kat, Mikki and I sent Jesus over to the little kiosk on the beach for beers. He returned with four cold bottles of Fix and we settled down on a rock to watch the show.

The groom and best man were arranged by the wedding planner so that they stood facing the sea. It was Greek custom that the groom should not see the bride's arrival. The wedding party stood in a semi-circle in the sand. There was no shade. A couple of guests fanned themselves with paper napkins. The wedding planner shielded her eyes against the sun and everybody waited patiently for something to happen.

After a few minutes we saw the local registrar from Kavindos town hall potter down the road towards the beach on his old scooter. Vangelis was a miserable little man who treated every tourist wedding as some kind of huge intrusion into his daily routine. He received extra money for beach weddings outside Kavindos but they clearly made his life an unholy chore. As well as his civic duties, Vangelis also ran the local DVD store in Elythia. He was merely a ceremonial token at non-Orthodox weddings which had already been rubber-stamped by the town hall.

Vangelis was typically unshaven and poker-faced. He parked his scooter near Stefanos' mini-bus and strolled across the beach towards the wedding party carrying a small leather briefcase. He ignored the groom and guests completely, nodded curtly at the wedding planner and stood with his arms folded waiting for the bride. Every few seconds he would tut and glare at his watch. Tourist weddings ran to a tight schedule. Generally the registrar allocated six minutes per wedding. It had already been at least 10 minutes since the groom and guests had first arrived on Magda beach and there was still no sign of the bride.

"Five euros says the bride's changed her mind," said Mikki.

Kat snorted.

"Fifty euros says the bride's too fucking fat to get into her dress!"

Jesus frowned and was about to say something to Kat but wisely changed his mind. Kat and Mikki chinked their bottles of Fix. The beer was already warm. The groom was getting twitchy and kept mopping his forehead with a handkerchief. One of the older women in the party walked over to the wedding planner and wagged a finger. The wedding planner raised both hands as if to surrender to events beyond her control. It was, after all, a bride's prerogative to be a selfish horse and leave her wedding guests and fiancé standing around in the scorching sand like sun-baked turtles.

Just as Vangelis the registrar looked like he was about to give up on the whole charade, we heard car horns blaring from the main road. It was a common fanfare in Greece and usually signalled a bride's arrival. Or victory for the local football team. Or the death of an important politician. Or the start of the fruit-picking season. In fact the sound of car horns blaring could mean practically anything in Greece. That afternoon, however, the fanfare did indeed herald the arrival of the ridiculous bridal procession.

The bride wore what appeared to be a large white cloud. It was difficult to tell not only from this distance but also because she was sitting side-saddle on a donkey. The donkey wore a straw hat and was led gingerly down the hill towards the beach by an old man. The five bridesmaids wore matching purple outfits and followed the bride on separate donkeys. A younger man with a stick followed the group. We could hear him yomping and grunting at the donkeys to keep them in line. A local violinist walked alongside the procession whilst a Greek photographer ran around the group snapping random shots with a cheap Canon camera. A white rental car driven by a distinguished-looking man with white hair followed the donkeys at a discreet distance. We guessed he was the father of the bride who had wisely opted out of the circus. Donkeys were uncomfortable, undignified and stank like sewers.

The four of us sat and watched the animals' laborious progress in awe.

"Outstanding!" said Kat. We had to agree.

The six donkeys, two minders, one violinist, photographer and rental car eventually made it to the beach. The bride and bridesmaids giggled as the minders helped them awkwardly dismount. The bride wore a sickly, serene expression to suggest that she had just been delivered to her betrothed by pixie spirits and choirs of heavenly angels rather than a flea-ridden donkey wearing a stupid straw hat.

The distinguished man with white hair took the bride's hand. The bridesmaids took up position in front of her like five purple skittles and together the group set off slowly across the sand. One of the bridesmaids was taller than the rest. The other four girls were as dumpy and squat and moon-faced as the bride. The tallest bridesmaid, however, carried herself like runaway royalty. A daring blue streak in her hair caught the sun. I smiled to myself. She looked like magnificent trouble.

The bridal group joined the rest of the wedding party and the bride was handed over to the groom. They were instructed by the wedding planner to turn and face Vangelis who read a brief welcome from a laminated sheet of paper, jabbed a finger at the best man to hand over the rings and then told the couple to kiss beneath the arch. Everybody clapped. The registrar thrust some papers at the couple to sign, slipped these into his briefcase without a word and strode back across the sand towards his scooter with a face like thunder. After probably months of preparation, thousands of euros and countless tantrums the whole ceremony had lasted maybe three minutes.

The wedding party, however, seemed delighted. The violinist began to play. The wedding planner snapped her fingers and summoned the Greek photographer for the official portraits. He arranged the bride and groom beneath the arch so that they were facing the bright sun and then seemed to get angry because they kept squinting like piglets. He pushed them around for a while until everybody was more comfortable and then spent maybe a million years fussing over the bride's voluminous dress. The couple looked stiff and awkward as they posed for photographs that would probably hang sadly over the mantelpiece in a dark little house a long way from Magda beach.

The rest of the party stood chatting in groups. The tall bridesmaid with the blue streak in her hair stood apart near the water's edge. She seemed graceful and aloof. I watched her idly pick the petals from her bouquet. Every now and then she would glance at the groom when she thought no one was looking.

It's a tradition at Greek weddings for the guests to line up and congratulate the happy couple. The British were never comfortable with such formal intimacy but they obliged nonetheless in the spirit of the occasion. The father of the bride kissed his daughter on the cheek and shook the groom's hand. The best man followed. One of the older women with a feather in her hat dabbed her eyes and hugged the beaming bride before kissing the groom and squeezing his arm. The violinist continued to play in the background as the line of guests gradually dwindled. After a while only the five bridesmaids remained.

"Sweet," said Mikki.

Kat and I stood up slowly and tugged gently on the dogs' leads. They yawned. I tried to roll a cigarette in the breeze whilst keeping one eye on the wedding. The guests began to drift slowly up the beach towards Stefanos' coach. The tall bridesmaid was the last in line. She bent forward and pecked the bride on the cheek. As she moved towards the groom, however, all hell suddenly broke loose.

The bride launched herself at the tall bridesmaid and knocked her to the ground. The groom instinctively recoiled in shock and tripped over his own feet. The wedding guests stopped and spun around to see the bride and bridesmaid wrestling in the sand like furious tumbleweeds. They were screaming and swearing, lashing out with claws and talons in clouds of sand. The groom picked himself up, dusted himself down and tried to intervene. The bride kicked him sharply in the shins and he fell to one knee in pain.

The best man arrived at the scene and grabbed the bridesmaid's arm. The bride took a split second to recompose herself before landing a punch on the side of her bridesmaid's head. The best man let go of the bridesmaid and held the palm of his hand out towards the bride.

"Enough!" we heard him shout.

"Fuck off, Gaz!" the bride yelled back and hurled herself once again at the bridesmaid. They continued to screech and scratch and scream in the sand as the younger guests ran back to help. The Greek photographer could barely believe his luck. He crouched down, pointed his camera at the tangle of limbs in the sand and managed to grab a couple of quick shots before the best man knocked him unconscious with a single punch.

The four remaining bridesmaids hiked up their purple dresses and waded into the chaos with brutal intent.

"Fucking slag!" one of them spat whilst aiming a kick at the tall bridesmaid's face. She missed the tall bridesmaid but connected with the bride's chest instead. The bride howled in agony and grabbed her assailant's hair.

The four of us sat back down on the rock. We barely dared to blink.

It was a typically disorganised brawl. The wedding planner ran around waving her clipboard in the air like a banshee. The old women with feathers in their hats stood rooted to the spot and watched the commotion in horror. The donkeys – who had been waiting patiently to be led back to their fields - began to fidget nervously. Stefanos the Duke leapt from his coach and ran towards the melee.

"Hey," he yelled. "No fighting! No fighting at the Duke's wedding!"

The violinist continued to play in the background as if this was all perfectly normal.

After several minutes the show began to wind down. Everyone agreed a truce. It was too hot to fight. The best man pulled the bride to her feet and they limped slowly back towards the coach. She was sobbing uncontrollably. The groom followed looking shame-faced and shaken. The four bridesmaids clucked around the bride like protective beetles.

The tall bridesmaid stood up slowly in the sand. Her dress was torn and her hair dishevelled but nothing had been broken except her dignity and grace. She made her way down to the sea and washed her bruised hands in the salt water before setting off after the others. The father of the bride waited for the tall bridesmaid at the top of the beach. As she approached he pointed to the rental car. She nodded and forced a sad smile. The distinguished old man with white hair shrugged kindly and put his arm gently around her shoulders. They walked back to the car together. We watched Stefanos' coach pull away from the beach and move slowly up the steep hill towards the main road. The little white rental car followed behind and pretty soon both vehicles had disappeared from view. The Greek photographer lay motionless where he had fallen in the sand. We didn't think he was dead. He was waiting for a round of applause. Sure enough after a few minutes he opened one eye and groaned theatrically.

We sat in silence for a while.

"Outstanding!" said Kat eventually. "Fucking outstanding!"

We laughed. Kat and I bid farewell to Mikki and Jesus and headed back to our little cottage. Later that evening I drove to the Kittyhawk club and offered to buy Marcus the goose for 50 euros. Tommy and Gina were appalled.

"No fucking way, man," drawled Tommy. "You can have the god-damn bird for free and with our blessings."

I tried to insist but Tommy and Gina would not budge. Instead I offered a compromise. I would put 50 euros behind the bar and when the cash was gone I could claim Marcus as my own.

"Deal," said Tommy.

So I now owned a giant goose called Marcus. He was the perfect machine. We all drank until dawn. It felt good to be prepared.

9

GOOSE

So for three days I kept the goose at the Kittyhawk. I didn't want to upset the bird unnecessarily. Technically it was a gander. It was male and it was a big bastard. It was always angry. Its bill was liquid black and the eyes looked as if they had been carved from flint. It was especially pissed off at that time because it was the molting season and it couldn't fly. It just ran around the yard honking and flapping like a furious bird-beast.

I never told Kat about the goose. It didn't feel appropriate and I was sure that the two would never meet. The goose scared Honey.

"You're crazy, Cal," she said one afternoon, as the bird tried to attack the wrecked helicopter around the back of the Kittyhawk.

"You're clever, but you're crazy. What are you going to do with a goose?"

I thought for a second.

"I'm going to set it free," I said. "It's a big bird. It should have a new life."

I was very well aware that the Kittyhawk was becoming my shed and my sanctuary. I went up there a lot. I went up there to get away from Kat. I went up there to get away from our bullshit day-to-day existence. I went up there to get away from tourists. I went up there to get away from ex-pats. I went up there to get away from Greeks. I went up to the Kittyhawk to get away from everyone.

I'd taken Kat up there once or twice. Everybody loved Kat. One night she danced with Honey on the tiny stage whilst Tommy and I cheered until we ached. Honey was so out of it that she could barely stand. It was a good night. But Kat understood that we both needed our space on the island. She was happy to let me potter about in the mountains if it kept me sane.

Personally I don't think I'm either clever or crazy. Some of the craziest people I've known have occasionally said the most sensible things. The cleverest people that run the world seem to come up with some pretty damn stupid notions on a regular basis. Concepts such as war and religion and stock markets and politics are not the fruits of giant intellects. They are the by-products of idiots. I was just a man caught up in the middle of it all like everyone else. I could not change the wheel of history. I could not predict the future. I had about as much chance of taming world events as I had of taming the goose. I was a lost cause. I was only human.

After three days we managed to stuff the goose into a sack. There was quite a lot of blood. Geese don't have teeth. They do, however, have serrated bills which can rip through flesh like a cheese grater. My goose also had a wingspan of about three feet. That was a lot of feathers. The goose could easily knock a man down and then saw through sinew just to prove its point. The point being that geese didn't belong in sacks. There was much hissing and spitting and bruising but eventually Tommy and I managed to get the damn thing into the bag. Once inside the sack the bird appeared to wilt and surrender. Occasionally the bag would twitch and buck but it seemed that the goose had given up the fight for the time being.

We dragged the bag to my car and placed it on the back seat as carefully as we could. I didn't enjoy driving the goose to its new home. The bag was too quiet. I thought that maybe the goose had died of a heart attack or something. It didn't look like a goose with much of a heart but you never know.

I introduced the goose to Jardine and she screamed. I suppose it was a perfectly natural reaction. The bird puffed out its sizeable chest and spread its enormous wings before strutting slowly to one corner of the little room. It dominated the space like a black hole. The goose stood perfectly still and stared at Jardine as if she and she alone had been responsible for such an undignified experience. I left the two of them alone to get better acquainted.

I drove back to the Kittyhawk and we toasted the bird's new life with beer and tequila. Tommy shook my hand. Gina hugged me warmly. It was certainly a lot quieter now that the goose – like Elvis - had left the building. In the morning I drove back to check up on the goose and Jardine. It was not a pretty sight.

After the fracas on Magda beach I ran into the bridesmaid with the streak of blue hair at Vito's Bar 69 in Kavindos. It was a tiny triangular bar tucked away at one end of the main cobbled street. It was a place to sit and watch the village trickle past. It was a warm evening but still early and the bars were quiet.

"Hi, Vito," I said.

Vito was standing alone behind his bar staring longingly at the bridesmaid. She was sitting at a table inside wearing a polka dot dress and black fishnet tights. She was his only customer. He sighed.

"*Ciao*, Cal."

Vito liked to keep everything as Italian as possible. Many Italians lived in Kavindos during the summer months. The richest had bought old Captains' Houses in the village and spent fortunes renovating them with the finest woods and marble. Some hired yachts and threw parties out in the bay for the vivacious elite. Vito, however, was neither rich nor vivacious. He hadn't been back to Italy for over 10 years but still rambled on forever about his stupid village outside Naples like it was the most beautiful place on earth. Strange and sinister forces, he insisted, kept him and his beloved village apart. Sinister forces who carried violin cases and switchblades. The Family. The Mob. Vito told everyone that he had broken the bond. The sacred oath that ties the *Cosa Nostra* together. His eyes would fill with tears as he explained to anyone who would listen why he couldn't go back to his village. Personally I thought the reason why Vito couldn't go back to his village was because he never had the fucking air fare. Bar 69 was never that busy and any profits always seemed to end up in Vito's face one way or another at the end of the night. During the winter he reeled around the village running up credit tabs in the few bars that remained open. Vito was just another stranded ex-pat who had never come to terms with his very dull existence. I was pretty sure the Mob had bigger fish to fry.

I stood at the bar for a while with a beer. A flat-screen television was playing old music videos from the 1970s. The bridesmaid seemed entranced. She had lost the princess poise I saw on the beach. Instead she looked deflated and sad. She was also very drunk. I asked Vito if he knew who she was. He sighed again.

"*Bellissima!*" he whispered. "Very beautiful."

"Right," I said.

Apparently the bridesmaid had been drinking vodka and tonics with shots of *Sambuca* since three o'clock that afternoon. I ordered more and walked over to her table to introduce myself. Just a regular guy shooting the breeze with a beautiful stranger in a Greek bar. No intrigue. No mystery.

You see, Honey? If I had been really clever I would have used a false name. I would have made something up. Something bland. John, maybe, or Dave. But I didn't. That would have been the clever thing to do. Throw in a false name to muddy any future investigation. Confuse the statements. Skew the paperwork just a little in order to undermine the reliability of any witness. But, then again, using a false name would have proved pre-meditated intent in the eyes of the law. That would have been crazy. So, Honey, strike one for logic!

The bridesmaid's name was Jardine. She was not having a good holiday.

I told her that I had seen the wedding on Magda beach. She groaned.

"I'm drinking to forget all that. What a fucking disaster!"

She told me the story over a few more drinks. I can be a good listener. The wedding party had arrived from Gatwick seven days before the ceremony. Everybody was in high spirits. None of the party had ever been to Greece before. No one really cared anyway so long as there was cheap alcohol and sunshine. They were not disappointed. It was, however, a lethal combination.

The groom had asked Jardine's brother to be his best man. They played in the same rugby club back in Croydon and had been beer-buddies since leaving school. Jardine was not related to anyone else in the party. The bride had asked her to be a bridesmaid because she didn't want Jardine to feel left out. Jardine had accepted and they'd spent many happy months together planning the wedding.

"If I see one more fucking wedding catalogue in my life...."

She left the sentence unfinished and downed another *Sambuca* shot.

Back in Croydon, she said, it had all seemed so simple. Everybody worked hard during the day and partied harder at the weekends. Everybody knew everybody else and it was a good crew. A close crew. Before the wedding was announced, however, Jardine and the groom had a brief affair.

"It was nothing, really," she told me. "Just one of those things. We was both single at the time. I didn't know he was gonna get hitched to that fat cow. She's got a lazy eye, you know? Anyway, we sent each other a few texts and the silly bastard forgot to delete them. Turns out the fat cow had checked his phone one night when they got here and went stupid. Proper bat-shit stupid! But why would you want to check your fiancé's phone just before your wedding? It's not real. I reckon she was just looking for a reason to tie him around her little finger for the rest of his natural born. Poor bastard. She'll never let him forget it. His life is over."

She shook her head slowly.

The night after the ceremony, she said, the wedding party blamed Jardine for everything. There was quite a lot of noise around the hotel pool bar. Everybody was drunk. There was some pushing and shoving. The bride ended up getting soaked. Someone threw the wedding cake at the groom.

Jardine giggled.

"A proper mess!"

Eventually she stormed out of the pool bar, packed a bag and walked out of the hotel. She left her bridesmaid's dress in the toilet. Only the bride's father – the distinguished old gentleman with white hair I had seen on the beach – had offered any support. Stan gave her some cash to tide her over in Kavindos until the charter flight back to Gatwick in a few days' time. She was dreading the journey. In fact, she said, she was thinking of re-booking her flight to avoid another bloodbath. Back at the hotel, however, someone had thrown her purse into the pool and her mobile phone was ruined. She said she was trying to contact the travel rep to make arrangements.

I listened and nodded and tried to make sympathetic comments. It did seem a little unfair to blame everything on Jardine. The groom, unless mentally deficient, wasn't entirely blameless. Jardine agreed.

"He was rubbish in bed 'n' all. Them two deserve each other. *Lazy Eye & No Dick*. Sounds like a cartoon!"

I laughed. We chatted for a while. She was pretty funny. I liked her. By now a few more people were drinking in Vito's bar. Tourists. Kat and I called them 'pebbles'. There were a million on every beach and they all looked the same.

"Anyway," said Jardine. "Enough about all that. I feel better. Tell me about yourself, James."

Sorry, Honey. I lied.

Eventually I suggested that we could meet later at the little white chapel overlooking the bay so that she could see where most people get married without incident every year.

"Thanks," she said, "I think I need that."

I told her I had a few errands to run and that I'd see her later at the chapel. Maybe an hour. I strolled around Kavindos for a while and made sure I was spotted in a couple of bars. Everybody seemed in a good mood. Even the old Greek guys who always sat at the ancient fountain with their worry beads and cigarettes seemed content. The air smelt of herbs and charcoal smoke.

Jardine was waiting for me at the chapel. She looked beautiful in the pale moonlight. We stood for a while just staring out across the bay. Several boats bobbed gently at the pier. The lights of the village reflected in the silent black water. We didn't see another soul. It was perfect.

"Are you going to kiss me"? Jardine said softly. I thought about this for a second.

"No."

Sorry, Honey.

Instead I smashed the bridesmaid in the face with a stone. I did it again. Just to make sure. Then I carried her to the car and drove up into the mountains. I parked outside the old abandoned sanatorium near the middle of nowhere. It was a ghostly building and an evil place. I sat for a while barely daring to breathe. It was so quiet. I looked up at the night sky. The stars were bright and pure.

I dragged the bridesmaid into the derelict building by her long hair. I shoved her down on the floor in one of the tiled torture cells and chained her hands to an old iron ring still attached to one wall. Presumably it had originally been fitted for that very purpose. The bridesmaid was still unconscious. Blood covered her face. I think I broke her nose.

I left her there in the dark and drove home. The following day I went back with the goose. The morning after that I drove back to the sanatorium with a beating heart. I walked carefully along the silent corridors to the little cell at the back of the building. The corridors became darker. Water dripped from holes in the ceiling. A small bird darted from the rafters and made me jump. I paused before pushing open the heavy cell door. The room was no more than five feet by four. It was a mess. I took a photograph of the scene on my mobile phone. It wasn't a very good picture. There was a lot of blood. It didn't look real. Maybe I could run the picture through some software later? Maybe it might look better in black & white? In times to come I could maybe sell it to a newspaper and make a lot of money.

The goose was sitting on the bridesmaid's chest. It ignored me completely. An eyeball hung from its beak. I took another photograph. The goose went back to work.

10

POLICEMAN

For one week every summer Kavindos played host to the *Rock On The Rock* festival. The festival took itself very seriously indeed. Every year around June a stage would be erected in the municipal car park above the little white chapel overlooking the bay. Trucks would bring the PA towers and lighting rigs down from Kolasios Town. Generators were hooked up to the village grid. Metal security barriers were placed across the dusty car park to prevent any unauthorized access. Licenses were granted for various concession stands selling everything from t-shirts to local crafts. A huge beer tent was assembled. Posters appeared across the island. It was a sizable production and one that attracted several hundred fans of Classic Rock from across Europe.

Rock On The Rock was organized by a man called Teddy Lightfoot from his home in Surrey. Teddy had made his fortune from a trucking company he later sold to an American consortium. He then moved into the real estate game which in turn brought him out to Kavindos for the very first time back in 1984. Over the years he had cultivated many contacts on the island which came in useful when the festival was first conceived. It had been a regular fixture on the island for a decade. Now in his sixties, Teddy ran *Rock On The Rock* as a money-making hobby more than anything else. Not only did he sell tickets to the festival but he also arranged travel and accommodation packages for the fans and musicians.

Teddy was quite a character. He rather fancied himself as an old-school concert promoter. Kat and I first met him at our landlord's hotel. Hercules encouraged us to use the pool bar whenever we wanted. It was a purely commercial invitation but Hercules knew no other way. We were sipping cold beers and listening to this ridiculous little man yelling into his mobile phone. It was Teddy.

"Tell Zeppelin they cannot go to Switzerland," he shrieked. "No fucking way! Just tell them. No...Bollocks...if Zeppelin go to Switzerland the I am fucked! There are no direct flights from Switzerland to this island which means I'm going to have to re-route them via Copenhagen and that will cost me a fucking fortune. If Zeppelin even mention Switzerland ever again I want you to personally shoot them all. Fuck them! I've got Bad Company and ZZ Top booked on the red-eye charter out of Doncaster. Tell Zeppelin to be on that plane like good little boys. Tell them they can look out of the window after a couple of hours and see Switzerland from a very great height. End of. Moving on...has David fucking Coverdale finished painting his front room yet?"

After maybe half an hour Teddy hung up and ordered a glass of water from Hercules' son behind the bar. He slumped into a chair next to us and mopped his brow.

"Bands!" he gasped. "Like children, really. God love 'em."

We nodded. His phone rang. He mumbled something we didn't catch. There was a pause. Then Teddy was off again at full volume.

"What? No! What's the fucking point of having Foreigner on board if half of Journey aren't going to show up? Jesus...!"

We left Teddy to his complicated world and thought no more about him. It was only days later when we saw the posters for our first *Rock On The Rock* festival that we understood the true horror of this monstrous delusion. Our hopes and expectations were instantly dashed right there on the jagged rocks of dark deception. The festival – the legendary *Rock On The Rock* festival – was no more than a fucking tribute show! Despite all the impressive hardware and staging down at the municipal car park, as well as the growing excitement in Kavindos, the festival was just a bunch of copycat gnomes and imposters pretending to be bands that most of the world had already forgotten. We were devastated.

"Holy fuck!" said Kat, reading the line-up on the poster out loud. "*ZZ Topless featuring Billy Baboon, Windy Hill, Frank Whisker & a bevy of local beauties?* What the hell is that all about?"

I stared at the poster. I was in shock. *Starship Airplane? Jukebox Heroes – featuring the songs of Foreigner & Journey?* Why would anyone want to combine those two particular bands? It was insane. That would be like adding rotten toffee to a pus-filled pancake! *AB/CD? The WhiteSnake Skin Gang?*

Naturally Kat and I had to go. We went to the opening show on Friday evening. We watched a couple of songs by a dopey, right-handed white guy pretending to be Jimi Hendrix for the benefit of a few hundred family rockers grooving sedately in rows of plastic chairs. To be honest we spent most of the evening in the beer tent. There's something about tribute acts which makes my skin crawl. If you were lucky enough to have seen Jimi Hendrix live on stage then you had your memories to treasure. If you never saw Jimi Hendrix then, you know, tough shit. Tribute shows are like inner-city farms. If you want to see a gazelle then go to Africa. Don't go to a muddy shed in Croydon expecting to be amazed by the beauty of nature. Go to a library and stare at a photograph or something.

It was at the *Rock On The Rock* festival, however, that Kat and I first met Police Captain Manolis Trelliosos. He insisted everyone call him Manni. Later we found out that Captain Trelliosos was in charge of appointing licenses for all the festival stall-holders. Naturally he had the largest stall in the car park. It was festooned with fairy lights and gaudy Greek icons. He was selling hot snacks and soft drinks as well as home-brewed *souma* and cheap Turkish cigarettes. Captain Manni was making a small fortune.

Over the years Kat and I got to know the policeman well. Some might argue that we were too close but I always maintained it was better to know your enemy than to live forever in fear. Captain Manni had been a policeman all his life. He knew no other way. Some insisted he was a corrupt, power-tripping Shylock with fingers in every island pie. Legend had it that he had also rigged every election in the village to retain his influence over the town hall and protect his varied business interests. Kat and I didn't really care. Captain Manni treated us well and even invited us to his house one year for an Easter feast of spit-roasted lamb and rabbit. We drank and danced until dawn. Mrs Trelliosos was long-suffering and very charming.

Captain Trelliosos was popular with the locals because he resolved their petty disputes and often turned a blind eye to rowdy bar owners and drunk drivers. When he was not on duty he could usually be seen cruising around the island in a brand new Toyota Hilux. He owned a lot of land. Together with the mayor of Kavindos he had shares in a holiday property company which rented out villas to summer tourists. He was very proud of those villas. Manni and the mayor had secured funding from the EU to build the villas as an environmentally-friendly project. The funds would only be released once the plans had been approved and showed that the villas would be energy-efficient and non-destructive to the local terrain. Captain Manni and the mayor were very careful to comply. The funding was approved and the houses were built. Everyone was very happy. Then they wired up the villas to the island grid and switched on all the lights, pool pumps and water boilers. The electricity bill for the heated pools alone was astronomical. At night the villas lit up the land like a funfair.

The Captain was also an important keystone to the local economy in other ways. He was able to rubber-stamp a project just as easily as he was able to block its path. He was the keeper of the stamps. He granted licenses to small businesses and ensured the smooth progress of any necessary paperwork for a nominal fee. There was always a lot of paperwork in Greece. This clandestine cash payment was described throughout Greece as the "speed tax". Paying the speed tax was infinitely preferable to the many lost and lonely years one could spend just wading through the various departments of the State's public sector.

In those early days I had no way of knowing whether Captain Trelliosos was a good policeman or just a great actor. After all there were very few crimes on the island for his small squad to actually solve. Sometimes they would be called out to investigate suspected cases of goat-rustling or illegal dynamite fishing but nothing ever seemed to stick. During the summer months they appeared to do little more than direct traffic and tourists in the main square.

Manni liked to talk at length about the time he spent in New York City as part of some police exchange programme. It was the '80s. He had been assigned to a precinct in Brooklyn and returned to Kolasios with his head full of De Niro. He came back with an accent. Suddenly everybody in Manni's squad was a "stoopit fuckin' mook!" Apparently the Big Apple's finest had also made him an honorary deputy. He still carried that little fake badge around in his wallet.

Manni also told us the funniest Greek joke.

"God comes down to earth to check up on his creation," he said, holding court in a bar with a glass of Ouzo.

"He decides to visit America. There he finds a man sitting at the side of the road. The man is weeping. 'Why are you weeping?' God asks. The man looks up and shakes his head. 'I have been drilling for oil for a very long time,' the man says. 'My land is dry and I have no food. My neighbour struck oil and he is now very rich.' God is silent for a while. Then he tells the man to go home to his family and all will be well. The following day the man wakes up to find his land spewing oil. The American man is very happy.

"The next day God goes to Germany. Again he finds a man sitting weeping by the side of the road. 'Why are you weeping?' says God.

The man explains that he can only afford a small car because his job is not well paid but that his neighbour drives a huge Mercedes and makes the man feel inadequate. 'Don't worry,' says God, 'go home to your family and in the morning you will have a new car.' Sure enough the man wakes up in the morning to find a brand new convertible Mercedes parked outside his house. He is very happy.

"Finally, God decides to visit Greece. He finds an old man weeping at the side of the road. 'Why are you weeping,' says God. The Greek man explains that he owns a donkey but that the animal is not very well. It is an old donkey. It is also the olive harvesting season and the donkey cannot carry many baskets. His neighbour, however, owns a powerful white horse that could carry many baskets at a time and would never tire or complain. 'Don't worry,' says God, 'go home to your family and in the morning you too will have a powerful steed to carry all your olives.'

"'But God,' says the man, 'I do not want a powerful horse of my own. I want my neighbour's horse to die!'"

The Captain banged the table and roared with laughter.

"That, my friends, is why Greece has a problem!"

When we moved out of Kavindos and headed up the road to our little cottage in Haraklos, Kat and I would often run into Captain Trelliosos. He would always stop and chat. I never really understood why he bothered to spare us his time. Kat was undeniably a striking woman and neither of us were typical of the ex-pats in the area. We tried to distance ourselves from the bars and cliques. Maybe Captain Manni just liked the fact that we listened to his stories. Sometimes I would visit Manni at the little police station in Kavindos. He would tell tall tales of local gossip. Once he told me how he had single-handedly managed to catch a well-known hoodlum who had fled the scene of a road accident.

"Easy," he said. "I just waited outside his mother's house until he came back for his evening meal! He was not such a bright fellow."

One day, however, Captain Trelliosos was not happy to see me. There was an unusual amount of police officers gathered inside the station. There was a lot of cigarette smoke and the sound of many telephones ringing. Such activity was not normal. The Captain was at his desk. He caught sight of me hovering at the door and waved me away. For some reason I was not welcome that day.

I overheard one word: *akrotiriasmena*

On the way home I repeated the word over and over in my head. I didn't want to forget it. My grasp of the Greek language was still pretty shameful. I asked Kat what the word meant. She thought for a while and made me repeat it several times. Then she consulted a dictionary.

"Strange," she said. "I think it means 'mutilated'."

We enjoyed a quiet evening together in the cottage with our dogs and a bottle of wine. I slept fitfully. In the morning I suggested we should move house.

11

EX-PATS

Jimmy the Stick.

Jimmy was a pensioner and a pest and a joker and a cripple. He only drank in bars with the prettiest staff. At the end of every evening he would insist they danced with him to some slow smooch on the radio so that he could touch them up. The bar staff were too polite to refuse or complain. He bought them Alcopops and gave them sweets he fished out of his musty pockets. Everybody laughed at Jimmy. He was a character. He was a lascivious old frog with oily hair and dandruff. He used his disability to bully and intimidate. He figured that no one would hit an old man who had to use a stick just to get to the toilet. The stick gave Jimmy a license to grope and leer and harass any female within his reach. The ex-pats thought Jimmy was hilarious. He was deemed harmless and rather salty. He would invite himself to a table and regale everybody with a stream of smutty blue jokes and revel in the embarrassment of his audience. Jimmy barely concealed his bile and ignorance behind the jokes. It was the comedy of petty hate. Jimmy always insisted it was just banter. Just end-of-the-pier kind of stuff. He meant no harm.

"Except the fucking blacks!" he snorted. The ex-pats all laughed.

He was a sour old man. He was Jimmy the Stick. He was a cunt.

Jimmy lived alone in one of the white houses up the road. He had never married. As far as anyone knew he had no family. He had a small pension which funded his retirement and he seemed to do no more than hobble through the local bars seeking out an audience to humiliate. He once referred to Kat as his "little German cockatoo" because she had red hair. He flapped his elbows and clucked like a chicken. Everybody laughed. So Kat stood up without a word, picked up Jimmy's stick and threw it in the sea. He was furious. He limped outside and hid behind a bush. He waited for an hour in that bush just so that he could shout abuse at Kat as we left the bar. We both laughed. Someone retrieved Jimmy's stick from the surf. We heard no more about the matter and Jimmy never said another word to either Kat or I. There was no love lost.

I was sitting in Billy's bar on the sea front one night. I was alone and flicking through an old English newspaper that somebody had left behind. There was a new barmaid working in Billy's. She was eastern European. Her name was Lena. She was very beautiful and a little nervous. Jimmy the Stick was soon pestering her with a barrage of innuendo. Billy himself was chuckling at Lena's discomfort and this only encouraged Jimmy.

"Four beers and a hand job, darlin'!" Jimmy said, pretending to unzip his flies. "Hang on, love, forget the beers! Only kidding. Jimmy's just glad to see you...look!"

He stuck his fist through his flies and waved at Lena. She blushed. I felt sorry for her. Jimmy picked up his beers. He winked at the barmaid and limped back to a table of ex-pats in the corner. Everybody laughed.

"He's an asshole," I said.

Lena smiled.

"Yes."

It was a quiet night in Haraklos. I smoked a cigarette on the promenade and waited for Jimmy the Stick. Eventually he emerged from

Billy's bar and struggled over the road to his little blue hatchback. He was whistling an old cockney tune. I waited for him to unlock the car before approaching. He was surprised to see me. His milky eyes narrowed imperceptibly. I punched him once in the throat before he could say anything. He hit the tarmac like a sack of mud.

Jimmy the Stick was a heavy bastard. It took a lot of effort to heave him into the boot. I picked up the keys and set off towards the mountains. After a few kilometres there was a lot of angry banging and thumping from the boot. The noise began to get on my nerves. So I pulled over, checked the road, opened the boot and punched Jimmy once again. He fell silent. I tied his hands and feet with plastic cable grips and continued my journey.

The mountains were dark and silent. I parked near the hole I had dug for Jimmy the Stick. It was a large, deep hole. I bundled the old man out of the boot of the car and left him wheezing and gasping on the ground. I dragged a heavy wooden crate out of the undergrowth and gently nudged it down into the hole. Then I pulled the old man over to the hole by his feet and rolled him into the crate. He was fighting for air. He was pathetic.

I tossed Jimmy's stick into the crate before securing the lid with a hammer and several heavy nails. The crate was bucking and jumping in the hole as Jimmy tried to kick himself free. It was pointless. I walked back to the car and fetched my bag. Carefully I unwrapped the road flare I had bought that morning from a chandler in Kolasios Town. I unscrewed the plastic cap at one end, tapped the ignition flint against the cap and stuffed the blazing tube into the crate through a hole I had drilled in the lid. Smoke and sparks poured from the hole. I could hear the flare fizzing and popping inside the crate. I peered into the hole and watched the sulphurous orange light burn brightly. It was like a window into hell. There was no sound from the old man. After fifteen minutes the flare expired. I shovelled earth over the crate, smoothed over the surface and then drove to Jimmy's house. I parked the car in the driveway, pocketed his papers and left the keys in the ignition.

Then I walked back across the fields to our little cottage in Haraklos by the light of the stars.

Kat was making soup. The house smelt good.

Larry.

Larry made his fortune as a sporting agent back in the 1980s. He'd enjoyed something of a career as a professional footballer in the '70s but his pot of gold was acquired later in life by trading other sportsmen between clubs for a hefty percentage. It had been a lucrative racket. Now Larry played golf every Sunday afternoon and owned a bar in Kavindos called the Churchill Arms. It was known as a British bar. Larry liked to keep it as authentic as possible. He served roast beef and mushy peas with pints of imported cider and pork scratchings. The TV screens showed nothing but Premiership football. Sporting paraphernalia hung from every inch of the ancient Greek building. Larry didn't care much for the local culture. He was the last remaining Englishman – king of a castle that he could no longer defend. The flag of St. George hung from the old oak ceiling and dominated the Churchill Arms.

Larry was worshiped by the little circle of ex-pats who hung around this sporting micro-legend like moths to a candle. He was admired for his gruff, manly, straight-talking demeanour. He had little time for the modern world which he viewed with deep suspicion. Ever since 1966 it had become a limp-wristed place, he insisted, full of benefit scroungers and immigrant scum. It was not a place in which he wished to live anymore and so he had brought his family out to Kolasios to enjoy a decent quality of life.

His wife, Jacqui, was a loud, ear-splitting banshee. She walked a high wire of ignorant indignation, small town outrage and poisonous conceit. Jacqui was deeply unlovable. Their daughter was no better. Nichola was just fat, aggressive and stupid. Simply due to the fact that

Larry had a pot of gold, the family were regarded by many as local royalty.

The king and queen lived in a huge house up in the hills which overlooked Kavindos and the surrounding area. It was a sprawling, vulgar estate complete with a miniature golf course, five-a-side football pitch and an Olympic-sized infinity pool. The house itself was stone-clad and faux-Tudor. The kitchen alone was bigger than our cottage. There was a separate outhouse for guests and an old Jaguar in the driveway. The basement games room featured a professional snooker table carved from solid mahogany, a 52" home-entertainment system and a private bar stocked with imported lagers and spirits. Larry and his cronies would spend many a happy afternoon down there in the basement whilst Jacqui and Nichola went shopping in town. In the evenings they would all reconvene on the giant, floodlit patio and sip cocktails and play charades. During the winter Larry and Jacqui would throw ex-pat parties to which we were never invited. I don't think Larry had ever forgiven Kat for both World Wars, Mercedes Benz and Franz Beckenbauer.

Occasionally Larry and Jacqui organised quiz nights and raffles in the local bar at the foot of the hill. Larry was always the master of ceremonies. Jacqui always over-dressed like a homecoming prom queen. Together they would hand out the prizes as if bestowing great magic to their loyal citizens. Quiz nights could be ruthless. Mobile phones had to be switched off. Conferring amongst team mates was hushed. Rumours that one team had enrolled a lip-reader resulted in answers being passed under tables on scraps of paper. Marking another team's score at the end of the night was a minefield. Half a point shaved off the final tally could result in victory and so any discrepancies were brutally punished. There were no heroes in battle. Only the winning team could claim the few prize pennies and a free round of drinks. Somehow Nichola always ended up on the winning team.

One night I burned down Larry's house. It was easier than I'd imagined because most of the house was made from wood. If Larry had spent just a fraction of his budget on a sensible security system then my solitary task that night would have been considerably more difficult. As it was, the trusty road flares and gasoline worked a treat. The fire was visible from Kavindos village. I joined the people piling out of the bars and restaurants and watched the flames dancing around the huge house on the hill. The fire raged for hours. Eventually the house collapsed in an enormous shower of sparks and in the morning there was nothing left except charred beams, scorched earth and the terrible smell of ruin.

No one actually died in the fire. Larry, Jacqui and Nichola escaped in their pyjamas with just a bottle of whisky as a souvenir. Larry died a week later. He had a stroke whilst playing golf. The coroner said that the stress of the fire probably induced the heart attack. He was dead before the ambulance arrived. Jacqui and Nichola bravely soldiered on but everyone could tell they were broken and defeated. After a few weeks they put the Churchill Arms up for sale and moved back to England. The fire was blamed on faulty electrics. Everyone was amazed.

The Churchill Arms is now a heritage museum for local culture. Larry is no doubt pissing bricks at this affront to his national pride. The world knows no greater fool than a fool with a flag.

Grace.

Grace was having an affair. I told Kat.

"With what?" she said. "A forklift truck?"

Grace was a big girl. She'd lost a couple of kilos since attending anger management courses last winter but she was always going to have problems with seat belts and swimsuits. Grace was having an affair with Louis Armstrong. Louis was young enough to have his own hair but certainly too old to still be living at home with his parents. Cyril and Sandra Armstrong had retired to Kolasios with Louis in tow. They gave Louis a weekly allowance to piss up the wall and Sandra brought him a cup of tea in bed every morning. Louis was an artist. Like any spoiled child with a weekly allowance he was hopeless. Yet his status as a Creative enabled him to charm the likes of Grace into believing that he was a man tirelessly suffering for his medium. It was the duty of every artist, Louis insisted, to be wildly misunderstood.

Grace was only 23 and stupid enough to fall for it all. She had the personality of a defective teenager anyway. She had a pretty moon face which was permanently hidden behind a floppy blonde fringe. Grace was embarrassed by her weight and frustrated by her shallow intellect and so took everything out on a world she imagined revolved around her giant shadow. She could be sweet and infantile but usually she was just defensive and sullen.

Grace was Terry the Squaddie's girlfriend. They had been dating for years. Grace and Terry were well-suited. He was a small man with a short fuse, a violent temper and a tiny brain. Grace was exactly the same except that she also had a fat arse. Together they grazed around the south of Kolasios like simple prehistoric beasts. Terry was a short-order cook. Grace was hooked on daytime television. It was an awkward relationship but symbiotic nonetheless. An utter cretin – just like a barnacle or a louse – depends on another cretin for survival.

It was not easy for Terry to return to the UK for one week in June to sort out some problems with his army pension. The micro-celled cretins were divided and Grace was a whale out of water. Terry left with one half of Grace's motor social functions. It was a miracle that Grace remembered to breathe let alone have an affair with a nonchalant, cosseted braggart like Louis Armstrong. He was only ever Terry's temporary replacement. Personally I thought Louis had a fucking death wish.

You could just tell by the way they played pool together in Billy's bar. Louis would cheat and Grace would giggle. Louis cheated at everything. He had the ego of a coward and hid behind his lofty aspirations like a little child. Pretty soon Grace and Louis were inseparable. They would drink alone together in a little simpering huddle, playing footsie under the table like a couple of bashful kids. It was kind of comical. They never left the bar together but Louis would sit in his parents' car outside and wait for Grace.

One evening Grace and Kat had a huge argument. It was over something stupid like Louis cheating at backgammon or something. Grace called Kat a "skinny little bitch". Kat threw a pool cue at Grace. Louis stood up and told me that my wife was being a liability. I told Louis that he could call Kat a liability only when he grew up, cut the apron strings and learned to stand on his own two feet without the aid of a baby buggy. It was quite a scene. Eventually everybody calmed down. I offered to buy Louis a vodka and tonic. He accepted. Grace snivelled and ordered a Malibu and low fat coke.

"It's a bit fucking late," Kat muttered.

The brief affair didn't last long. Terry returned from the UK at the end of that week and remained none the wiser until Grace's death a few days later. It was a shock. It was certainly a shock to me because I had planned to kill Grace myself. I had everything planned out. I was going to hang her from a tree in the mountains one night and then set fire to her. I had the rope. I had the gasoline. I had even found a suitably sturdy tree. My plans, however, were prematurely curtailed when the silly fat cow was found dead in the bath tub like some self-ish, bloated suicide. For a while I was angry. Apparently Grace had drunk herself into a coma and passed out in a puddle of tepid water and bath salts. She would have been unconscious when she drowned. It was a pointless, painless and uncomplicated death and nothing to do with me. Death could be so unfair. At least if I'd been allowed to sacrifice Grace up in the mountains then her death would not have been completely in vain. Certainly her death would have been very painful. It would also have been an event. A victory. The gods might even have smiled.

12

GHOSTS

I t was late October. Kat and I sat outside the Terrace Cafe in Kolasios Town drinking strong coffee and iced water. Kat was checking her e-mails. I was not in a good mood.

Greece was screwed. Whichever way you cut up the papers and re-arranged the news the story always remained the same. Another bailout. Another strike. Another power cut. Another petrol shortage. Another riot. Another assault. Another old religious man holed up at the feast behind the barricades. Another pointless Euro summit and another motherfucker in a motorcade. It was an old country. It was run by old men. No Greek over the age of twenty five, it seemed, really wanted anything to change. It was an empire built on nothing firmer than shifting sands and grand deceit.

I stared out across the boat yards and watched the traffic. The *Nautilus Elite* had docked earlier that morning. The cruise ship dominated the horizon like a glittering city. She was a regular visitor to Kolasios and she was enormous. She easily dwarfed the luxury yachts in the marina, the old grunting naval frigate moored nearby and the Blue Star ferry alike. You could see the *Nautilus Elite*'s twin yellow funnels from clear across town. I watched the armies of ants up there on the gleaming decks. Some jogged around the swimming pools. Some played tennis. Some stood waving at each other on the observation platforms and some just stood gazing down from the sky like pin-prick puppets.

The bravest of the brave had ventured off the ship and out from the commercial port towards the walls of the ancient Old Town. You could clearly see the targets painted onto the backs of their Hawaiian shirts. Once inside the medieval city the polite folks from Winnipeg and Wichita ran the gauntlet of cocksure waiters in the main squares waving shabby menus and shouting to be heard above the din and chaos of commerce. Grandparents, small children and even parrots were strategically deployed along the way to lure the luckless visitor into a particular establishment. It was an exhausting battle. Many had died. The Forgotten Martyrs of the Microwaved Moussaka.

Kat folded her laptop and lit a cigarette.

"Look on the bright side," she said, "your mother might die."

It was cruel but it was the truth. Not that I particularly wanted my mother to die or anything, but a good funeral would solve the impending winter malaise. A good funeral would cheer us up. It would certainly give us something to talk about.

My mother would enjoy Kolasios Old Town. She might not approve of what I had become but she would love the city's history and architecture nonetheless. Away from the tourist traps, the Old Town was a maze of cobbled streets and fairy tale squares. Little old women sold fruit and cakes from their front rooms. Stray dogs and cats limped through the alleys searching for scraps. Gypsy children wandered the bars begging for pennies with tuneless instruments. It was easy to imagine another world in the Old Town. A world in which princes rubbed shoulders with pirates, painters courted their muses and spice traders stabbed gunsmiths for their powder and brass. At night, after the cruise ships had sailed and the moon had risen above the turrets and spires, the Old Town was as quiet as a dark star.

It was unlikely, however, that my mother would ever make the trip. My sister had phoned a few days ago to tell me that Rose was not as strong as she used to be. The winters were always harsh. I really should phone her or something.

It was a beautiful day in Kolasios Town. The boat yards were bathed in golden sunshine. Kat and I had been living up here now for almost three months. My father used to say that a new address was like a new beginning. A clean slate. A chance to put the past to rest and start again. I doubted very much whether he actually believed his own words because he had been a very logical and cautious man. The idea of needlessly up-rooting from one house to another was anathema to a man who itemised his domestic bills in alphabetical order. Yet it felt that we had left the ghosts of Haraklos and Kavindos behind.

We had rented a little house in the old Italian quarter behind the university. For the first time since moving to the island we had a proper address with a street number and a letter box. Our neighbours were very old and very Greek. We could see the walls of the Old Town from our front porch and watch the sun go down behind the university campus. Kolasios Town itself was no bigger than any average market town in Europe but, compared to Haraklos, it felt like a future-world of noise and light. Even the university had an energy of protest about it that Kat and I both admired.

The beige-brick walls of Kolasios University were daubed with graffiti. Anti-establishment slogans and political posters blared from every lamp post and noticeboard. It was a long way from the miasma of village life. A small contingent of self-styled anarchists had squatted a campus building on the far side of the car park. The collective of punks and skaters and jugglers and junkies had turned the place into an unofficial commune and club house. The only objection to the squat was raised by the miserable local priest whose chapel overshadowed the ramshackle building. The authorities, however, were powerless to intervene.

Greek law states that the police cannot enter any academic premises without the consent of an elected student council. As a result most universities were no-go areas and off-limits to the police.

Riots on the mainland nearly always started at major universities before spilling out into the cities and suburbs. The initial spark of any uprising is always the most important and the most difficult to extinguish.

Not all the students were quite so disaffected with the system. The majority of them were largely drawn from the offspring of Kolasios' merchant elite and ambled around the campus with the air of those who had not been born to suffer. Academic study was simply a way to pass the time before entering the family business. Most of the students at the university looked too groomed, pampered and well-fed to scale the ramparts of social injustice. They sat in the sun outside the university canteen and sipped chilled frappes and smoothies whilst comparing mobile phones and designer labels. Nothing combats change more effectively than new money and fresh coffee.

Most weekends the student anarchists would organise free gigs at the club house. Kat and I would load up with beer and stand happily in the spray-painted building watching teenage garage bands play songs by Green Day and Rancid on the makeshift stage. It was a good scene. Some of the older guys would pass around a bucket for some cause or another and everybody would donate a few coins. It was a clatter of feedback and home-made distortion. Some kids dressed in ska and skinhead-chic with boots and braces. Others danced manically wearing wiped-out t-shirts and baggy combat pants. The bands had nothing to play for and that was a unifying rage.

It was impossible for those young bands to get any other exposure on the island. They didn't stand a chance. The live music scene in the bars and clubs was dominated by a handful of experienced musicians. It was a scene protected with malice. The older guys were happy to play the same songs by the same popular artists every night as if caught in a trance by American FM radio. This old herd had failed abroad to set the world on fire in any way and now they didn't want to dance. They just wanted to get paid. Club owners wouldn't even consider hiring an alternative because that would involve taking a risk and no one in

Greece had taken a risk since 1974. So the established scene simply rotated around itself like a fat, dead planet.

No one at the squat ever asked why two middle-aged immigrants from London would want to join their party, but Kat and I were made to feel more than welcome nonetheless. We were thrilled. Anything was better than recycled R.E.M and the over-familiar patchwork of anodyne radio hits.

For a while we lived a normal life in Kolasios Town. The house was owned by a simple Welsh woman who had left the ashes of her dead husband in a box under the stairs. We put him out on the porch with his golf clubs. It wasn't a big house but there was enough room for us and the dogs. The whole street had been built during the Italian occupation as living quarters for lower ranking officers. The light switches were made of Bakelite plastic. There were orange curtains in our tiny kitchen and a courtyard shaded by two papaya trees from Mexico. We sat outside every evening listening to the chatter of the neighbourhood.

We could walk to the shops in the New Town and run the dogs in the park over the main road. We went to the cinema for the first time in years and watched *Piranha 3-D* at midnight. Kat enrolled in two weekly Greek classes. She was determined to conquer the language.

"How difficult can it be?" she said. "It's just letters. Letters that don't make any sense, letters that don't translate into anything and letters that have six different meanings for everything anyway, but it's just letters nonetheless. I've just got to learn to re-arrange them in the right order."

We found bars and cafes hidden in the walls of the Old Town. We found sprawling markets selling fresh fruit and herbs. We drank coffee and Ouzo with garage mechanics and scrap merchants in the oily *souvlakias* behind the boat yards. No longer did we have to struggle out of the house and drive for maybe a thousand miles just to buy a light bulb or a pint of milk.

Most of the ex-pats from the south considered Kolasios Town to be another universe. A fear of anonymity kept the majority away. In a small and fragile community it was easier for the meek to be heard and the loud to be seen. The arrogant always need the oxygen of attention and most ex-pats would simply suffocate in Kolasios Town. No one would care. Recently the dreams of an idyllic island existence in the sun had been falling apart on a regular basis. The ex-pat community was dwindling. Some had returned home to find work. Some had returned home to try and sell their grand bungalows and daft business ventures. Kat and I never thought about returning home. We were home.

October turned into November and the curtain came down on another season. Kolasios took a deep breath and exhaled the toxic fumes. There was a mass exodus to the mainland. Hotels and restaurants were hastily locked down and left to fall into disrepair. Rental cars were parked in rows underneath derelict buildings. Taxis were hidden in fields. Even the little train that drove tourists around the walls of the Old Town during the summer was mothballed in the central bus station. No one, it seemed, had any desire to remain on Kolasios for a second longer than was necessary. The summer had been strictly business. Nothing personal. See you.

The island fell silent. She would hide her secrets throughout the winter under crystal blue skies and heavy storms alike. The island always hid her secrets. I spent a lot of time in the mountains. There wasn't much else to do. The trick to surviving the winter was to keep occupied. Kat and I planned to spend a few weeks photographing for an exhibition in Brussels the following year. I drove to the Kittyhawk club. Tommy was looking older.

One night he was perched on a bar stool as I pushed open the door. The place was dark and quiet. Honey was playing pool with a priest. She was barefoot as usual. The jukebox was playing Dolly Parton's *Jolene*. Tommy handed me a beer.

"Tell me, Cal," he said, "why do you stay on the island?"

It was a difficult question.

"How do you mean?"

"I mean, why this rock? This particular rock? There's a whole world out there and yet you've never left this island for almost four years. There must be something special to keep you here?"

I thought about this for a while.

"Well," I said, "I guess you are what you are, Tommy. Everybody needs to find a home. I think this island is my home now. I don't think I could ever go back."

Tommy was quiet. Honey looked up and smiled.

"Never say never, Cal" he said. "Only a dying man is allowed to say never."

I nodded. We sat in silence for a while. All of a sudden Tommy's mood seemed to brighten.

"What the fuck?" he drawled. "Listen to us. Mooching about like old men in the mud! Let's get us another beer and go find Honey some goddamn shoes!"

In December the university squat burned down. It happened late one night and in the morning there was nothing left except a pile of smoking rubble and the stench of kerosene. Luckily the squat had been empty at the time of the blaze. The anarchists blamed the fascists. The fascists blamed the communists. The communists blamed the merchant elite. There was a lot of talk about recriminations and vendettas. Ultimately, however, the only real benefactor of the disaster was the miserable old priest next door. By some remarkable coincidence, within days of the fire a corrugated metal fence had been erected around the site and work began on a fancy new extension to the chapel. God really did move in mysterious ways. The anarchists staged their final free concert in the university quadrant.

Kat and I celebrated Christmas Day on the beach. We drank wine from plastic cups and watched the sun go down behind the Turkish mountains in the distance. On New Year's Eve we went to a bar in the

Old Town and ate pizza with three brothers from Baltimore. At midnight we braved the cold to watch the firework display over the moonlit harbour. The sound of church bells rang out across the town. We stamped our feet to keep warm as total strangers handed us shots of whiskey and homemade cakes. It really was a beautiful island. We went to bed that night feeling happy and full of hope.

In the morning we awoke to a message from my sister on the answering machine and the news that my mother was dead.

13

FAMILY

The flight to London was uneventful. I left Kolasios on the little commuter jet to Athens as the sun rose proudly over the Aegean. Later that day, as the scheduled flight from Athens banked steeply over Windsor Castle and dipped towards Heathrow, I recognised the familiar patchwork landscape of gunmetal green fields and grey suburban streets. I enjoyed flying. There was still a tiny, minuscule grain of glamour attached to the concept of speeding through the skies drinking coffee and dreaming of a destination far away.

The plane touched down in a cloud of spray. The Greek cabin crew wrapped themselves in coats and scarves before opening the doors. I was greeted by an icy blast as I stepped out of the aircraft and set off along the endless miles of connecting tunnels towards immigration. I was nervous. After four years spent living on a Greek island I had long forgotten how to face official scrutiny with any conviction.

The immigration officer flicked open my passport and looked up at me with a stern expression.

"What is the purpose of your visit to London today, sir? Business or pleasure?"

"A funeral," I said.

The officer nodded, scanned my passport and handed it back.

"Bit of both then, sir," he said. "Welcome back to the United Kingdom."

I felt like cheering as I walked through the customs hall and into the arrivals concourse. The noise was overwhelming. I picked up a copy of the local London newspaper and smiled at the front page. SACK THEM ALL! screamed the headline above a photograph of the Prime Minister. Back in Greece the editor would have been shot before the ink had even dried.

I collected the keys to something cheap and Japanese from the car rental kiosk inside the terminal. A courtesy bus drove me to the car park on the far side of the airport. A vicious wind whipped across the acres of dull municipal tarmac. It began to drizzle. For some reason I had ordered a car with a sun roof. I shivered as I fiddled with the keys and glanced up at the swollen clouds rolling across the miserable charcoal sky.

It was already getting dark as I joined the traffic on the capital's orbital motorway. The little car was warm and hummed along smoothly behind the kaleidoscope of tail lights which stretched out in front of me for mile after mile. After a while I left the motorway and headed south towards the coast. The local London radio signal began to fade. I stopped for petrol and chocolate at a service station in the middle of nowhere. The young cashier was bored and keen to please.

"Bad weather," he said. I nodded.

"Have you come far?"

"Greece," I replied.

"Wow!" said the cashier. "You've driven all the way from Greece?"

I laughed.

"No. I've just flown into Heathrow. I left Greece this morning. On a plane."

The cashier grinned and handed me a receipt for the petrol.

"If I lived in Greece you'd never get me off the beach," he said. "Have a safe journey,"

I pushed on through the relentless drizzle until I reached the Drive Inn motor lodge just outside Arundel. I parked outside reception and sat for a moment listening to the engine tick as it cooled and the patter of rain on the roof. The Drive Inn shared a car park with a plastic family pub on one side and a neon-lit diner on the other. I counted just three vehicles scattered in the shadows. The lodge itself was shapeless and anonymous. It didn't look like much fun but it served a purpose. It was a convenient bed for a few nights. I couldn't face staying with my sister in Brighton. We had never been that close.

The receptionist looked up as I pushed open the glass door. A gust of wind ruffled a few papers on her desk.

"Damn!" she said. "That always happens."

She was a middle-aged woman with a kind face and a neat smile. She wore a rather pointless blue uniform that matched the carpet as well as the abstract pictures on the wall. It was obviously a corporate theme. The tiny reception area smelt of air freshener and cheap floor polish. I watched her type my details into a computer to confirm the booking. I wondered whether she liked her job. Did she have a husband somewhere nearby? Or was she recently divorced and stepping out into the employment jungle for the first time in years – grateful for the income and the independence? I stared at her name tag. Hello Brenda.

The room was compact and stuffy. There was a bed, a kettle and a bathroom. I pushed the window open as far as it would go, rolled a cigarette and exhaled through the tiny slot. I was too tired to care whether anyone was out there snooping around in the dark. Let them tear my lungs out. See if I cared.

It was getting late. After a shower I went to the pub next door. The place was bland and cavernous. Cheap paintings of Arundel hung on the walls alongside posters advertising meal deals and local ales. I ordered fish and chips from the menu and a bottle of beer.

I sat down in a corner booth and phoned my sister. Liz had organised the whole funeral herself and that, I suspected, was something I would not be allowed to forget in a hurry.

"Where are you?" she asked.

"I'm in a pub waiting for some fish and chips."

I listened to one long second of disapproving silence.

"Yes, well, just don't turn up tomorrow with a hangover," said Liz. "The service starts at ten thirty and I want us both to be there early to greet people. By the way, we're singing hymns."

I groaned.

"I don't sing hymns, Liz. You know that."

"Well, just open your mouth and mumble something. You don't have to sing the words."

The barman appeared with a plate of food that looked as if it had been incinerated in hell.

"My fish and chips have sort of arrived," I said. "See you tomorrow."

"See you, Cal," said my sister. "I mean it, don't turn up hungover."

I glanced at the till receipt.

"I doubt that very much indeed."

The battered slab of cod was as crisp as concrete and tasted of salt. I stabbed a few chips but the plate was a hopeless case. I rolled a cigarette and skulked just outside the front doors like a refugee. The rain had stopped. The streetlights threw a sickly orange glow across the glittering car park. I could hear the rhythm of the dual carriageway in the distance.

It felt strange. I missed Kat already. I missed our house and the dogs and the golden chaos of our ridiculous little island which lay mournful and quiet almost two thousand miles to the south. My mother had died just one week shy of her eighty fourth birthday. Not a bad innings, people had noted, as if Rose's life had been little more than a game of cricket. I never thought it was particularly helpful to measure the success of someone's life by how long they had survived. Just because one person was prised from the planet before another didn't make anyone's life less important. Death was just a fleeting moment of destruction. Kurt Cobain was no more a hero than my father. My father had a greater intellect and better shoes. Cobain had better timing and more guns.

The barman rang last orders on a brass bell and began to clear away the empty glasses. It had been a long day. I was exhausted. I headed back to my room, turned off the lights and sat on the window sill smoking a final cigarette. I set an early alarm on my mobile phone and fell asleep to the sound of the radio in the room next door.

My mother's funeral was a damp and chilly affair. I wore my father's overcoat and scarf with a white, Nero-collared shirt, pin-striped trousers and 12-hole Doc Martens boots. It was the smartest outfit I could assemble from my meagre island wardrobe. I met my sister, her effeminate husband and their nine year old son at the tiny church in a pretty village just a few miles outside Chichester. Liz wore a black suit with a silk shawl which made her look older and more severe than I remembered. We rubbed our hands together to keep warm and chatted through clouds of condensation. My young nephew studiously handed out song sheets as the family began to arrive.

My mother's relatives were a disparate group. I recognised my roguish old uncle Arthur as he strode up the gravel path towards the chapel flanked by his fourth wife and youngest daughter. My cousin Samantha had made her fortune from some dubious pyramid scam in the City and today looked every inch the sleek, sassy assassin in her black, fake fur coat and spiked red heels. They were followed by a cantankerous aunt who had frittered her savings away on the dogs and now lived nearby in one of the alms houses built by the church for the bereft and destitute. Aunt Viv was a tough and humourous old boot. She walked in front of her sister who had emigrated to Canada and married a fat man whose company made fridge magnets and mousetraps. Aunt Jane was a pointed, owlish woman with horn-rimmed spectacles and a timid voice.

Other relatives appeared through the freezing mist. My mother's younger sister Joy gave me a warm hug. She had sensibly moved to Germany in the early seventies, married a lawyer and currently worked as a translator in the European parliament. Aunt Joy kept herself removed from the family circus, preferring instead to cackle heartily from the side lines. She was a clever, quiet woman with a mischievous sense of humour. I had always considered Aunt Joy to be an ally. Her German husband was a stiff and fidgety man with a blunt vocabulary and impeccable manners. Their teenage son Rolf had died some years ago after falling into the river Rhine. His body had never been recovered. Joy had fought hard to successfully overturn a verdict of suicide and never spoke about the tragedy to anyone again.

It was quite an occasion. Friends from the village mingled awkwardly with my mother's wayward family. Some brought flowers. Some shook my hand and offered their condolences. The old church smelt of faded incense and mothballs. The priest gave a reading and described Rose as a colourful woman and a valued member of the community. I heard Aunt Viv cough loudly in a nearby pew. The two sisters had never agreed over anything. The situation had exploded a long time ago when Viv sold their mother's house to pay off a fearsome gambling debt. It had been the last straw for my mother and resulted in a brittle Cold War between the two of them which had lasted for years.

My nephew sung a song about a frog in a trembling falsetto. Liz beamed proudly in her seat as the congregation clapped politely. I stood up and bowed my head as hymns were sung and prayers recited. The priest's voice was a toneless drone and the service itself seemed to last forever. My eyes grew heavy and the back of my neck began to itch. After maybe forty minutes, as the organist struck up some baleful lament, my mother's mahogany coffin was picked up and carried slowly out of the church by six burly undertakers. Liz and I led the procession through the neat little cemetery between rows of ancient headstones. Rose was buried next to my father under an old apple tree. My sister and I threw a handful of gravel onto the casket as it was lowered by ropes into the grave. After a few words the priest closed his bible and smiled benignly. The congregation began to disperse.

I hung back for a moment and stared into the godless, muddy hole. If only we could all be buried with our secrets intact. It was a liberating thought. Kolasios would keep my secrets safe until she sank in shame. Right now I could disappear and simply never return. I didn't have to go back. Kat would be distraught and that would be unfair. I would feel bad. But Kat and my sister would soon tire of the search if no clues were ever unearthed. There was nothing more pointless than chasing a ghost. Life was too short. I could take my secrets anywhere in the world. My mother's inheritance would provide the funds. I would have to work out a way to access those funds with my new identity. I should probably wait until the inheritance was transferred into my account before withdrawing everything in one lump sum. The bank would be suspicious. Fuck the bank!

Right now I needed a master plan. I needed a plan so fool-proof and watertight that the greatest detectives in the land would never be able to unravel its mysteries. It would have to be a snake-headed hydra of deception and duplicity. By the plan's very nature I would have to work alone without the aid of any accomplice. I would have no safety net. If my plan ever began to crack then I would plummet back to earth like a broken bird. I would rather take my own life.

The cemetery was a desolate place. I walked back alone to Rose's little house in the village where the family had gathered for canapés and wine. My plan would have to wait. Fortune rarely favoured the hasty and I had all the time in the world. The cottage was warm and homely. I watched my aunts and uncle circle around each other like scorpions. Beneath the smooth surface of shallow bonhomie there was an undertow of resentment and rivalry which was hard to ignore. For the sake of circumstance they had obviously called an awkward truce but it was uncomfortable nonetheless. Only my cousin Samantha seemed able to flit between the factions with any confidence. Together we designated the kitchen a smoker's zone and held our cigarettes under the oven's extractor fan.

"Smoking's harmless," Sam said, "it's the small talk that'll kill us."

We sat on the counter and swung our feet as we smoked. Sam was four years younger than me. Her long black hair framed an angular face and magnetic green eyes. Without her red heels and fur coat she reminded me of the tiny gothic princess I had known as a teenager.

We were joined in the kitchen by Joy and the family solicitor. Donald Timms was an avuncular, pastry-faced man. He shook my hand and suggested I might want to stay in the country until the reading of my mother's will before returning to Greece.

"It would certainly be of interest for you and Liz to attend," he said. "Your mother's will was relatively simple and so the whole thing shouldn't take too long."

He passed me his business card.

"Call me in a day or two and I'll arrange everything."

"How exciting," said Joy, stubbing out her cigarette in the saucer that we were using as an ashtray. "You see, Cal, every cloud and all that."

She followed Donald Timms back to the front room. Sam and I sat alone in the kitchen listening to the muted conversations and occasional hoots of laughter.

"So what are your plans?" she asked. "You want to come up to London and stay with me for a while?"

I dragged on my cigarette and glanced at my cousin.

"Really?"

"Sure," she said. "Why not? There's plenty of room and it would be good to catch up after all these years. Anyway, let's face it, you'll die of boredom in that motel."

I smiled. She wrote her phone number on the back of the solicitor's card and jumped down from the counter.

"Call me," she said brightly. "Anytime."

After a couple of hours I managed to duck out of the party blaming jet lag from the previous day's journey. I told my sister I would see her in a few days at the reading of Rose's will. Later that evening I phoned Kat from my motel room.

"How's it going?"

"Deathly," Kat said. "Simply deathly. How was the funeral?"

"Similar," I replied. "I left my family drinking wine and arguing over the spoils of war. The solicitor is reading the will in a couple of days so I might stay on for a while."

"Come back rich or come back dead," Kat said cheerfully.

The following afternoon I called Samantha, checked out of the Drive Inn and headed north towards London. The skies had cleared overnight and the air was cold and brittle. I was glad to leave the endless green fields and strangled, sleepy villages behind. Power lines crackled overhead. The tapestry of the countryside began to slowly unravel as I approached the city's dormitory suburbs and soon I had disappeared into the familiar, pulsing arteries which fed the capital's beating heart.

14

My cousin's address turned out to be a riverside wharf conversion just north of Greenwich. I parked the rental car next to a row of sleek German convertibles and looked up at the building. The three-storey, red brick Victorian grain depot was a slick development. The original iron winches remained intact on the side of the building and hung ominously in silhouette above the renovated loading bays like gallows against the blue sky. Balconies groaned under the weight of flower baskets and wind chimes. Even the vintage Vespa VBB scooter standing outside the entrance looked as if it had been placed there purely for ornamental effect.

The old storehouse was one of many similar buildings along the river to have been saved from demolition by an army of sharp-eyed property speculators. The area had changed dramatically over the years. The stagnant, oily waters of the creeks and canals had long since served their purpose as commercial tributaries. Russian yachts now docked in modern marinas built from the silt banks and mudstone on which the rotten cargo barges had once run aground. Factories that had produced everything from weapons for the empire to leather aprons for the meat market porters were now prestigious properties for the city's bachelor elite. The good old boys from the

Creek-side smuggling gangs had been consigned to folklore. These days the pirates of the 21st century wore pink, pin-striped shirts as they looted helpless postcodes from the back of glossy magazines.

Samantha buzzed me into the building and answered the door to her third floor apartment wearing a skinny red t-shirt and black leggings. She held one hand over a mobile phone and kissed me on the cheek.

"Sorry," she said, "got to take this call. Make yourself at home."

The open-plan loft was bright and spacious. I put my bag down on a long, blue sofa as Sam spoke rapidly on the phone in a language I guessed to be eastern European. The place was sparsely but tastefully furnished with a mixture of cold chrome fittings, unvarnished wood and warm fabrics. A huge framed movie poster for *Run, Lola Run* hung on one bare brick wall beneath a metal spiral staircase leading to a mezzanine level. Piles of books, Cds and magazines were stacked neatly on the floor next to a spot-lit kitchen with a breakfast bar and red vinyl stools. Potted indoor plants and a bamboo screen separated the office area in one far corner of the ground floor. Nothing, however, could detract from the panoramic views which dominated the entire apartment. I stared out across the great river towards London's postcard skyline as the setting sun caught the glass towers of Canary Wharf. For a moment the whole city seemed to reflect the burning sky.

"What do you think?" said Sam.

I turned from the window and grinned at my cousin.

"No pinball machine? I thought it was the law that every wharf conversion in London had to have a pinball machine somewhere? And a mountain bike. And a dead Cockney gangster buried in the foundations."

Sam laughed and headed for the kitchen.

"Yeah, well, no pinball machine, I'm afraid, but Phil Collins and Sade are popping round for tea in a minute. Yuppie icons work on rotation, you know? Yesterday the whole of Dire fucking Straits turned up and played *Money For Nothing* at me. It was really inconvenient. You want a drink?"

She returned with a can of beer from the fridge and curled up on the sofa.

"It's a company lease," she said. "I don't pay as much rent as you might think. I certainly don't own the place. Oh, that reminds me..."

She reached into the bag at her feet and handed me a set of keys.

"Spares. Just in case I'm not here and you want to go out or something. Don't forget to double-lock the front door."

I nodded and put the keys in a pocket.

"So who owns the building?"

"Villains," Sam replied in a flash. "Villains with shooters."

She held my gaze with her emerald eyes.

"Really?"

"No, not really," she said, throwing back her head and hooting with laughter. "To be honest, I've no idea who owns the building. The company I work for leases it from another company who probably leases it from another and so on...blah-blah-blah. I doubt very much whether any of them are related to Harold Shand!"

I smiled.

"Sounds like Greece."

It was getting dark. I glanced out of the factory windows. The cityscape on the horizon was a black ocean studded with a million white diamonds and laser beams. Sam stood up and stretched. She had the body of a ballerina. I watched her walk to the fridge to fetch another beer. Despite her elfin beauty and obvious good fortune, as far as anyone in the family was aware Sam had remained resolutely single. The apartment itself was strangely androgynous. It was neither masculine nor feminine. It was almost as if the place had been styled by a computer. The loft was undoubtedly elegant and impressive but there was little to indicate that it was actually a home. It was too orderly and precise. It felt more like a luxury hotel. The music, movies and magazines on the floor looked as if they had been ordered from a pop-culture catalogue. Even the unopened packet of Gold Label Lavazza coffee on the breakfast bar seemed to be no more than a prop.

Sam handed me the beer and switched on a row of chrome birdie spotlights hanging from a gantry secured to the ceiling beams. The living area was bathed in a soft, diffused glow. I felt like an actor on stage awaiting his cue from the wings. We talked about the funeral for a while. Sam asked if I had any plans for my inheritance. I shrugged.

"I hadn't really thought about it. I don't even know what half a house is worth. I guess I'll find out when they read the will in a couple of days."

Sam suggested I invest the money overseas. I said I'd think about it. Moving the money abroad would certainly make it more difficult to trace. I needed anonymity to effectively submerge and off-shore accounts were rumoured to be discreet. I could authorise my new identity to withdraw the funds on my behalf. With a new passport I could travel and trade as two separate people. It was an interesting plan.

"I can help you with some numbers," Sam said. "I know a few people."

As if on cue her mobile phone rang again. She glanced at the screen, tutted irritably and took the call in the private office area. I tried not to eavesdrop as she spoke quietly and tersely in the same European language as before. I didn't understand a word.

Later that evening we took a cab to a Thai restaurant in New Cross. It was a secret, intimate place behind Goldsmiths College. We were the only customers. Sam was easy company and, despite several phone interruptions, we chatted casually as the staff brought us warm rice wine. I asked her about the only boyfriend I had ever met almost twenty years ago.

"Oh, Christ!" Sam shrieked. "God's gift to my hairspray and several Japanese cosplay models? I'd forgotten about him. The band moved out to Tokyo to live the rock star dream but they came home after a couple of months. He told everyone that he had to leave Japan in a hurry because he had slept with an unsuitable Yakuza girl but that was horseshit as usual. I know for a fact that they all came home because they ran out of money and couldn't afford to eat in McDonalds any more. He even phoned after we'd split up and asked me to wire him some cash. I sent an invoice instead for the money I'd leant him when we were dating. Last I heard he was teaching primary school kids in Twickenham how to play the recorder."

She grinned.

"So there you go. I don't think I was really cut out to be the dating type. But I have my moments."

I took a sip of wine.

"I can believe that."

Sam picked up the bill and pulled some notes out of her purse. I tried to protest but she held up one hand and winked.

"It's on me, Cal," she said. "You can owe me out of your inheritance."

I suggested we move on to a bar for a nightcap. Her phone rang again. She groaned and took the call outside. When she returned to our table she looked distracted.

"Listen, Cal," she said, "I've got to go back to the flat and sort out some shit otherwise this fucking phone is going to ring all night. Do you mind? I'm really sorry. I'd love to come with you but maybe tonight is not a great time?"

I felt deflated but tried not to show it. We agreed to meet back at the apartment later. She flagged down a passing cab and waved from the back seat. I heard the sound of live music coming from a pub across the road and pushed my way inside. The place was peeling and stained but obviously a favourite with the college students who jostled for position in front of the tiny stage. I ordered a pint of lager from the barman and watched the band from the back of the room. Four thin kids dredged up old Stooges' riffs and delivered them with an affected, art school boredom as if it was the greatest chore in the world. Just for a few minutes I felt as if I had never left London. It was reassuring to know that the phantoms of Johnny Cool still prowled the sticky back-rooms of the capital's dwindling music clubs long after the scene had eaten its own head. I stayed until the end of the minuscule noise storm.

It was after midnight as I walked back through the rows of deserted market stalls along Deptford High Street towards Sam's apartment. I heard sirens in the distance but otherwise the streets were quiet. A stray cat darted from the shadows and ran past the lines of pawnbrokers and betting shops. The last train to Greenwich and the dull flatlands beyond clattered overhead. A solitary figure stood at the station entrance. He glanced up as I approached and crossed the road. I smiled to myself. One of the city's many unwritten laws stated that no two strangers should ever meet at night on the same side of the street unless drunk, destitute or damaged. We walked parallel along the High Street for a while until the stranger disappeared into the flats above a video shop.

I let myself into Sam's apartment with the spare keys. The kitchen light was still on. An empty wine glass stood on the breakfast bar next to a folded laptop. The flat was quiet and I guessed that Sam had gone to sleep in the mezzanine bedroom. She had made up the sofa in the living area. I switched out the lights, took off my boots and climbed under the quilt. The space was silent and ghostly with only the sound of my own breathing for company.

It was still dark when I was vaguely aware of a muted alarm. Seconds later I heard footsteps on the spiral staircase. I opened one eye and saw Sam's pale, naked body heading towards the bathroom. I heard the sound of running water and drifted back to sleep. Later I was woken by someone gently rocking my shoulder. Sam stood over me wearing a smart black business suit. I could smell her perfume.

"I've got to go to Paris," she whispered. "Work stuff."

I propped myself up on one elbow and squinted at my cousin. "Paris?"

She smiled.

"I should be back tomorrow. Make yourself at home and don't forget to double-lock the front door if you go out."

It was getting light. I lay back down and stared at the grey dawn unfolding outside. The apartment felt empty. I heard water gushing through the pipes in the wall and realised that it was time for the city to rise and greet another day. Just for a second I was tempted to get up and do something constructive. Instead I went back to sleep. For some reason I dreamt that I was pushing snow and slush through a letterbox.

Later the sound of someone knocking on the front door began to seep through my subconscious. I heard muffled voices outside in the corridor. I ignored them. The knocking became more aggressive. A telephone rang somewhere in the apartment. I heard keys scraping in the lock. Suddenly I was wide awake. I was gripped by a moment of panic. I dared not breathe. There was nowhere to hide. Open-plan loft apartments were not designed with the fugitive in mind. Eventually the sound of a power drill outside made me bolt for the door.

I was greeted by the sight of two uniformed policemen, a locksmith holding a drill and two men wearing grey suits. They stared at me for a second with expressions suggesting they had better things to do than wait for people like me to get out of bed.

"Police," said the older of the two suited detectives. "We were just about to drill a hole through your front door."

He held up his identity wallet and stepped into the apartment. The second, younger detective followed whilst the two uniformed officers waited outside with the locksmith.

"We have a warrant for Samantha Martin." said the older man. "Where is she?"

"Paris," I replied.

The two detectives exchanged glances.

"Paris? What the hell would she be doing in Paris?"

"I've no idea," I said. "She left early this morning. Said it was work related."

"And who are you?"

"Callum Colyier. I'm Sam's cousin. What's this about?"

The younger detective glared at me.

"You're coming with us," he said. "Have you got any ID?"

I pointed to my bag on the sofa.

"And you might want to put some shoes on."

The two detectives drove me to the station in an unmarked saloon car. No one spoke. My mind was racing as I stared out of the window at the gridlocked traffic. If the police only had a warrant for Sam then I assumed that Greece had not yet surrendered any awkward evidence in my absence. I had a bad feeling in the pit of my stomach. Police checks could slowly unravel the unpalatable truth and whatever Sam had done would soon pale into insignificance. This was not part of my plan.

The detectives parked the car at the back of the police station and led me to an interview room on the ground floor. I noticed the younger detective hand my bag to a uniformed officer sitting at a desk. The officer glanced in my direction and reached for some paperwork. The interview room was small and airless. There was a table in the middle of the room and a tiny window set high on one wall.

"Right then," said the older detective. "First things first. Do you want a cup of tea or something?"

I must have looked confused. The detective tapped his watch.

"It's lunchtime," he said. "No point trying to sort this all out on an empty stomach."

He left me alone in the room. I sat down at the table. I listened to the everyday sounds of the office outside and tried not focus on the situation. The door opened after a few minutes and I recognised the officer who had been sitting behind the desk with my bag. He asked me whether I knew which airline Sam had taken to Paris that morning. I shook my head and he closed the door. I presumed the police were checking passenger lists.

After maybe thirty minutes the two detectives returned with plastic cups of tea. The older detective sat down opposite me at the table whilst the other stood silently by the door. The older man opened a thick brown folder and flicked through the pages as he sipped his tea. Eventually he put the file down and looked up at me.

"Paris?" he said carefully. "Samantha definitely told you she was going to Paris?"

I nodded. My throat was dry.

"Then do you have any reason whatsoever to explain why Samantha Martin landed in Bratislava almost two hours ago? Bratislava is in Slovakia and, according to my notes, about eight hundred miles from Paris. That's quite a detour whichever way you choose to look at it."

I had to agree. It didn't make much sense at all. It might, however, explain the phone calls yesterday evening. There was an awkward silence in the room.

"According to our records," the detective continued, "you arrived in England from Greece three days ago. Why?"

"For my mother's funeral," I said.

The detective stared at me for a second.

"Sorry to hear that. It's always unfortunate."

He picked up the file again. The detective at the door stared at me intently.

"Look, what's all this got to do with me?" I asked after a while. "What's Sam actually done?"

The detective put the file down and sighed.

"Well, to be honest with you, we don't really know," he said.

"Then why are you trying to arrest her?"

"We're trying to arrest her for fraud," the detective replied. "At least that's what it says on the warrant. But we would also very much like to talk to her in connection with an eastern European syndicate responsible for aggravated extortion, kidnapping, torture and ..." he glanced down at the file, "...thirty six murders. On the whole it's a rather messy and somewhat complicated affair."

I laughed. It was a nervous over-reaction. The younger detective at the door folded his arms and frowned.

"Murder?" I said. "That's ridiculous."

"I suppose it is," the older detective replied calmly. "But there's always been money in murder. More tea?"

He stood up and both detectives left the room. I stared at the wall and tried to absorb all of this new information. I knew that I was being selfish but I began to relax nonetheless. If anything had been discovered concerning my darker human traits then by now there would have been a lot more shouting and a lot less tea. So murder ran in the family? We were genetic monsters. A killing clan. Outstanding! Although the detectives hadn't actually accused Sam of murder. It was only murder-by-association. Murder by association with a bunch of Slovakian mobsters and assassins. I remembered Sam's interest in my future inheritance and her offer to help out with some contacts. Gradually the realization dawned like a brick that I had been set up. I had been no more than a target in an elaborate and potentially violent scam. I smiled. Sam had gone to great lengths to conceal her real motives. The motive was always the money. My younger cousin – the tiny, ballerina princess with raven hair and heart-breaking green eyes – was undoubtedly a class fucking act.

The police released me later that afternoon. It was obvious that I was not in a position to help with any investigation. I signed endless statements to the effect that I had absolutely no knowledge of Sam's business concerns or immediate plans. I couldn't even really offer much in the way of background information. Sam and I had exchanged more words during the past twenty four hours than we had for nearly twenty years. The older detective apologised for any inconvenience. He gave me his card and requested I get in touch should I hear anything from my cousin. I agreed. His younger colleague handed back my bag and scowled at the floor like a spoilt child.

I walked out of the police station and never looked back. I caught a cab to Sam's apartment, dropped the spare keys through the communal post box and drove straight to the airport. I paused inside the busy terminal building and looked up at the departure boards. I was standing at the edge of the world and facing an infinite sea of possibilities. Destination overload. I held my passport in one hand. It really didn't matter. Deep in my heart and soul I knew I could never return.

15

THE LONG AND WINDING ROAD

The forest held my secrets safe and I was furious. The shallow graves lay undisturbed. I had placed large rocks in the earth to mark the last resting place of the entertainer, the bridesmaid and the old cripple. A smaller rock marked the goose's grave. I had a detailed mental diagram of the area should the four rocks ever disappear. I knew every inch of sacred soil and the broken bones that lay beneath. Nothing had moved in my absence. Under normal circumstances this should have been a cause for quiet celebration. Undetected I stood alone in the shadows of death. Instead I was angry.

It was an elemental afternoon up in the mountains. The storm last night had battered the island. Neither Kat nor I had much sleep. Hail stones had smashed into the courtyard like bullets as thunder rolled overhead. Sheet lightning strobed a murderous sky. The rains came soon after with a vengeance. Torrents of water gushed from our house's flat roof and before long the drains were blocked with debris. The dogs hid under the furniture and whimpered with fear.

In the morning the storm had abated a little. Heavy clouds still scudded across an ominous sky but the air smelt fresh and clean. The West coast beaches were wrecked. The winds had turned the sea into a dark, malevolent swell that crashed over sections of the road as I drove south. Old women swept the water from their tumble-down houses and surveyed the damage with an air of resignation. They had probably seen worse over the years. Small fishing boats had been dragged from the sea for safety. They would remain ashore until the waters had calmed. Children danced happily in puddles as tractors negotiated the water-logged farmland along the coast.

I turned off the main road and headed inland. The forest was a menacing place. The trees stood barren and skeletal against the sombre sky. The storm winds hammered my face as I walked towards the clearing and surveyed the four graves. I stared at the ground for a very long time. It didn't make any sense. It was an atrocity. A sheer, unadulterated, fucking atrocity!

I would find whoever was responsible and suck their brains from their skull through a straw. I would tie their arms to a catapult and hurl them into the ocean from the top of a cliff. I would mince their muscles through a fucking blender and force-feed them alive with their own skin. It was not possible. It was simply not possible.

The wind howled through the trees and I felt spots of rain. I knelt down beside someone's grave. I couldn't remember who was buried beneath the rock. It didn't really matter. They had all been willing accomplices. Except for the old cripple, I suppose, but Jimmy the Stick had been a monster long before I set him on fire inside a box and buried him alive. And the goose. The goose had been a liability anyway. It had been an aggressive and noisy bird. The goose could not have been trusted at all. But at least the entertainer and the bridesmaid had been willing accomplices. I couldn't remember their names.

I placed the palm of one hand on the damp earth.

"Tell me," I said quietly, "what's happening? What the fuck is going on?"

There was a silence broken only by the wind and the distant sound of thunder. The storm had retreated but it would soon return. The forest was not a place in which to get trapped. I trudged back to the car and set off home. The sky was turning black. I switched on the headlights. A bolt of blue lightning illuminated the forest either side of the road. Before long I was driving blind through sheets of violent rain and hellfire. The windscreen wipers made little difference. I pulled over and considered my options. Driving back to the city in this weather was dangerous. I decided to ride out the storm at the Kittyhawk Club instead. It was not far.

The Kittyhawk was surprisingly busy. The jukebox was playing *Bad Moon Rising*. I recognised a few familiar faces at the bar. There was the old priest who always drank alone as if seeking absolution from the bottom of a bottle. A girl from the local village sat with her hand resting in the lap of some faggotty hep-cat. She wore a pretty dress and daring ballroom heels. Two woodcutters played backgammon in one corner. A small group of local bikers chatted with Honey and Gina at the pool table. The place was full of smoke and the atmosphere was warm and friendly. Tommy grinned as I approached the bar and handed me a beer.

"I fucking hate this island," I said.

Tommy laughed like an old lizard.

"Yeah, well," he drawled, "better get used to it cos you ain't going nowhere for a while. At least not until this storm is over anyway."

I sat down next to the old priest. His face was the colour of concrete and cracked with age. His beard looked as if it had been made from silver twigs and dead insects. I guessed the old man must have fallen from grace a long time ago. He stared into space and chewed his thin lips as if rolling mud around his mouth.

It was February. I had been back on Kolasios for three weeks. I had spent hours at London airport just gazing at the departure boards as they were constantly updated. I could have gone anywhere in the world. It was just a matter of money. Ultimately, however, I could never leave Kat. We had come too far together. I could never leave the island. Kolasios was the one place where I would like to be buried. To lie in peace beneath the island's ancient, scorched earth by the shimmering waters of the grand Aegean.

I called my sister from the airport and told her about the day's events in London.

"I don't want to get involved, Liz," I said. "Can you let me know what happens with the will?"

Liz was shocked and sympathetic. Kat found the whole thing hilarious.

"Let me get this straight," she said, trying hard not to laugh. "Your cousin is wanted by the Serious Fraud Office, Interpol and God knows who else for extorting money to help fund a Slovakian crime gang who kidnap, torture and kill people when they get annoyed? Jesus, Cal, that is fucking priceless! It's like a bad movie plot."

Naturally I left out a few details. They didn't seem important. I left out the details of my overnight stay in Switzerland. I left out the details of my aborted plan to abandon my wife in order to evade arrest by the Greek police for the murder of three people and a goose. Every married couple had their secrets. It was only human nature. I'm sure Kat had her own secrets too.

Yesterday we had driven south to help Steve and Amanda Bedlam lose a pub quiz in Haraklos. Kat thought it might help me relax. There was nothing else to do and the old Cornish punks were always good company. Steve and Amanda had moved out to Kolasios around the same time as us. They had bought a small white house in a muddy field just outside Elythia. For one year they had lived without either electricity or cash-flow as they waited for the house to be completed. They were a popular couple. Steve once told me that the only grief he had ever encountered on the island was from the English ex-pats who had sneered at the sight of his triumphant Mohican and renegade tattoos. I was not surprised. During the summer months he cleaned pools and odd-jobbed around the island. Amanda helped out by cleaning villas and together they struggled through the winter like everybody else. They survived on Amanda's vegetable soup and Steve's good humour. There was talk of Steve's old band re-releasing an album they had recorded back in 1983. Bedlam & The Kneejerks had once been revolting local heroes. Steve still insisted that the Revolution was just around the corner and he wanted a song on the soundtrack.

Billy's Bar on the beach front was crowded and noisy. A storm was forecast. The heavy plastic sheeting which protected the outside area was already snapping in the wind. We could hear the surf crashing onto the beach outside as we sat down with Steve and Amanda.

The bar was popular with the local ex-pats. It was open every night during the long winter months and the same faces could be seen there every day. The fat, emperor bullfrog and his bottle-blonde shrew would always be the first to arrive. They would sit there until the burping great turtle fell over and had to be carried home in a wheelbarrow. The hopeless artist and his startled, slow-witted parents would always be the next to arrive. They would sit in a little group and read the English newspapers to each other like home-sick simpletons. A trio of mean-faced hags would always commandeer the same table in one corner. They would spend every evening sipping gin and surveying their domain like razor-bladed sticklebacks. Often they would be joined by the bland, oily Lothario who laboured under the illusion that he could schmooze the pants from a piranha. Middle age and alcohol, however, had conspired to scupper his charms. The acidic old women much preferred the attentions of the loud and crazy-eyed buffoon who had once driven his motorcycle through a plate glass window in a fit of drunken pique. All of them had one thing in common. They all depended on the oxygen of petty gossip for their survival.

It wasn't long before Kat and I heard the rumour which had apparently gripped the island for the past few days. Amanda leant across the table.

"They found a body," she whispered conspiratorially. "A dead body."

Steve stared at his wife for a second. He took a sip of beer and burst out laughing.

"A dead body? Not a body that was alive, then? Like half a dead body with living arms and legs? Not a dead body with a talking head still attached or something? It was definitely a dead body? Fucking hell, Mand!"

Kat was enthralled. I feigned indifference. I hated gossip. I hated the trivial trickle of misinformation which seemed to fuel the island for most of the year. I hated the jealous way in which gossip was guarded and embellished as it oozed through the dull conversations and saccharine parties. Gossip was a weapon to be wielded with competitive authority. Gossip was god.

"Where did they find the body?" I said.

Steve shrugged.

"No idea. Probably down the back of the same sofa where they hid all the Nazi artwork!"

That evening there was talk of little else. The story had taken on a life of its own as it spread through the villages and bars like a super virus. The dead body was headless. The dead body was African. The dead body was found spread-eagled like a starfish.

The limpet Lothario sat down at our table and fixed us all with his most serious expression.

"I heard they never found his cock," he said. "Some proper nutnut chopped off his cock, threw it away and then buried the poor chap without his knackers. Hard to believe, I say. Very sad."

We lost the quiz and drove back to town in silence. The storm was closing in above us. We made it home just in time. The following morning I drove back down the island to find Captain Manni Trelliosos. I had spent the night fighting to suppress the rising tide of panic and nausea. If there was a single grain of truth in the rumour then I needed an exit strategy and I needed one fast. Rumours, however, have a knack of acting as a distraction. More than anything else I needed reliable information before I could take any action.

The police station in Kavindos was an old, converted captain's house. I parked on the wasteland overlooking the village and walked down into the jumble of whitewashed houses and cobbled streets. The village was quiet. Captain Manni was nowhere to be seen. Instead an unfamiliar officer sat at the front desk. He looked up as I entered.

"Yes?"

The police station looked different. There was an unfamiliar air of industry and authority.

"I'm looking for Captain Manni?" I said.

"He is on holiday," the officer replied brusquely. "Who are you?"

I looked around and noticed the charts and graphs on the wall. Computers had replaced the old typewriters on which Manni had bashed out his fabricated traffic reports. A team of smarter, more agile officers had replaced the old rogue's former crew of misfits and cronies. They wore guns on their hips and actually looked as if they knew how to use them. They stared at me with barely concealed suspicion. It was undoubtedly a mainland murder squad.

"Just a friend," I said.

I walked back to the car and drove into the mountains. I had to be sure. I found the clearing in the forest and stood staring at my four graves as it began to drizzle.

It was unthinkable. It was the action of a mad man. I would find and feed whoever was responsible to the fucking sharks! Who in their right frame of mind would want to test the mettle of a multiple killer? A coward? A competitor? A demon? He was playing a dangerous game. It didn't matter. Friend or foe he was going to die. I would make it my life's mission.

I went to The Kittyhawk.

The old priest sitting beside me raised his withered hand to order another whiskey. Tommy poured a generous measure and slid the glass across the bar. The jukebox played Johnny Cash. I felt a hand on my shoulder. Honey smiled and draped herself across the bar stool next to mine.

"Cal, *mon amour,*" she crooned, "*mon cherie,* the love of my life. I am so bored. Will you buy me a drink?"

She looked like a little raggedy doll with her black, haystack hair and sheer white dress. She gazed up at me pleadingly with wide, cartoon eyes and pursed her lips like a petulant child. I laughed.

"How could I refuse?"

We drank shots of tequila until the storm had passed. I shrugged into my coat and was about to leave when I paused.

"Do you mind if I ask you a question?"

"Anything," said Honey.

"Do you have any secrets?"

Honey frowned.

"Of course I have secrets. I am Romanian. We all have secrets."

I smiled.

"I mean, do you have any secrets that you could not tell another living soul? Secrets that you will have to take to your grave?"

She thought about this for a minute. The old priest yawned.

"Yes," she said eventually. "I have a secret that I will take to my grave. I could tell you my secret but then I would have to kill you. That would not be right."

I leant forward and kissed her forehead.

"It would just be another secret."

16

WRITER

Some years ago an old man wrote a book about his travels across the Greek islands. The book was called *Windmills & White Houses*. It was first published in 1978. The old man had retired from the civil service some years previously. He wanted to buy property in the Dodecanese. His mind was set and he would consider no other place on earth. The book documented his search for a suitable house. Eventually he found a ruined windmill on the island of Rhodes. He immediately fell in love with the building and spent years renovating the windmill until finally it was safe to inhabit. The author lived happily in the windmill on Rhodes and wrote his memoirs. *Windmills & White Houses* became a television series. It was broadcast every Sunday afternoon for six weeks.

I had read a few chapters of the old man's book. It was a sunsoaked journey through an innocent country. Greece was a land of olive groves and donkeys, tiny chapels and blue skies. Old women wept with relief as the author strode into their village. He was invited to eat roast lamb at every family table. There would be so much food. These feasts would invariably last for maybe a thousand years. In exchange for such generous hospitality the author would help fix the villagers' ancient sedans and rusting scooters. Farmers and shepherds were so thankful that they would offer him livestock and the hand of their ravishing daughters in marriage. He would always politely decline but accept some local cheese and a loaf of delicious, home-baked bread instead. This would keep him going until the next village. He was always humbled by such acts of kindness.

The author was just a desk clerk from England yet the simple island folk had taken him into their hearts nonetheless. Entire communities would turn out to wish the author a safe journey. Even those so old and infirm that they could hardly walk managed to totter out into the sun to pay their respects. Everybody wept as he strode out across the fields in search of his idyllic island home. As the author disappeared from view the grief-stricken villagers would all fall down and die. Without the author their lives had lost all meaning. The olive groves withered. The skies turned black. Life without the author was a godless apocalypse.

The old man's book became a huge success on the back of the television series. He died in his windmill before he could complete a sequel. He left no will. So the Greek authorities re-appropriated the windmill and gave it to the wife of the deputy prime minister. She was a stubborn and unpopular woman. The windmill was one of several properties the politician forgot to declare during the weeks leading up to his resignation from government.

Many more books from a variety of writers appeared in the wake of *Windmills & White Houses*. Most were self-published. None achieved much success. A boyish, ex-pat priest from Oxford published a picture book of old Greek doors. It was called *The End of the Doors – A Life in Wood*. He was planning another about windows. A mad woman wrote an entire book about Greek island cats. A slightly sinister divorcee based her novel around a rugged Greek fisherman's torrid affair with a slightly sinister divorcee. It all ended in tragedy. The fisherman choked on an orange. The fictional divorcee wept at his graveside. She resolved to wear black for the rest of her life. She would call their unborn child Giorgos in memory of the fisherman.

It seemed as if everyone was writing books about some fanciful paradise far away. The poets and the painters joined forces with the writers and the word-smiths. Together they conspired to eradicate every trace of Greece's troubled history. Centuries of brutal occupation had been replaced by armchair observations and plastic prose. Three thousand years of culture reduced to mangled travelogues hanging by a thread from the fringes of the internet. No wonder the country was confused. The simpering word-junkies had turned her into a fucking cartoon!

Emanuelle Lagarde was a tall and elegant woman. I met her late one afternoon in March. I was sitting in the courtyard of the Glass Bottomed Boot bar in Kolasios Old Town. Tucked away in the maze of medieval back streets behind the three main squares, it was not an easy place to find. The Boot was run by three Greek-American brothers from New Jersey who bickered constantly like trolls. They argued about everything. They argued about the pizza toppings and the menu designs and the décor and the cash flow. The only time the brothers ever presented a united front was when faced with the Old Town's army of petty licensing officials. There were strict by-laws and these were diligently enforced. Everything from noise levels to sidewalk table arrangements had to be agreed with the authorities. Sometimes it seemed as if you needed a license just to apply for a license in order to run a business in the Old Town. The three brothers took turns to contest the frequent violations in court. Money changed hands and the disputes were usually resolved.

It was almost Spring. Another long winter of isolation and inertia was drawing to a close. It hadn't rained for several days. There was an air of gentle industry around town. The more ambitious proprietors were already returning from the mainland to prepare for the season. Restaurants and bars which had remained padlocked for months were being cleaned and painted. Bar owners chatted amicably with their neighbours and rivals like great warriors before the battle. It was hard to believe that within a few weeks the tranquil streets and pretty squares would again be awash with the blood and bile of psychotic commerce.

I was trying to decipher an email from a Russian hotelier who had commissioned us to redesign his marketing brochure. My new reading glasses were not helping. Recently I had noticed that my eyes were straining to focus on the laptop screen. I was getting old and cranky. Kat had picked out a pair of glasses from a chemist. She said they made me look intelligent. I doubted at that moment whether the Russian hotelier would agree.

I was aware of the woman sitting at a table in the courtyard. She was alone and seemed deep in thought. She poured herself a last glass of white wine from a carafe and smiled in my direction.

"Are you on holiday?" she said. "If you don't mind me asking?"

Her cut-glass accent was precise and too exact to be English. I removed my glasses and rubbed my eyes.

"No," I replied, "I live here."

She seemed surprised.

"You live here? My darling, how wonderful! Do you mind if I join you?"

The woman stood up before I could reply and walked unsteadily towards my table. She wore a white linen suit with a yellow silk scarf and fussy Greek sandals. Despite the wine she carried herself with the unmistakable air of either the aristocratic or the insane.

She held out one hand.

"My name is Baroness Lagarde," she announced. "But you can call me Emanuelle. May I sit down?"

It seemed churlish to refuse. To be honest I was glad of the distraction. The Russian hotelier was making even less sense than usual. The Baroness arranged herself at the table and lit a menthol cigarette with a gold lighter. Her silver hair was tied back in a bun and framed an inquisitive face with sculpted cheekbones and bright, grey eyes. Undeniably she had once been a very beautiful woman.

"I am a writer, darling," she said, exhaling smoke towards the ceiling. "I am writing a book about this beautiful island. I am writing a book about this beautiful house in which I live and I am writing a book about all the charming characters I have met and who have been so very handsome and generous."

I felt my heart sink.

"You're writing three books?"

She patted my hand and laughed.

"No, silly, of course not! I am writing just one book but I must encapsulate everything about this magical place within the pages of my book. I must capture the flavours, the sights, the sounds....I must capture the delightful sense of freedom I feel whenever I am alone. I must capture the fireflies and the crickets as they chirrup in the woods. My book will be very beautiful. My book will be adored."

"Right," I said. "Would you like some more wine, Emanuelle?"

The Baroness sighed theatrically.

"Yes, darling, that would be very pleasant."

I walked inside to order the drinks. The youngest brother was alone behind the bar. As usual he was stoned.

"See you've met the Baroness then, dude?" said Sammi.

I nodded.

"Who is she?"

Sammi shrugged.

"Not too sure, dude, but she's Belgian. She's, like, the queen of Belgium or something. I think she's writing a book."

Emanuelle Lagarde, I discovered that afternoon, was a lonely woman. She had inherited the title from her third husband. Baron Henri Lagarde had been a wealthy industrialist and completely besotted with Emanuelle. After a whirlwind courtship they had married at Bolland Castle near Liege. Together they had enjoyed a grand life. They moved in rarefied social circles and counted noblemen and even royalty amongst their friends. A recent stroke, however, had left the Baron paralysed and bed-ridden. Rather than burden his wife with worry the old man had signed over the majority of his vast fortune to Emanuelle. He encouraged her to use the money to travel and explore the world before it was too late. He owned property across Europe and the Caribbean including a sixteenth century merchant's house in Kolasios Old Town. She planned to stay in the merchant's house and write her book.

The Baroness said she had a happy childhood. She told me stories of her father who used to own a flower stall in Antwerp. Every weekend she would help him gift-wrap the flowers and then dance in the markets until dusk. Her first marriage to a local boy had lasted barely seven months.

"We were just children," she said wistfully.

Her second husband was a good man but an awful bore. It wasn't, she insisted, until she met Henri Lagarde in 1979 at the age of thirty that she understood true love. She had been swept off her feet by the charming industrialist. His power and wealth apparently made no difference.

"I would have loved him even if he had been a penniless farmhand," she said. "I hardly noticed the castle in Vienna or the mansion in Mustique or the private jets or the cars or the hotels or the horses or the caviar. I only had eyes for my darling Henri. I was blinded by love."

By now the Baroness was a little drunk. It was already dark. She insisted on paying our bar tab and in exchange I offered to escort her back to the merchant's house.

"You have been most patient," she said, as we linked arms and swayed through the dark, uneven streets of the Old Town. The old gas lanterns had been replaced by modern lamps. They cast an eerie, orange light over the fairytale houses that loomed overhead. After a while we stopped outside a heavy wooden gate set into a high stone wall covered with creeping vines.

"Come," said the Baroness, "at least let me offer you some champagne?"

She unlocked the gate and we stepped into a large, pebbled court-yard. Like many properties in the Old Town, appearances could be deceptive from the street. An ornate fountain stood in the centre of the courtyard. Tall palms and fruit trees lined the walls. An old brick water well stood in one corner with a white bucket hanging from the iron winch. A pile of logs lay stacked against an old wooden wheelbar-row. It was like stepping back into another century.

The two-story house itself was calm and cavernous. A huge stone arch dominated the entire ground floor and supported the oak-beamed ceiling. Middle Eastern rugs lay scattered across the polished marble floor tiles and heavy wooden banquettes. A mottled brick fire-place took up one corner of the main living area. I noticed a croquet set standing next to the fireplace. An ugly, rusted hunter's trap hung from one wall above a solid staircase leading to the upper floor. Soft lighting helped to warm the old wood and cold stone. The house felt secure and homely.

"Come, come, come," said the Baroness with a flourish. "Champagne!"

She led me by the hand to a spacious, spot-lit kitchen. A long wooden workbench stood in the middle of the room. There was a basket of fresh fruit on the table and chequered curtains were drawn across the little window above a deep basin sink. She opened the stainless steel fridge and handed me a bottle of Veuve Clicquot.

"Would you?"

She giggled as the cork popped from the bottle and hit the ceil-ing. I poured the champagne into two crystal flutes and handed one to the Baroness. We chinked our glasses.

"Isn't this just the most wonderful house?" she said. "Henri owns a lot of houses but I think this is my favourite. I would very much like to be buried in this house one day. So much space! So much history! Look..."

She put her champagne down on the workbench and I followed her to the far corner of the kitchen. She knelt down beside the fridge and pointed at the floor.

"Can you see?"

I looked down and noticed a wooden panel set into the floor. There was a large iron ring bolted to the panel.

"It's a secret trap door," the Baroness whispered. "It leads to a passageway which runs under the walls of the Old Town. The original owners built it as an escape route should foreign armies ever invade. Isn't that romantic?"

I smiled and helped the Baroness to her feet. We took our champagne back to the living room. The Baroness fussed around lighting candles and arranging cushions. I went to the bathroom. I gripped the black marble sink and stared at my reflection in the antique mirror.

What a fucking shambles, I thought. What a fucking mess! The old Baroness was a lark. A martyr. Holed up in this fucking museum like a raddled old sponge. Love? Champagne? Secret tunnels? What a fucking mess!

I stared at the ghosts in the glass.

You had better be prepared. I tell you now. You had better be fucking prepared!

I took a deep breath and walked back out into the living room. The Baroness stood up and held out both arms.

"I must read for you..." she began to say.

Fortunately she got no further. I knocked her unconscious with one swift punch to the temple. The Baroness never saw it coming. She collapsed at my feet and lay motionless. I looked around the room. The house was silent. I picked up the wooden croquet mallet from its rack beside the fireplace and laid it on the floor next to the Baroness. I needed something sharp. Not a knife. Something sharper than a knife. Eventually I found a small scalpel in a sewing kit on a bookshelf.

I was no surgeon and I made quite a mess. I wouldn't know whether I had been successful until after the Baroness regained consciousness. I dragged her body into the kitchen. She was as light as a feather. The trap door was heavy and took quite a bit of effort to open. There was a small flight of stairs leading down into the dark tunnel. I found a light switch on the wall. A single naked bulb illuminated the dank, stone cellar. I rolled the Baroness down the stairs and propped her up against one wall. I took a moment to catch my breath. The Baroness was still unconscious. I untied the yellow silk scarf and placed it over her eyes. Gently I tied the scarf in a knot behind her head. Satisfied, I sat back and stared at the Baroness. I had a few more things to collect. When I was finished I sat on the stairs and waited.

After maybe one hour the Baroness began to moan. I stubbed out my cigarette and leant forward on the staircase.

"Baroness Lagarde," I said, "please do not try to make a sound. It would be most uncomfortable."

I tried to speak as calmly and as slowly as possible.

"It is very important that you understand what has happened. I will try and explain as best I can so that you won't feel alarmed. I have broken your jaw in three places. Maybe four. I used the croquet mallet that was standing beside the fireplace. I have also tried to remove your larynx with a scalpel but I'm not too sure whether I succeeded or not. There was a lot of blood. The scalpel is sticking out of your left leg just above the kneecap. I don't know why.

"At the moment you are sitting in the secret tunnel under the kitchen. You are not blind. I have merely covered your eyes with your yellow scarf. There is a fresh ream of blank white paper next to your right hand. On top of the pile of paper is a silver biro. I think it would be a good idea if you finished your book down here before you died."

The Baroness' hands began to twitch. Her breathing sounded like a mountain mudslide.

"Not that it really matters," I continued. "I mean, no one's going to read it or anything like that. God knows there are enough books in the world already. I just thought that maybe if you finished the book before you died then all this might not have been in vain. You probably have a few hours left. I hope you understand.

I don't even particularly dislike you as a person. But you have to understand that I am at war and all war is senseless. Your death, I'm sure, would be described as collateral damage in the grand scheme of such things."

I stood up.

"I'm leaving now. Good luck with the book, Baroness. Thank you for the champagne. I will leave the light on but obviously I am going to close the trap door behind me."

I took one step and paused.

"There is just one more thing I nearly forgot to mention. Your right leg is currently chained to the iron hunter's trap that used to hang on the wall over the staircase. The trap is spring-loaded and quite delicate. I would be very careful."

I closed the trap door and picked up the house keys from the kitchen workbench. The Baroness did not survive. The following day I returned to the Old Town and let myself into the merchant's house. It was as quiet as a church. I heaved open the trap door and stepped down into the cellar.

The hunter's trap had severed the Baroness' leg below the knee. She sat upright and rigid with her chin resting on her blood-soaked chest. The paper and pen were untouched. I sighed. I picked up the severed limb and placed it inside a heavy black plastic sack. I had brought many sacks for the task ahead. I climbed the stairs and went outside to the courtyard. There was an axe embedded in the log pile. I wrenched it loose and returned to the cellar.

By the time I had finished there were eight sacks sitting in the kitchen. I placed the sacks in the old wooden wheelbarrow and pushed the Baroness through the narrow streets. An old man smiled and stood aside as I struggled across one of the bridges that spanned the city's medieval moat. I put the sacks into the boot of my car and returned the wheelbarrow to the courtyard. Having secured the trap door in the kitchen, I poured the champagne into the sink and carefully placed the empty bottle into another plastic sack along with the two crystal flutes. Very neat. I switched out the lights and locked up the merchant's house for the last time. That afternoon I stopped for gas and threw the keys into a trash bin before heading up into the mountains once again.

17

KAT'S WATCH

Kat and I went to the beach to celebrate with pizza and champagne. The weather was hardly ideal. Last night's gale had swept across the island from the mainland and that afternoon the sea was violent. Angry waves crashed against the empty shoreline and a vicious wind whipped across the deserted beach. Even the old Greeks who swam regularly were nowhere to be seen. But the sky was blue and we could feel the sun's warmth on our faces. We sat down on the sand in the lee of an old army pillbox which had stood derelict and abandoned since the end of the Second World War. There were bullet holes in the concrete around the narrow gun slits.

I poured the champagne into two glass flutes and handed one to Kat. We chinked glasses.

The celebration was double-edged. On one hand my mother's inheritance would provide a roof over our heads for the foreseeable future. It was not a huge amount of money. It was not as if I could afford to buy an oil company or anything. But it was enough to ensure that Kat and I would not starve. On the other hand our good fortune would always remind me of my mother's death. It was money that came with ghosts attached.

We ate the pizza and laughed as clouds of sand swirled around the pillbox. After all these years I still loved Kat from the pit of my soul. I couldn't imagine a life without her. This year we would both turn fifty. We were getting old. Sometimes it seemed as if Kat had barely aged. That afternoon I sat and watched her idly throwing pebbles into the surf. The wind blew her shock of red hair into crazy shapes and pressed her orange gypsy skirt against her legs. I had always loved Kat. The first time I met her I knew my heart had crossed over into another place and that I could never return.

Kat and I were introduced at a vocal audition to read audio porn for the blind. A mutual friend had been commissioned to organise the project and she had rented my place for the auditions. An odd assortment of friends and misfits turned up and we drank cider and ridiculed the whole project. Not that audio-porn for the blind was a particularly bad idea. It just made us laugh. Blind wankers jerking off to a bunch of piss-heads and punk rockers. The project was doomed from the start and hastily abandoned by all concerned. Only Kat and I survived. Our mutual friend fell pregnant and was immediately sucked into the vortex of motherhood. Kat and I moved in together. We got married. We left the country. I never got to meet her parents. She told me her parents had never married.

"Free-loving German assholes," she said. "I wish they'd been members of the Baader-Meinhof Group instead and blown shit up. That would have been pretty cool. But my parents just dropped out and sat around naked. Yuch!"

Kat told me she fled to London at the very first opportunity. She fell into the city's squat scene and wore a lot of black leather. For a while she played bass guitar in some free-form punk cabaret collective and sold vintage clothes in Camden Market. Back then we had inhabited a parallel world of murky music clubs and pubs that felt like lungs. We breathed the same air of chaos and cacophony with our desperate convictions and a tattered instinct for survival. Back in the 1980s it had been the survival of the skinniest. No fucker survived the '80s with any innocence intact. The '80s ruined us all. Kat still had the tattoos to prove it. She had three separate bands inked around her upper left arm to remind her of the friends who never made it out alive.

Kat and I hadn't known each other at the time but we later figured out that we had many common acquaintances. We had been at the same clubs and bars. We had enjoyed the same noise pollution. We had walked home through the same dead-end streets. We had stolen food from the same shop in Islington and knew the same old soaks that could get you cheap cigarettes and salt-cured hams. It had been a pointless struggle. A million people took to the capital's streets and the City boys threw photocopied fifty pound notes out of their office windows into the crowds below. It had become a conceited city of make-believe and deceit. Even the fireworks over London on the eve of the new millennium made little difference to our spirits. We were simply exhausted.

Greece had been Kat's idea. She wanted to live on a beach some-where and raise chickens and dogs and grow herbs and vegetables. She wanted to live a life without rules and interference. Personally I always wanted to move to Dublin but the weather was shit. For a while we talked about converting an old shack on the west coast of Kolasios. It was just a tumbledown cafe on a deserted stretch of road but we had hopeless plans that inevitably turned to dust. Even the simple practicalities of renovating a humble shack in the middle of nowhere were mired by the legal Greek malaise and quicksand. Kat and I spent just one night on the beach behind the shack before ad-mitting defeat. We retreated to Kavindos village instead and rented a little house which leaked like a sieve. The shack was still there. It was still derelict. The old tin roof still flapped in the wind and the weeds still kept the hut from falling into the sea. Occasionally we passed the shack heading south and we always wished it well. It would be a sad day when nature finally reclaimed the land.

We stayed on the beach until sunset. The wind had dropped. In a few days the clocks would go forward and the scenery would change.

Not that it really mattered. There were only two seasons on the Greek islands. The summer season was all about money. The winter season was all about survival. Everything else was just a shade of compromise. Everybody learnt to live like pirates. Everybody learnt to ride out the calm seas in the winter and exploit the summer trade winds.

We packed up our stuff and headed back to the car. Kat suddenly stopped.

"Shit," she said, "look!"

She held out one hand and waved it in my face.

"What? What am I supposed to be looking at?"

"My fucking watch!" Kat replied. "My watch has stopped. My fucking watch is broken!"

I laughed.

"It doesn't really matter, Kat. It's Greece. It's always 1986 in Greece."

Kat looked at me and burst into tears.

"Fuck you," she spat. "It has sentimental value. It always works. It always fucking works and now it's broken."

I was dumbfounded. Kat was inconsolable. She began to scratch at the watch strap. Personally I'd never regarded the watch as anything special. Kat had found it on a beach at the end of our first summer. It had been forgotten by its previous owner and lay glinting in the sun. Kat retrieved it from the sand like a thieving magpie and had worn it proudly ever since. It wasn't a particularly pretty watch. It was kind of fat and round like a stainless steel boiled sweet. It was the only watch either of us had ever owned.

Kat was sobbing uncontrollably. She looked wretched. I held her tightly as she trembled in my arms.

"It's OK," I said quietly. "It's OK. I'll get it fixed tomorrow. It's probably just the battery."

That evening Kat took to our bed early with a bottle of vodka. She didn't eat and she couldn't sleep. She lay there all night snuffling into the pillow. In the morning I took the watch to a shop in town. It was a tiny shop owned by a large man. He looked like an ogre in a matchbox. I held out the watch.

"Is broken?" he asked.

"I think it's just the battery."

The ogre smiled kindly and pointed to a small chair in the corner of the shop.

"Please," he said. "Sit. I will fix it for you now. It is not a big problem."

He disappeared into a back room. The shop was full of watches in glass cases. I noticed an almost identical watch to Kat's in a case next to a rack of Zippo lighters. I was tempted. Not by the watches but I had always loved Zippos. There was something about the smell of petrol. But I had lost more Zippo lighters than I cared to remember and I'd vowed never to inflict any more disappointment on myself than was necessary.

The ogre returned after a few minutes.

"Now it's OK," he said with a grin. "Battery."

I breathed a sigh of relief as I left the shop and headed home. Kat was delighted. She insisted we go out and celebrate. We ate fresh sea food in the Old Town before dropping into the Boot for tequila shots and a bottle of wine. Sammi asked after the Baroness. I told him she had gone to visit Kos for a while.

"Who is the Baroness?" asked Kat.

"A writer," Sammi replied. "She's, like, the queen of Holland or something. She's writing a book. I haven't seen her for a while."

"Fucking writers," said Kat.

In the morning the watch had stopped working. Kat's initial shock soon turned to anger. She spent the morning stamping around the house and cursing the watch.

"I will kill it!" she shouted. "I will take it apart and throw it into the sea. It must die!"

Later that morning I returned to the ogre's little shop in town. He was apologetic and perplexed. I sat and waited as he disappeared into the back room once again. This time he returned looking glum.

"It is big problem," he said. "The battery is good but the mechanism has failed. Maybe you have dropped the watch?"

"No," I said. It was really only a white lie. Kat had kicked it around the house but she hadn't actually dropped it.

"Can you fix it?"

The ogre shrugged sadly. He looked at the watch which lay in pieces on the counter.

"I cannot fix this," he said. "I will have to send it to Athens. I know a man in Athens who can repair the watch. Maybe three days. Maybe five. I will call you."

Kat was furious. She spent the afternoon in a dark mood with a bottle of wine. I invited Mikki and Jesus over to help Kat commiserate. I suggested that maybe just for once Jesus should leave his stupid guitar behind. We sat in the courtyard and tried to cajole Kat. We were all a little drunk.

"Athens?" Kat suddenly snapped. "Why the fuck does my watch have to go to Athens?"

"He cannot fix it here," said Jesus helpfully. "He has to send it to Athens."

"Then why the fuck is this man allowed to run a shop that repairs watches when he can't repair my watch and has to send the watch to Athens? He is a fucking liar! He tells everyone he can mend watches but in fact when you take him a broken watch he just shrugs like a fucking goat and tells you he has to send it to Athens. What's the fucking point? You may as well send your own watch to this other man in Athens yourself. This other man in Athens is probably the goat-fucker's cousin! Nothing happens on this island without somebody sending something to Athens. Can you repair my watch? Can you fix my washing machine? Can you mend my car? No, I fucking well cannot, but I know a man in Athens who can help. That will cost you a thousand euros and maybe take several months if you're very lucky. Is that OK?"

She paused for breath.

"Well, no, it is not fucking OK!"

We sat in silence for a while. Eventually Jesus tried to lighten the mood.

"Come on, Kat," he said. "It's only a watch."

I winced. Mikki picked up her wine glass. Kat glared at Jesus.

"Fuck you!" she yelled. She stood up and threw a bowl of salad in his face. Jesus didn't move. He sat there with lettuce and cucumber hanging from his long curly hair. He looked confused and completely terrified.

Kat picked up a fork.

"Don't speak," she said. "Don't speak again."

Mikki and I stared at Kat. For a second I thought she might actually stab Jesus in the face. Instead she sat back down and burst into fits of uncontrollable laughter. It was contagious. Fuelled by relief and the ridiculous look on Jesus' face we doubled up and laughed until it hurt. The dogs began to howl. Only Jesus remained unamused. I felt sorry for him. Salad Boy.

Kat and Jesus were sworn antagonists. Kat hated Jesus because she thought he was a useless bum trading on his Norwegian charms and flippancy in order to secure himself a smooth passage at Mikki's expense. Jesus was scared of Kat because she didn't believe a word he said. He considered himself to be somewhat exotic and heroic. His tall travel tales of daring adventure were designed to impress. Kat scoffed at his stories about giant land crabs in Polynesia and diving for lobster with nothing but a spear and a loin cloth. She openly sneered at his nautical affectations. He had recently taken to wearing a thick, roll-necked fisherman's sweater and a heavy naval jacket.

"He looks like the captain of a submarine," Kat said. "He's only twenty five. I wouldn't trust him to steer a plastic boat in a bath."

Jesus was unused to such scepticism. He had spent the winter living on a boat moored in Kolasios Town's main harbour. He had been employed by a local shipyard to protect and repair the old wooden schooner which had apparently once belonged to the king of Norway. It was an easy job but one that Jesus failed to appreciate. He felt the shipyard didn't value his sailing skills. He kept threatening to quit.

The boat was beautiful. It sat in the harbour surrounded by bulging, ostentatious super-yachts like a rare painting. Jesus was supposed to live permanently on board. Instead he spent most nights with Mikki at her little house up in the hills overlooking Skataki. When he wasn't eating Mikki's food and washing his clothes in her sink, he would stumble around the Old Town bars in an argumentative stupor. He had never been able to hold his beer.

Mikki was getting tired of the abusive phone calls in the middle of the night.

"The last time he called," she said, as Jesus cleaned himself up in our bathroom, "he told me I looked like a crack whore but with better teeth. I woke up to find thirty seven missed calls on my phone."

Kat told her that Jesus was just trying to push Mikki over the edge so that she would initiate a permanent separation.

"He's a coward," Kat said. "He's just playing games. He hasn't got the balls to tell you to your face."

Mikki nodded and helped herself to another glass of wine.

"I know, Kat, but he can be really sweet when he's sober. He keeps promising to sort himself out and I don't want to be alone. I wish you two would try and get along."

Jesus returned from the bathroom and sat down in the courtyard.

"Is everything OK now?" he said.

Kat stood up and hugged Jesus. He flinched.

"Everything's OK," she laughed and winked at Mikki. "But you stink of salad."

In the morning I returned to the ogre in his little matchbox shop. He looked at me with sad eyes.

"Forget Athens," I said. "My wife is upset. I don't think she's prepared to wait."

"But what can I do?" said the ogre.

I pointed at one of the glass cabinets.

"How much for the identical watch over there? And a Zippo?"

The ogre glanced at the cabinet. He looked relieved.

"Two hundred and twenty euros. Two hundred. It's a fair price."

I nodded and reached for my credit card. He placed the watch in a carrier bag and held the door open for me as I left.

"Sometimes," he said with a kindly smile, "the quiet life is the easiest life."

18

BOMBS

A general air of panic had gripped Skataki. The faded resort which had remained dormant, dilapidated and forgotten for almost six months had suddenly woken up with a heart attack. It was as if someone had just remembered where they'd dropped the keys after the frantic stampede to flee the island at the end of last season. The chaos was entirely predictable. It was the same every summer. It wasn't as if the shylocks and hucksters who owned Skataki were completely unaware of the changing seasons. There were unofficial channels of communication between the shylocks, the tour operators, the airport and the cruise companies. There was no such thing as an unexpected arrival on Kolasios. In a matter of days the island would be open for business whether Skataki was ready or not.

A small army of local labourers and contractors had invaded the resort. Everywhere you looked there were flat-bed trucks laden with plastic furniture and potted plants. Peeling facades were hastily splashed with paint. Shops re-stocked with fake luxury labels and inflatable beach tat. The red sand and winter debris was hosed out of the bars and into the street. The beaches were levelled with bulldozers. Plagues of feral animals were poisoned with anti-freeze and dumped into skips. There was a lot of noise and cheap cement.

There was even more urgent activity behind the flimsy wooden scenery. Fleets of rental cars were wheeled out of the nearby fields to be re-plated and insured. One million taxi drivers jumped down from the trees and began to argue amongst themselves. The larger hotels to the north of the resort filled their pools with ten tonnes of chlorine. The water parks were tested for safety by sending rats down the slides in plastic bags. Seasonal staff were beaten with sticks and trained in the ways of all-inclusive service. It was not a good day to be a tourist in Skataki.

I was looking for a man called Mollusc. He owned the Prick Tease Tattoo Parlour on Bar Street. Mollusc wanted some advice on his new designs for the season. He was nowhere to be found. I went to see Tubby Tony who owned the fish and chip shop next door. Tony was a squat, irascible old ex-pat who lived nearby with two bulldogs and an alcoholic wife. He was pouring oil into his deep fat fryers from an enormous yellow barrel.

"Have you seen Mollusc?" I asked.

"Nope," said Tony.

"Do you know where he might be?"

"Nope."

I paused.

"Are you looking forward to the season, Tony?'

"Nope."

I sighed and headed for the door.

"Thanks, Tony, always a pleasure."

"Aye."

I drove slowly around Skataki in search of Mollusc. Chances were he'd be hunched over a beer somewhere. He was a well-meaning man but a lazy sod. The land behind the two main streets was strewn with builders' rubble and piles of rotten rubbish. Broken plastic chairs and long-forgotten menu boards lay abandoned amongst the overgrown weeds. Flies buzzed around the old car tyres and hub caps which sat in stagnant puddles of fetid water. Skataki was a cheap illusion.

Behind the atmosphere of piercing party hysteria, the resort was just a shit-hole and a shanty town.

I never found Mollusc but I nearly ran over Captain Manni Trelliossos. The police chief was ambling back from the beach with a can of beer in one hand and a cigarette in the other. He grinned as I slammed on my brakes.

"You drive like a fucking mad man!" he bellowed and pummelled the roof of the car with his fist. "English fucking mad man!"

"Hi, Manni," I said. "How are you?"

He shrugged.

"I am cleaning sun loungers in Skataki," he replied. "What can I say? They pay me to watch the beach now. Why? What is the beach going to do?"

I parked the car and we adjourned to Fatty's Bar. Fatty himself was nowhere to be seen but his paint-spattered brother served us drinks and a bowl of nuts. The captain was not a happy man. He had been relieved of his command by the mainland detectives who arrived as soon as the dead body was reported. Manni's squad had been dismantled and scattered in the wind. Most of them were now writing out traffic tickets to village farmers. Manni himself had lost a little weight along with his crooked empire. His khaki uniform was ill-fitting and crumpled. With only his badge, holster and gleaming aviator sunglasses as props, he looked like a tin-pot dictator in exile.

In Manni's opinion the authorities had made a mistake.

"All they think about are the tourists," he said. "Tourists and money. They want to clean this mess up quickly so they can pretend it never happened. The tourists must never know what has happened. Murder is bad for business. This squad from the mainland has the computers and the money. But the *malakas* do not have the local knowledge. They are used to street crime in Athens. They are not used to fishermen and shepherds. No one in Kavindos will talk to them."

"How do they know it was murder?" I asked.

Manni rubbed his eyes and sighed.

"We found the body in a cave."

"Maybe they were pot-holing or something? Accidents happen?"

The captain sipped his beer and wiped his mouth.

"Accident? Sure it was a fucking accident. We found the body in the cave with its spine broken. In several places. They drowned when the tide came in. Maybe they did this to themselves? Maybe it was suicide? Ha! Accident!"

He waved his empty glass at Fatty's brother and frowned at me.

"What is this pot-holing?"

I thought for a moment.

"Pot-holing is when people go exploring small caves and stuff. It's usually raining and no one ever finds anything. You wear hard-hats and take torches."

Manni looked at me blankly. I shrugged.

"Maybe it's not a Greek thing."

"Of course it's not a Greek thing," he said. "It's a fucking stupid thing! What is the point? Crawling around in a cave looking for something that isn't even there. Fucking stupid English!"

I smiled.

"Mainly Welsh."

Manni nodded and stared out of the window in silence. He was a proud man but his authority had been undermined. It took a billionaire Arab playboy almost four years to buy six Greek islands. It would take Manni considerably longer to regain his standing in the local community. He had been deemed incompetent as a professional policeman. It was a slap in the face. Right now he looked like an old bison whose days on the prairies were numbered. Manni would spend the summer breaking up bar brawls in Skataki and posing for photographs with fat girls in bikinis. But he still had his more lucrative commercial ventures to keep himself occupied. The eco-villas he owned just outside Kavindos were fully booked for the season. The Russians and eastern Europeans were negotiating to buy land across the island. Old goats like Manni would never starve.

"What have they done with the body?" I asked.

Manni glared at me with bulging eyes.

"My body!" he hissed and slapped his hand on the table. "It was my body! I found the body. They are fucking body snatchers!"

"But I don't know what they did with the body. They first took it to the hospital here on Kolasios. Then they took it to the mainland. Now maybe they have lost the body. Who knows? They are the experts. Maybe they have swapped the body for another. Maybe they have removed the body's internal organs and sold them on the black market. This is Greece. We are poor. It can happen."

I laughed and ordered another beer. Everyone knew the story of the dead British tourist and his missing kidney. After all these years there was still no explanation from the hospital concerned. It would never be resolved.

We finished our drinks and shook hands. Fatty's brother waived our bill. It was a customary gesture. All the bar owners knew that such hospitality would be repaid during the summer season. License applications could be sped through the courts by sympathetic officers. Local curfew infringements could be ignored. Verbal warnings could be issued instead of fines. Complaints could be muddled and mislaid. A few beers and a bowl of nuts was a small price to pay.

I drove back to town. Kat was in the shower when I got home. She emerged naked and dripping from the bathroom with her hair wrapped in a towel.

"You have a message from your sister on the machine," she said. "I think you'd better call her. It's about your cousin Samantha."

I played back the message and called Liz.

"Samantha's been arrested," Liz said bluntly. "It gets worse."

After maybe thirty minutes I hung up and helped myself to a beer from the fridge. Kat was sitting in the courtyard wearing a t-shirt and sarong. She raised an eyebrow.

"Don't laugh," I said. "Will you promise not to laugh?"

Kat nodded.

"Samantha's been arrested. A judge is dead. There are riots in central Bratislava. Oh, and the media are calling for the Prime Minister to resign."

There was silence. Kat stared at me for a long time. Her bottom lip began to tremble.

"Holy fuck!"

I sat down and lit a cigarette.

"It's not funny," I said. "It's pretty serious."

Kat began to cough uncontrollably.

"No shit!" she spluttered. "I need a glass of wine."

I waited for Kat to compose herself before trying to explain as best I could.

"So Sam was arrested just outside Bratislava," I began. "She was charged with extortion and tax offenses. Nothing too serious but enough for the police to keep her in custody. They try and make a deal. A lighter sentence can be arranged in exchange for Sam's co-operation with an on-going State investigation into organised crime. Sam refuses the deal and opts instead for a slick city lawyer who fronts up her bail and whisks her out of custody."

I lit a cigarette.

"A date for the trial is set and a circuit judge appointed to mediate the whole circus. Sam's lawyer is convinced he can get the case over-turned on a technicality and lack of evidence. The police and politicians, on the other hand, are desperate to be seen to be tackling the problems of organised crime. It was going to be a huge trial. And then it all went pear-shaped in Slovakia."

"How?" said Kat.

"Someone blew up the judge."

Kat looked amazed.

"Someone blew up the judge's car?"

I shook my head.

"Nope. The judge's car was fine. It was in the garage or something. Someone actually blew up the judge. In fact someone broke into the judge's house in the middle of the night, strapped an explosive waistcoat around his chest and threw him out of a helicopter over central Bratislava. The waistcoat was triggered remotely with a mobile phone. The judge exploded in mid-air. They're still finding body parts across the city."

Kat looked at me with wide eyes.

"You're fucking joking?"

"No," I said. "Apparently it's all over the news. A bit like the judge. So now the government has an embarrassing problem because it's patently clear to everyone that the politicians cannot control anything in Slovakia. Understandably no other judge wants to take over the trial. The citizens take to the streets to vent their frustration at the government. The police try to contain the angry crowds and someone gets shot. So now the mob goes on the rampage and the police are overwhelmed. The media blame the government for the judge's murder as well as the riots and call for the Prime Minister to resign. The Prime Minister is photographed taking his dog for a walk as if he hadn't a care in the world. This picture enrages ordinary Slovakians so much that they set fire to local tax offices and municipal buildings."

I paused.

"Where's Samantha?" asked Kat.

"No one knows. Her legal team are saying nothing. Apparently my uncle Arthur is very concerned. In fact he's furious. I suppose it must be pretty disconcerting to wake up one morning at the age of eighty three to discover that your own daughter's arrest and involvement in organised crime has de-stabilised an entire fucking country. There's probably a moral to the story somewhere."

"Politicians should never be photographed with animals," Kat said. "It makes them look like idiots. 'Man with nuclear bomb takes puppy for a shit!' It's stupid."

Later that evening Kat went out to her Greek language class. I phoned my sister to check on developments. Apparently Arthur was now apoplectic with rage and threatening to sue Slovakia. He had been advised not to travel by the Foreign Office. There was still no sign of Samantha. Her lawyer had issued a statement to say that Sam was not only safe but entirely innocent. The trial had been suspended indefinitely. Under the circumstances it would be impossible to find an impartial jury. Emotions were running too high and tempers were shredded. There was talk of moving the trial to another country altogether.

"It's a bit of a mess," said Liz, with an academic's understatement.

"I wish our family could be normal. Other families manage to get through life without sparking a single international incident. Most normal families just read the news over breakfast. Our family *is* the bloody news!"

I laughed.

"At least you and I are pretty normal?"

"Don't say that," Liz replied. "Chances are I'll now get hit by a meteorite in the morning."

I was almost asleep when Kat returned. She sat on the edge of the bed and patted the dogs.

"You smell of smoke," I mumbled into my pillow.

"We had a barbecue," said Kat. "We sang children's songs with a guitar. Apparently it's a good way to learn a language. It's good to learn like a child."

She leant over and kissed the back of my head.

"Now go to sleep. It's late."

The bed was warm. I heard sirens in the distance. It was probably nothing.

19

FIRE

Early the following morning we drove south to Pilafkos. Kat and I were on a mission. We intended to destroy the yellow plastic elephant which stood outside the Kleftiko Music Bar & Happy Snak Cafe. Pilafkos was not the prettiest resort on the island but it didn't deserve the elephant. The elephant belonged in a skip. It deserved to be crushed and incinerated. No one liked the elephant. They just defaced the elephant with graffiti. It was a problem for Nikos the owner and it was a problem for Pilafkos. That morning Kat and I intended to solve the problem with a large sledgehammer and a can of kerosene.

The elephant served no purpose whatsoever. It was an ugly and useless monolith which stood unloved and ridiculed outside the Klef like a circus freak in the rain. Nikos once told us that he'd bought it for the children. The plastic elephant was supposed to keep the children amused whilst their parents sipped over-priced cocktails at his bar. The children, however, preferred the internet computers inside. We tried to explain to Nikos that he was not dealing with normal children. Pilafkos was primarily a British holiday resort. He was dealing with British children. He was dealing with the retarded spawn of slow-brained adults who barely knew how to use a knife and fork. A yellow elephant was never going to work.

"They don't want an elephant, Nikos, they want sugar, they want sun and they want omelettes."

Nikos was a stubborn man. He shrugged.

"Fuck them," he said. "Now they have an elephant! The elephant stays."

Over the years the elephant had become symbolic of the resort's inevitable decline. A decade ago Pilafkos had been a thriving holiday destination. The bars were cheap. Accommodation was basic. The food was familiar and untroubled by flavour. It was easy money. Money for the old rope the restaurants served on toast. No visitor expected too much from Pilafkos. It had no history. It had a beach in the sun. It was hot. Pilafkos owed its success to little more than the weather, a fridge full of cold beer and a microwave oven.

A few years ago the writing was on the wall. The writing was on the elephant. The writing was everywhere. The first all-inclusive hotel was built just outside Pilafkos. Another soon followed. Business in the resort began to dwindle. To over-compensate for free-falling revenues the bar owners raised their prices. Trade deteriorated further. A grim cull of local establishments ensued. Many bars and restaurants were abandoned by the all-inclusive tourists and left to fight each other for the remaining scraps. Very few had the foresight to adapt. They had never seen the need to adapt. Pilafkos simply could not compete with itself.

Kat and I stopped for coffee and water. It was a mistake. We were too late to destroy the elephant. Nikos and five cousins were already standing outside the Klef staring at the elephant as we arrived. The winter storms had not been kind to the plastic beast. Nikos poked the elephant's broken trunk with his foot. It hung by a thread of fibre glass from the elephant's face. It was a big, happy, yellow face with human eyes and enormous ears. The elephant looked very simple.

We joined the little group standing in a circle around the elephant.

"Your elephant is broken," said Kat rather unnecessarily. "It looks like a lunatic."

Nikos glared at Kat.

"It can be fixed," he said. "It needs glue."

"It needs dynamite," Kat replied. "You should put the elephant out of its misery. We can help."

Nikos held out the palm of one hand in a dismissive gesture.

"This elephant cost me a fortune," he said. "It is from China. The children love my elephant."

The cousins nodded in agreement.

"Oh, come on, Nikos," I said. "The children laugh at your elephant. Everybody hates it. It's ugly."

"It is good for business."

"Drunk people draw on it," said Kat. She pointed to the elephant's back leg.

"Look! There's a penis!"

Nikos and his cousins peered at the crude doodle of a cock. Nikos shrugged.

"I will clean the elephant. It will be as good as new in no time."

"It's broken," said Kat. "Burn it."

After a while the cousins disappeared on their rattling, smoking scooters. Nikos invited us inside for coffee. He was keen to show us the Klef's new music system.

"Very expensive," he said. "Latest thing in Athens. No more DJs."

"Ever?" said Kat.

"No more DJs ever in the Klef. They want too much money. They play shit music. They drink all my beer. Fuck them!"

Nikos' ancient mother was scrubbing the kitchen floor on her hands and knees. She looked up and waved cheerfully.

"*Mama*," said Nikos. "Bring us coffee."

The old woman struggled to her feet and hobbled dutifully towards the cooker. Greek boys were tied to their mother's apron strings from birth until marriage. There was nothing more useless in the world than an unmarried Greek man.

Nikos' new music system turned out to be a laptop computer and a library of stored music. He stood behind the bar and looked at Kat.

"Ask me to play a song," he said. "Pretend that you are a customer and you would like to hear something. Ask me for anything."

Kat thought for a second before replying.

"Can you play something that wasn't written 20 years ago by a small American man with long hair wearing leather trousers and a cowboy hat?"

Nikos stared at Kat for a second.

"Ask me for something sensible," he said. "Ask me to play a song."

"OK, have you got any Greek music?"

Nikos beamed.

"Yes!"

He fiddled with the laptop for a few minutes. There was silence.

"I mean, no," he said eventually. "I have not yet programmed the Greek songs."

Kat sighed.

"Have you got any Bon Jovi, Nikos?"

"Yes!" he said and slapped the counter. "I have plenty of Bon Jovi. See? How simple was that? Even a fucking monkey could be a DJ!"

"If you like Bon Jovi," Kat said. "If I didn't like Bon Jovi then I'd probably go out and write something offensive on your elephant."

Nikos frowned and lit a cigarette.

"Everybody likes Bon Jovi," he muttered. "It is the law of Pilafkos during the summer. It has been the law of Pilafkos for the past ten years."

"I know," said Kat. "That's my point. I think you should hire another DJ."

Nikos' decrepit mother shuffled out of the kitchen carrying three tiny cups of strong Greek coffee on a tray. She nodded and beamed at Kat and me as we sipped the hot black syrup. She was very old. Her face was lined like the desert. Soft white whiskers covered her chin. Nikos gulped his coffee. He drank too much coffee. It was bad for his nerves. He placed his empty cup on the tray and waved his mother back to the kitchen. The old woman turned and limped slowly back to her chores.

I watched the frail old girl as she rubbed the base of her spine with one gnarled hand.

"Why can't your cousins help your mother in the kitchen?"

Nikos snorted.

"They are fishing," he said. "The kitchen is no place for them."

"Your mother is very old. Your cousins are fit and strong. It wouldn't kill them to help your mother."

"They are fishing," Nikos repeated. It was the end of the matter. His mother would scrub the floors and the hopeless cousins would lie on the beach drinking beer whilst staring at a cheap fishing rod. If by some miracle the cousins managed to catch anything at all then Nikos' mother would clean and cook it so that the boys would not go hungry. The old lady would eat fruit and go to bed early. In the morning she would be back in the kitchen.

We moved outside and sat smoking in the sun.

"It is very bad news about the fire," Nikos said quietly. "You have heard?"

Kat and I glanced at each other and shrugged.

"No," I said. "What fire?"

Nikos shook his head slowly.

"Last night there was a big fire at the harbour in Kolasios Town. Three boats were destroyed. There is much damage. I think they have the fire under control but a boy is still missing. He was working and living on one of the boats."

"Jesus!" I said.

"Yes, it is bad," said Nikos.

"No, no, the guy is called Jesus. Well, not really, but we call him Jesus. His real name is Anders. He's been living on a boat in the

harbour and trying to fix it up for the summer. The boat used to belong to the king of Norway or something."

I looked at Kat.

"Call Mikki. See if she's heard anything."

Kat nodded and reached into her jacket for our mobile phone.
There was no reply. We smoked another cigarette and tried again.
The line was dead.

"Shit," I said. "Jesus told me that Mikki sometimes stays over on
the boat. Do you think they're OK?"

The colour had drained from Kat's face. She suddenly looked ill.

"I didn't know Mikki stayed over on the boat," she said in a voice
that was barely a whisper. "How could I know that?"

"I suppose you would stay over if you were Mikki," I said. "I mean,
it's a nice boat. It's probably quite cosy when it's not on fire."

"Don't joke," said Kat. "This is not funny."

She punched the keypad and held the phone to one ear. She was
shaking.

"Nothing," she said. "Fuck!"

She stood up and handed me the phone.

"I have to go to the bathroom."

Nikos and I stared at the ground in silence. After a few minutes I
went inside to find Kat. Nikos' mother looked concerned and pointed
towards the bathroom door. I could hear Kat retching and coughing
inside. I knocked gently on the door and listened to the sound of running water. When Kat eventually appeared she looked wretched. Her
face was ashen and she'd been crying. She wiped her mouth with a
paper towel and forced a thin smile.

"Sorry," she said. "I have a bad feeling about all this."

We drove back to town via Mikki's little house in the hills overlooking Skataki. She had only recently moved in and the garden was
still a tip. A coffee cup and ashtray sat on a table beside the front
door. Mikki's ginger cat emerged to greet us. The cat didn't really
like any humans at all but at least he tolerated Kat and me with surly

bad humour. He rubbed himself around our legs and began to purr. There was no sign of either Mikki or her car. We heard dogs barking in the distance. The house felt as silent as space.

Kat shivered in the breeze and tried the phone once again. It had become a pointless exercise. Our battery was running low. Mikki was obviously not going to pick up. It was getting late. The cat stretched and ambled slowly across the garden towards the flap in the back door.

I drove back down the dirt track towards the main road. Kat lit two cigarettes and handed one to me.

"We have to do something," she said. "We have to know."

We headed back towards Kolasios Town. There wasn't much of a plan. All we could do was hope that Mikki would find her phone and notice the missed calls. I thought about trying to locate Manni Trelliosos. A fire at the harbour, however, would stretch the island's emergency services. Every policeman within fifty kilometers would have been ordered to fight the blaze. Mikki would not be a priority.

I remembered hearing the sirens late last night as I fell asleep. It was unusual to hear sirens during the winter and spring months. In the summer it was more common as drunken tourists fought with the local boys in Skataki and the Old Town. During the off-season it was usually just an ambulance on its way to treat the frail and elderly in the middle of the night.

I parked the car in the usual space and we walked up the alleyway towards the house. There was a figure sitting on the steps leading up to our porch. It was too dark to make out any features. It could just be a kid waiting for a lift. The alleyway was narrow and cars frequently had to manoeuvre around each other on the way out. It was only when we were just a few steps from the house that I recognised the hood of Mikki's jacket.

Kat burst into tears. She ran ahead and threw her arms around Mikki. The two women stumbled backwards under the force of Kat's embrace and held each other tightly for several minutes. Kat sobbed into Mikki's shoulder and smothered her face with little kisses. The dogs began to howl. Mikki was laughing and crying at the same time. Eventually they agreed to separate and stood staring at each other in amazement.

Kat wiped the tears from her face.

"Where the fuck have you been?" she blurted. "I've been phoning all day! We've been so worried."

Mikki took a hold of Kat's hand.

"I gave my phone to Anders," she said. "The silly bastard dropped his down the toilet and he has to call the shipyards every day. He was going to buy another one this morning but no one knows where he is. There was a fire last night. His boat exploded. I've been at the harbour all day but I couldn't stand there doing nothing any longer so I came here to wait for you guys. I didn't know what else to do. Shit! It's a big fucking mess."

We sat in the courtyard with a bottle of wine. Mikki told us that according to one policeman the boat had caught fire just after midnight. A couple of passing street cleaners had tried to douse the flames with buckets of sea water but the fire spread rapidly. The old wooden hull and heavy masts were soon ablaze. The flames destroyed the mooring ropes and the boat began to drift out into the harbour. The fuel tanks exploded long before the rescue tugs with their water cannons could be launched from the nearby commercial port. It was almost dawn before the schooner was safe for the fire marshals to board. There was no sign of Jesus.

Mikki helped herself to another glass of wine.

"I just hope he wakes up in a bar somewhere with a head like a fucking brick."

Later that evening the three of us walked down to the harbour. The police had cordoned off the pretty waterfront promenade. Yellow tape stretched all the way from the grand Italian church at the far end to the Mirrorball Lounge at the other. Floodlights had been appropriated from the town's football stadium. The harbour was bathed in a ghostly white light. The thick, acrid stench of wet embers and scorched plastic hung in the air.

We joined the crowds drinking in a bar opposite the marina. The fire had attracted quite a circus. The aftermath had turned into something of a social event for the city's night birds and debutantes. There was a carnival atmosphere in the bar. The city's young elite jostled to be seen and heard above the music and laughter. Bar staff sashayed between the tables carrying trays of champagne and cocktails. The place felt like a macabre costume party for the benefit of the pampered, adolescent aristocracy. It was strange. The fire had become a mere backdrop for more important political concerns.

We squeezed into a table in one corner and ordered a bottle of wine. The bar was directly opposite the empty space where Jesus' boat should have been moored. The modern yachts either side of the space looked charred and badly damaged but they were both still afloat. We sat in silence and looked out across the dark waters of the ancient harbour. We could see the arc lights of the port authority's two iron fire tugs bobbing gently near the harbour entrance. They would wait until dawn before dragging the smouldering wreck of Jesus' boat to one of the shipyards along the coast.

At this time of year the marina was not busy. Mainly it was used to keep the seasonal tourist boats and island-hopping ferries safe from the winter storms. Only a few private yachts were moored in the harbour on a permanent basis. During the summer months, however, the marina became choked with the space-age vessels of the super-rich. Flotillas of towering wealth sat glinting in the sunlight as some of the richest old men in the world cavorted on deck wearing snug bikini trunks like slippery Sumo crabs. Topless blonde crack-heads gazed serenely down on to the promenade from lofty observation decks like silicone gazelles. Itinerant serfs like Jesus served caviar and crystal-meth. Yet even these gilded palaces of playboy pomp were no match for the true goliaths of the Mediterranean.

The largest yachts from Israel and Russia resembled battleships. The polished, gun-metal hulls and huge acres of dark glass lent them a slightly sinister presence. Helicopters perched high up in superstructures that bristled with radar and satellite antennae. Dark-suited security men guarded the gangways and gunwales. No one ever emerged from these monstrous black temples which seemed to loom over the port like menacing war machines. There was never any activity on deck. No one ever laughed or sang or tossed a beach ball around just for a laugh. The ships seemed as air-tight as coffins. They glided into port like a nuclear terror strike and just disappeared a few weeks later in the middle of the night. It was a level of luxury way beyond mere ostentation. It was the luxury of isolation. Billions of dollars buys some people an awful lot of paranoia.

The evening was warm. The three of us sat and watched the local boys tearing up the strip on their bored-out scooters. The noise was all for show. The rich girls in the bar affected disinterest. The local boys combed their hair and tried to smoke like Jimmy Dean. The promenade was a movie set. Teenage hearts beat as one under a silver moon. The same old blue denim dreams. The same drama of distraction. The same movie was playing out around the world in every parking lot and cinema, every night club and shopping mall, and it was the greatest movie in the world. Everybody knew the ending. The bad guy dies. The good guy gets the girl. They kiss.

It wasn't until months later that I heard Jesus had washed up on a beach in Turkey. He had been nailed to a cross and tossed into the sea. The crucifixion didn't kill Jesus. They found salt water in his lungs. Jesus had drowned on the cross. I didn't care. By the time I heard the news it didn't matter anyway.

20

AIRPORT

A magical air of turmoil gripped the island. The fire could not have happened at a more inconvenient time. The port authorities were still struggling to camouflage any evidence of the blaze even as the first charter flights began to appear in the sky overhead. Not that any visitor would be any the wiser. The fire was never reported in the media. The island had survived for thousands of years. She was a tough old bitch. She had survived earthquakes and hurricanes and storms and the endless summer furnace. She had survived invasions and wars and she had fought back like a tigress. But these days the island could not survive without the regular flow of tourist cash. A fire at the main marina was simply bad for business.

Jesus' schooner was towed to a quiet boatyard on the other side of the island where she lay abandoned for months. Eventually she was sold for scrap. The two yachts which had been moored either side of the old schooner were moved to the main shipyards just out of town. The Russian and Turkish owners agreed a generous and fast-tracked insurance pay-out in exchange for their silence. It was a fair deal. It was a deal, however, which sparked rumours that the fire might have been a desperate ruse to defraud the underwriters. It didn't make much sense. Insurance companies employed their own investigators.

They were fastidious and ruthless. One tiny discrepancy could stall a pay-out for years. The Kolasios port authority knew this. The island could not afford a lengthy legal battle which could easily tarnish its reputation and undermine the local economy. A private settlement was agreed within a matter of hours.

One of the smaller island ferries was moved from the commercial port into the empty space at the marina. The promenade was re-painted. The stalls selling ice cream and soda re-appeared. The beggars and time-share touts returned. The old Catholic priest took his daily stroll along the seafront as usual. Lovers walked arm-in-arm as the crystal waters sparkled beneath the blue skies. Life went on. There was life in the old bitch yet.

That morning the little island airport was a riot of activity. It was hot. I parked the car in the shade and watched from a distance as the crowds spilled out of the terminal building. They stood there punch-drunk and happy like herds of innocent cattle. Young transfer reps wearing cheap plastic shirts hung around like flies. They ticked names off lists with an irritable energy and steered people towards the muddle of multi-cultured coaches as quickly as possible. It was all about the turnaround. The turnaround was god. The coaches delivered the tourists to the resorts around the island. They picked up more tourists returning to the airport. They dropped those tourists off at one terminal and then waited in the coach park for another flight to arrive. It was supposed to run like clockwork. One late arrival, however, could screw the entire operation. One fucking piss-head who couldn't find his passport could tip the schedules into oblivion. If the turnaround failed then the law of the holiday jungle was invoked and it was every man, woman and piss-head for themselves. It was in the small print which no one ever read.

The coach park itself was a sprawling concrete expanse of diesel haze and rumbling vibrations. I got out of the car for a cigarette. A heady mixture of fuel and heat hit my lungs. The lines of new arrivals snaked from the terminal building to the coach park. They struggled the short distance dragging their suitcases behind them like mules. Most were already dripping with sweat.

I helped a young woman heave her suitcase into the cavernous underbelly of a nearby coach. She couldn't have been more than twenty three. She had a tattoo of a bird on one hand. Her eyes were blue and bright. But her head was too small for her body. The head belonged to someone sleeker and fitter than the young woman who stood there gasping for oxygen. Her shapeless body was wrapped in rolls of excess flesh which hung from her arms and hips like rancid butter. She looked like a dumpling. A monstrous troll who had waddled down from her lair to gorge on the unborn children of her village.

"Very kind," she wheezed. "Hot, innit?"

I smiled.

"It gets hotter."

The troll rolled her eyes and lit a cigarette. She stood smoking and staring at the ground in silence like a stun-gunned heifer. Her breathing sounded like wet sandpaper. I thought for a second that she might be shy. But she wasn't shy. She was just stupid. After a while she stubbed out her cigarette with one porky hoof.

"Best be off," she said. "I'm on holiday."

I nodded and watched her plod laboriously towards the front of the coach. She paused at the door and looked back at me.

"By the way," she said. "Where the fucking hell am I?"

I laughed.

"You're in Greece."

Her face lit up like a simple child with a cheap toy.

"Bloody brilliant!" she said. "I love Greece."

"Ever been before?"

The shapeless fat mule cackled merrily.

"Nah, but I've seen the film. The one with Abba in it. I love Greek men!"

She hoisted herself up into the coach. I heard the sound of people singing. The driver winked at me and closed the luggage bay doors before hopping back on board. I stood back as the air brakes hissed and the coach edged out to join the chaos of traffic which circled the airport.

I strolled back towards the terminal building. There was a lull before the next scheduled arrival. Transfer reps huddled together in jittery groups. They were wired on energy drinks and confusion. Taxi drivers drank coffee and played backgammon in the sun. A small army of cleaners swept cigarette butts into the gutter and emptied the bins. Everybody kept one eye on the information screens. There were no delays.

The little airport was a busy machine. A machine designed to deliver hundreds and thousands of people safely to a single destination. A machine to process and identify and reference and tag those people with the minimum of interruption. A machine to organise the constant stream of human data and jumbled tera-bytes of personal information which passed through its systems every day. It was unthinkable that such a machine could ever malfunction. The machine was both as formidable and fragile as the human brain. A tiny system failure could result in anarchy and meltdown. The machine would collapse. People would die.

It was cool inside the terminal building. I bought a coffee from the kiosk on the ground floor and sat in a metal chair near the arrivals hall. I scanned the rows of car rental counters. The staff looked tired. Everybody looked tired. It was only May. The season had barely started. No one could predict the future but it was safe to assume that the cloudless blue months ahead would take their toll.

I heard a muted roar in the distance as the Gatwick charter flight touched down on the runway. There was time for a cigarette outside. I didn't know what I was trying to find at the airport. I was hoping for a grand gesture. A gesture so huge and pointless that it would be impossible for anybody to comprehend. That would make me happy. I looked around at the cleaners and the taxi drivers and the tourists and the transfer reps. Somewhere here was a solution to the puzzle.

"Please?"

There was a young woman at my side. She held out a cigarette in one hand.

"Do you have a light?"

I smiled and handed her my new Zippo lighter. She was very beautiful. Her accent was maybe Italian. She wore tight blue jeans and a red checked shirt which was tied in a knot around her slim waist. She looked comfortable and stylish. Her long, dark hair framed a perfect face with olive eyes and sensual lips. She exhaled gratefully and handed back my lighter.

"*Grazie*," she said. "Thank you."

She took a sip from a bottle of water.

"Is hot today. Is very hot."

I nodded.

"It gets hotter. It's only May."

"Yes, yes," she said. "This I can believe."

We smoked in silence for a while. I admired her vampish red nails and the curve of her neck.

"You're in Greece," I said. The young woman stared at me for a second. She seemed unsure whether she had heard correctly. Then she laughed. The sound of her laughter could melt a thousand hearts.

"Yes, I know. I come here all the time. It is very beautiful."

I smiled and stubbed my cigarette out on the floor.

"It's just that some people don't seem to know where they are when they get here. It's very important to know where you are."

The young woman nodded.

"*Ciao*," I said. "Thank you. Have a good holiday."

I stood at the back of the concourse and watched the new arrivals as they emerged from the baggage hall. Taxi drivers jostled for position with the holiday and hotel reps. The new arrivals looked flustered and fearful. Some scanned the rows of hand-held signs and placards searching for a recognisable name. Others simply strolled through the sliding doors and stopped in their tracks. Soon there was gridlock. Faces reddened with frustration. People barged into one another. Suitcases became weapons.

I watched and waited for a signal. Anything at all. At that moment it was still an homogenous wave of pale skin and drab clothing. It was impossible to identify an individual. But just like the safari big game hunters I had patience and gradually the machine began to filter the crowds into manageable groups. After a while I noticed a family of four extricate themselves from the main herd and head towards a car rental counter near to where I was standing.

The short man-bull wore a blue football shirt under a polyester shell-suit. His hair was closely cropped and his eyes were wild and crazed after the long flight. His wife looked nervous and pinched as if her tatty blonde hair had been too tightly attached to her skull. Two teenage children stood dumbly in the background with dull faces and bad skin. The man-bull dropped his bag on the floor and barely glanced at the girl behind the counter.

"Shirley," he said.

The girl looked at him blankly. There was a silence. The man-bull sneezed.

"I'm sorry," said the girl. "Do you want to rent a car?"

"No, luv," he replied. "I don't want to rent a car. I've already rented a car. You have my credit card. The name's Shirley. Dave and Janet Shirley. From London."

The girl behind the counter smiled at the man-bull in front of her.

"Excellent," she said. "Let me check."

"You do that," muttered the man-bull. He fumbled with some documents as the girl tapped her computer keyboard.

"Come on, Dave," said the man-bull's wife in a voice like salt. "I'm fucking exhausted and I'm dying for a fag."

"Do one, Jan," said Dave. "I'm dealing with it."

After a few moments the girl behind the counter looked up at Dave.

"Everything is fine," she said. "We have reserved a Hyundai for you and your family. I will get the keys."

Dave's face began to bulge.

"You mean an Audi, right?" he said. "I ordered an Audi. I did not order a bloody Hyun...whatever you call it. Don't mess me about. I want an Audi and I want it now."

The girl behind the counter looked bewildered.

"But we do not have an Audi left, sir," she said. "They have all been rented out. We only have the Hyundai."

"Then I suggest you phone your manager," said Dave ominously. "I am not sitting in a box built by slit-eyed monkeys who eat food with sticks. It's not right. I want a car that I can at least bloody spell! This is a liberty. Typical of you lot. Take the money and then don't deliver. Don't try and tell me that you would actually want to drive one of those things yourself?"

"I wouldn't know, sir," said the girl. "I don't drive. But the Hyundai is a very reliable vehicle."

Dave snorted incredulously.

"I don't give a toss, luv. I don't care whether it could get me to another planet and back again. I don't want it. *Capice?* Now why don't you be a clever girl and phone Stavros or Pedro or whatever your manager is called and get this sorted? We're supposed to be on bloody holiday."

The girl stared at Dave with an icy calm. I could hear the heavy iron doors of superficial civility closing forever in Dave's face. Very slowly the girl picked up the telephone on her desk.

"Of course, sir," she said. "You may wait over there."

She pointed towards a row of uncomfortable seats.

"Dad," whined Dave's tubby young son. "Have we got an Audi?"

The man-bull spun around and glared at the boy.

"No, Daryl, we do not have a fucking Audi!" he said. "Now sit down over there and shut it."

It took someone almost two hours to find Dave and his family a suitable vehicle. Dave was not a happy man. His face had long since morphed into a frozen state of impotent frustration and rage. He sat scowling and fidgeting impatiently whilst his family skimmed idly through a pile of celebrity magazines. Eventually the girl behind the counter handed him the keys with the sweet smile of revenge.

"Enjoy your stay on Kolasios, sir," she said.

"What's left of it," snarled Dave. "Fucking disgrace!"

The VW Golf was parked in a bay on the far side of the airport. It was painted a sickly shade of lilac and looked to all intents and purposes like a big toy. Dave had stopped caring long ago. I watched from a distance as he shoe-horned his family and their luggage into the car. Janet got behind the wheel. Dave slammed the passenger door shut. The car didn't move. After a few seconds Dave and Janet got out again and they swapped sides. It was an easy mistake to make. Especially for a fucking moron like Dave Shirley.

I followed the family out of the airport. They headed south along the busy coast road. Dave drove slowly and erratically, drifting over the centre line and touching the brakes every time he was overtaken. He was overtaken a lot. I watched with interest as Dave's wife unfolded a huge road map inside the car. It was impractical and rather unnecessary. There was really only one road to follow. The map itself kept flapping in the breeze and threatened to smother Dave. He gesticulated wildly and veered towards a ditch. I kept two vehicles between us at all times. The little lilac Golf was difficult to lose. I whistled a tune as we trundled down the island towards Kavindos.

I tried to guess where Dave and his family might be staying. We had already passed the party slums of Skataki and, anyway, Dave didn't look the type. Maybe in his cocky youth. These days he had the brusque impatience of a self-made man. He didn't strike me as a man who would settle for a disturbed night's sleep. He also didn't strike me as a man who would appreciate Kavindos. He had a family to entertain and the old village was hard work. Kavindos was popular with dotty matriarchs and newly-weds. The cobbled alleyways and steep paths were cramped and claustrophobic. Dave looked like he needed to relax in familiar surroundings. The family needed televisions and computers to keep themselves amused. They needed recognisable food and cheap wine. They needed a sandy beach and plenty of bottled water. All of which meant they were probably staying in Pilafkos. The resort was perfect. It had no soul.

The family stopped for supplies at a supermarket just north of Kavindos. The two adults got out of the car and left the children arguing in the back seat. I parked in the shade and waited. After about fifteen minutes Dave and Janet emerged pushing a trolley laden with tins of baked beans, cartons of cigarettes and frozen family meals. They tipped everything into the boot and dumped the trolley beside the curb. They climbed back into the car and consulted the map once again. Dave pulled out onto the main road directly in front of a quad bike. The rider panicked, swerved and stalled the machine. He sat there cringeing with shock as the Golf disappeared around a bend in the distance. A transfer coach bore down on the quad. The rider jumped from his seat like a hare. He stumbled, tripped and fell into a hedge. The coach tore past just inches from the stricken quad. The rider picked himself up and stood there dumbfounded. He shook his head sadly.

I set off after Dave. Sure enough, as we approached the steep hill leading down into Pilafkos, he slowed to such a snail's pace that I had to overtake. I caught a glimpse of his bewildered face as I passed. He was hunched over the wheel searching for signposts that didn't exist. Janet sat beside him jabbing a finger at the map. The two children stared blankly out of the window like surly toads. I pulled over at the bottom of the hill and watched the Golf in my mirrors. As the car crawled past me I saw Janet point to the main drag on our left. Dave turned slowly onto the sleepy strip of burger bars and restaurants. I waited for him to get far enough ahead so as not to arouse any suspicions. It was now a game of stealth. I had the benefit of local knowledge and patience. Dave had the advantage of unpredictability.

I followed the car through Pilafkos and out into the wilderness beyond the Klef. I noticed Nikos had repaired the yellow elephant's broken trunk with black tape. The tarmac began to disintegrate. Soon the road was little more than a track. I followed the clouds of dust ahead as Dave's car bounced over the terrain towards a remote development of four modern villas overlooking the sea. I stopped the car on the crest of a hill and switched off the engine. The journey was over. There was no where else for Dave to go. Beyond the white villas there was nothing except a barren expanse of shrub and rock. It was dead land in a godless location.

I climbed out of the car. The only sound was the persistent pulse of the cicadas in the grass. I knew the villas quite well. They were named after Greek gods. They were clean and bright and well-equipped. Each had their own private swimming pool surrounded by sun loungers and umbrellas. The two old English queens who owned the villas took pride in every detail. They flew over several times a year to add yet more artefacts and ornaments purchased from European auction houses. Paul and Patrick could be quite menacing. You wouldn't want to cross the boys. Rumours of their shady criminal connections circulated amongst the ex-pats and rival property owners on the island.

I waited for a while as Dave Shirley and his family negotiated the main compound gates and parked in front of Villa Helios. The windows were shuttered and the place looked airless. The family disappeared inside with their luggage. I climbed back into the car.

On the way back to town I stopped at a hardware store.

"We have rats," I said to the clerk behind the counter.
"Rats?" he said. "Maybe you need pellets?"
"No," I replied. "We have big rats. I need razor wire."

21

ELVIS

The following morning I woke early and made breakfast. It was a beautiful day. Kat and I sat in the courtyard eating scrambled eggs and drinking fresh coffee. We showered, dressed and went our separate ways for the day. Kat was heading for the beach. She packed a rucksack with a towel, a bottle of water and a packet of cigarettes. After she had gone I picked up the car keys and headed out of town.

I found the car rental company situated on the main road a few kilometres from the airport. Rows of identical cars were arranged neatly on the forecourt like sweets. The Greek flag fluttered from a pole on top of the showroom. I parked in a bay behind the store and walked inside.

"I have a car reserved," I said to the salesman.

"Sure," he said and took my papers. He entered my details into his computer and glanced up.

"An Audi, right?"

I nodded.

"The Q5."

"No problem," said the salesman. "Give me a few minutes to print out the paperwork. There's a coffee machine if you want to help yourself."

The showroom was quiet and cool. I had deliberately chosen the company because it was a new venture on the island and probably still keen to impress. They needed customers. I figured they might be less picky than the major airport chains.

The salesman handed me the keys along with my passport and a bunch of documents.

"There you go, Mr. Rampling," he said. "Have a good trip."

He shook my hand and held the door open as I stepped outside onto the forecourt. I had to smile. It was probably the closest Johnny the Stick had ever been to an Audi Q5 in his life.

The car itself was stately and luxurious. It felt calm and peaceful inside the leather-padded cocoon. I sat high up in the clouds and surveyed the universe through polarized glass. I turned the key in the ignition. There was only the slightest sensation as a million micro-systems came alive. I revved the huge engine and felt the car purr beneath my feet. I drove slowly around the showroom to where my car was parked. I transferred a few things including a hold-all with a change of clothes. The heavy coil of woven sackcloth was awkward and cumbersome.

I pulled out of the forecourt and headed south down the island's West coast. The roads beyond the airport were clear. Pretty villages and farm land passed in a soft blur through my velvet vision. I felt remote and disengaged. I was driving effortlessly through my own silent movie. I had no sense of speed or direction. There was only the immediate moment of opiate motion. The world outside had ceased to exist.

After maybe an hour I turned inland and drove up into the mountains. I parked near the clearing in the forest. The graves lay undisturbed beneath the sun-dappled canopy of proud old trees. I glanced at the digital clock on the dashboard. It was almost midday. I stepped out of the car and walked around to the boot. I needed to make my preparations with the greatest care. I had allowed myself one hour. I pulled on a pair of heavy-duty gloves and began to cautiously untie the coil of woven sackcloth. The whole operation was painstaking. It took longer than I had anticipated. I cursed my own miscalculations but dared not panic for the sake of my own safety. I felt the sweat trickle down my face and into my eyes. But I carried on. It had to be perfect.

After maybe two hours I had finished. I stood up and surveyed the clearing. Satisfied that everything was neatly camouflaged, I wiped my face with a towel and changed my shirt. I threw my old t-shirt into the bag along with the gloves and the empty sackcloth. I climbed back into the Audi and headed south. It was two-seventeen. I had forty three minutes to reach Pilafkos.

The roads were mercifully clear and I made the journey with three minutes to spare. I pulled over on the crest of the hill over-looking the four villas and waited until exactly three o'clock. Only one villa appeared to be occupied. I could just make out the bright-ly coloured beach towels which lay strewn across the sun deck and loungers. A tiny figure drifted aimlessly around the pool on an in-flatable lilo.

I set off down the hill towards the villa. The gates to the complex were open. I parked next to the ugly lilac Golf and rang the doorbell. I heard the sound of a television from inside the villa. There was a splash as someone dived into the pool. I waited outside in the searing heat. A lizard sat motionless on a wall. It was a fine specimen with a long tale and heavy lidded eyes. Its body was dark green and flecked with yellow spots. Its head was the colour of blue marble and looked like a rubber mask. I stared at the lizard for a long time.

Paul and Patrick adored this place. Personally I could never really see the appeal. At the end of the day the villas were just another pile of white bricks and concrete under a huge blue sky. It was, however, the Greek dream to which everybody else seemed to aspire. The per-fect island postcard. Lazy days spent soaking up the sun with noth-ing but the wind and the cicadas for company. Balmy evenings spent drinking wine under the vast tapestry of silver stars. I think Patrick liked the place more than Paul. Patrick liked the simple life. Paul's tastes were chintzier and more ornate.

I first met the boys a few years ago when they had flown out to oversee the final stages of the villas' construction. It was March. The land was a mess. The boys arrived wearing long overcoats and carrying briefcases stuffed with cash. The Greek site foreman was demanding a speed tax in order to finish the project on time. Without the tax being paid to the foreman directly he could not guarantee the project. The foreman spent four weeks with his right leg in plaster. The villas were completed and signed off in record time. The boys spent the cash on new bathrooms.

Paul and Patrick told me the story over a glass of red wine one night. They had invited Kat and I over for a meal.

"Speed tax my big arse," chuckled Patrick. "Never has my jaded old sense of queenery been so affronted."

"We got a good deal on the bathrooms as well," said Paul. "They practically threw the whole store at us for pennies."

"I can't think why," said Kat.

The boys roared with laughter and topped up our glasses. That night we ate and drank until dawn. The boys regaled us with stories of Italian opera and Soho jazz, Victorian architecture and East End dance halls. They asked Kat and I about our new life as ex-pats on a Greek island. Back then we had been full of hope.

The lizard shifted on the wall. I rang the bell once again. The door opened and the bull-man stood in front of me holding a can of beer.

"What?" said Dave Shirley.

I smiled and held out my hand.

"My name is John Rampling," I said. "I am the Vice President of the Kolasios Car Company."

Dave's eyes narrowed imperceptibly. He ignored my outstretched hand.

"So what?"

"I would like to offer my sincerest apologies on behalf of the company concerning the unfortunate misunderstanding at the airport yesterday. I have driven down here today to make that apology in person."

There was a pause. I could almost hear Dave Shirley's brain trying to digest the information and relay the appropriate reaction. He shook my hand cautiously.

"Yeah, well..." he muttered.

"I would also like to offer you an upgrade at no extra cost."

I turned and pointed at the gleaming black Audi parked in front of the villa.

"No extra cost?" Dave repeated.

I nodded.

"No extra cost."

Dave's wife appeared in the doorway. She wore an orange bikini and flip-flops. Her body was pale and bony.

"Who is it, Dave?" she said.

I held out my hand.

"John Rampling," I said. "Vice President of Kolasios Cars."

"He wants to give us that big bloody Audi," said Dave.

Janet glanced over my shoulder at the car.

"Well, in that case," she said, "you'd better ask the man inside for a cup of tea or something."

I smiled my winning smile and followed the couple over the threshold. The villa was cool and dark. It smelt of bleach and sun cream. Piles of clothes lay scattered around the living room as if hurled by a dervish. Dave and Janet's frumpy daughter lay slumped in front of the television. She stared expressionless at a cacophonous Greek cartoon. I glanced out of the window. Daryl sat on the lilo in the middle of the pool eating a kebab. He looked like a little fat emperor. I watched as he picked out a clump of salad and dropped it disdainfully into the water. He took a bite and chewed vacantly. A greasy slice of meat stuck to his chin.

"Cup of tea?" said Janet.

"Get the man a beer, Jan," said Dave. "He's driven a long way."

"Please," I said. "I have a better idea."

I leant casually against the kitchen counter and looked at Dave.

"It would make my company very happy if you were to allow me to show you something of our little island. It's a beautiful afternoon. It could also be helpful if you were to familiarise yourself with both the Audi and some of the roads. Driving in Greece can be something of an experience."

Dave rolled his eyes to indicate that he knew all about that particular experience.

"Too right," he said.

"I have food and plenty of beer in the car," I continued gently. "We could stop somewhere for a picnic and then later I could take you to my favourite taverna for a meal. The owner is a good friend. He will not charge you a single euro."

Janet and Dave exchanged glances.

"So this would be totally *gratis* then?" said Dave. "Essentially you'd be paying for all this just to keep us *stumm*? So we wouldn't be awkward buggers when we get home?"

I smiled.

"Exactly," I said. "I hope you won't take offense at my transparent suggestion?"

Dave took a hearty swig of beer and tossed the empty can towards an overflowing pedal bin. The can hit the lid and clattered to the floor. Dave burped loudly.

"Not at all," he said. "It all sounds bloody perfect."

He walked over to the sliding patio doors and called out to the fat kid in the pool.

"Oi! Daryl! We've got the fucking Audi and we're going out for a meal. Get out of the water and look lively!"

He turned and glanced at the comatose lump on the sofa.

"You too, princess," he said. "We're going out."

The young girl sighed.

"Do as your dad says, Whitney," said Janet. "It'll do you good to get some air."

"Give us a minute," Dave said to me. "I suppose we'd better throw on some clothes."

I sat down on the sofa and waited. The television was hypnotic. I tried to make sense of the cartoon. For some reason a giant green frog was hitting an alligator over the head with a plank of wood. I turned to look at the shapeless young girl beside me.

"What are you watching?" I said.

"Dunno," said Whitney in a flat monotone. "It's in foreign."

I glanced back at the screen. The green frog was now splashing about in a puddle.

"Well, actually," I said, "it's in Greek. That's because you're in Greece."

I paused. There was no reaction. The young girl's eyes remained glazed.

"Do you like Greece?"

"Dunno," said Whitney.

I watched the fat kid from the pool squelch barefoot across the living room and disappear into one of the bedrooms.

"Dad!" he whined. "My kebab was wet."

Dave emerged wearing a short-sleeved shirt and blue jeans. A cloud of aftershave filled the room. He clapped his hands and tapped Daryl's bedroom door.

"Come on, son," he said. "Chop-chop. Don't hang about."

Janet appeared wearing khaki slacks and a white t-shirt. Two gold hoops hung from each ear. Dave grinned and grabbed her waist.

"Come on, Jan, give us a twirl!"

Janet giggled. He began to waltz his wife around the room.

"*I love-a the Greece,*" he sang. "*I love-a the Zorba, I love-a the feta, I love-a the...*"

He paused and frowned.

"What else is Greek?"

"George Michael?" said Janet.

Dave laughed.

"Don't be daft. George Michael's a poof not a Bubble!"

I stood up and motioned towards the front door.

"Maybe I should drive to begin with," I said. "It's a big car and the handling takes a little getting used to. I can let Dave take over the wheel on the way back when the roads will be quieter."

"Sure, sure," said Dave. "Whatever you say, Parker."

He ushered his family out of the villa and double-locked the front door. He put the key in the right-hand pocket of his jeans. We trudged across the gravel towards the Audi. Daryl gawped at the machine in awe.

"Does it go fast?"

I smiled.

"It can, yes, but it's probably safer if we take it easy to begin with."

Janet and the two children climbed into the back seat. Dave settled in the front and patted the dashboard like an old friend.

"Now this is more like it," he said. "Proper bloody class."

It was three forty-seven. I started the engine and we rolled forward towards the gates.

"Buckle up, kids," I said. "It's a bumpy road."

I drove through Pilafkos and headed north up the coast.

"Oh, Dave," said Janet wistfully. "It's beautiful, innit?"

Dave stared out of the window at the blue sea beyond the sun-baked fields and olive groves.

"Bloody paradise," he said.

After a few miles he turned to look at me.

"You live out here?"

I nodded.

"My wife and I moved out here five years ago," I said. "It's where we belong."

"Always fancied it myself," said Dave. "A little place in the sun. Living the good life. Nothing fancy. A bit of golf. A bit of swimming. I've put a little money aside for my old age and the kids ain't getting any younger.

"London's a shit-hole these days. All the gangs, the drugs, the Blacks, the Poles, even the football...it's not England any more, is it, Jan?"

I looked at Janet's face in the rear view mirror. She wrinkled her nose.

"It's a sewer," she said. "They treat England like a sewer."

I frowned.

"Who does?"

"The Pakis, the Romanians, the immigrants...all the scum of the world. It's a real shame."

We drove in silence for a while. The radio played a little Elvis. Janet sat in the back seat smiling serenely into space. The two children stared blankly out of the windows. Dave tapped his hands in time with the song and glared at the road ahead as we turned inland and headed towards the mountains.

"*You make me so lonely baby, I get so lonely, I get so lonely I could die...*"

The clearing in the forest was as I had left it earlier. I parked the Audi carefully and turned off the engine.

"Thirsty?" I said.

Dave turned in his seat and looked at his wife.

"What do you reckon, Jan? Beer o'clock?"

"Just the one, Dave," said Janet. "You're driving later. You know what I think about drinking and driving."

"I'll spill it," Dave replied and grinned at me. "Come on, kids, look alive."

I fetched a chequered table cloth from the boot of the Audi and laid it on the ground in the middle of the sun-dappled clearing. I went back to the car and returned with a wicker picnic basket. I opened the basket and handed cans of beer to Dave and Janet. I tossed a yellow frisbee at Daryl. The frisbee hit Daryl in the face.

"Ow!" he said, rubbing his head.

Dave laughed, picked up the frisbee and threw it across the clearing. I watched the yellow plastic disc glide across the grass until it hit a tree.

"Fetch!" said Dave and everybody sniggered. Daryl waddled off to retrieve the frisbee.

"Careful," said Janet. "Don't go too far. And take Whitney with you."

The children wandered morosely off into the undergrowth. Dave popped open his can of beer and took a hearty swig.

"Cheers!" he said.

I smiled at them both and raised my bottle of water.

"*Yamas.*"

I heard the kids crashing happily through the shrubbery. It wouldn't be long. It couldn't be long. One wrong footstep was all it would take for the heavens to split open and the sky to implode. I smiled at Janet. She was sitting cross-legged on the ground above the remains of the bridesmaid.

"So this taverna?" said Dave greedily. "Can you get a decent bit of steak or is it the usual muck in sauce?"

Before I could reply there was a squeal from the undergrowth. Janet sat bolt upright. No one moved. Then a piercing scream cut the air like a laser. I saw real panic in Janet's eyes.

"Jesus, Dave," she said. "What's happened?"

Dave stood up stiffly and squinted at the undergrowth. He took one step towards a large tree. He saw his son. Daryl was trying to walk and hold his ankle at the same time. The young boy was in shock. He crumpled to the ground and lay there moaning.

Janet sprang to her feet and ran across the clearing. She knelt down beside her son and stared at his foot. She looked up at Dave.

"He's cut his foot off," she whispered. "He's only gone and cut his own fucking foot off!"

"Where's Whitney?" said Dave. They scanned the undergrowth in vain. Janet began to sob.

A small figure suddenly appeared from behind a twisted tree. Whitney was pale and shaking. She didn't say a word. She held one hand around her wrist. Her arm was covered in blood.

"Princess?" said Dave. "Are you okay?"

Whitney shook her head very slowly. She let go of her wrist. Janet screamed. Whitney's hand had been neatly severed. The stump was bubbling with blood. The white knuckle of bone protruded like an ivory peg. Dave and Janet stared at their daughter in horror.

I stood up.

"There's a first-aid kit in the car," I said. "Don't move them."

I opened the boot of the Audi and pulled up the carpet covering the spare wheel. I found what I was looking for and strolled back towards Dave Shirley.

"What the fuck has just happened?" he said.

I glanced at Whitney's hand and then at Daryl.

"Well, Dave," I said evenly. "They've cut themselves on the razor wire which I laid out this morning around the clearing. You were probably still asleep. Don't worry. They'll bleed out and die pretty soon."

Dave swung around with a look of disbelief and rage on his face. His mouth was half-open and his eyes were bulging. I swung the heavy tyre jack at his head and it connected with his temple. He fell to the ground and lay motionless. Janet was on her feet in an instant and flying towards me like a venomous insect. A mother's fury. I batted her back with the jack and she stumbled to her knees. I raised the jack above my head. She held out one arm towards her daughter.

"Princess," she moaned.

"No, Janet," I sighed. "That is not a princess. That will never be a princess. Your family is a fucking disgrace."

I swung the jack down onto the back of her head.

German engineering, I thought. You always know where you are with German engineering.

I walked up to Whitney and punched the young girl in the face. I dragged her over to one side of the clearing and laid her down beside a large hole in the ground. I went back for her brother. Daryl's foot was dangling from his leg by a single blue tendon. I grabbed his arms, dumped him next to his sister and went back to collect Janet and Dave.

After arranging the family around the hole, I pulled on the heavy gloves and headed into the undergrowth. I had already cut the razor wire into manageable strips. Gingerly I pulled them out of the ground and went back to the family. I wrapped all four in the razor wire. It was a tricky business. Dave was still twitching. Every time he jerked I saw blood seep through his jeans. I pulled the keys to the villa from his pocket and coiled the wire around his face.

Dave was the last to go into the hole. Suddenly his eyes popped open. I jumped back in shock. He struggled in the lethal wire cage and tried to say something to me but he cut his own throat and died in a pool of blood. I scraped a layer of earth over the family before throwing the gloves and empty sackcloth into the hole. The forest was quiet. It was getting late. I shovelled the rest of the earth into the hole.

I drove back to the villa and let myself inside. I packed the family's belongings into several suitcases and checked everything at least four times. I cleaned up the dishes in the sink and emptied the pedal bin into a plastic bag. By the time I had finished there was no trace of Dave Shirley and his family.

I washed my face, changed my shirt and drove back to the car rental company near the airport. Along the way I threw the family's suitcases into the sea. The same salesman took back the keys and asked if I had enjoyed my trip.

"Yes," I said. "It's been just fine."

`We shook hands. I walked around the showroom to where my car was parked. It felt like a toy compared to the Audi. I pulled out into the anonymous flow of evening traffic and headed home.

22

MONDO FANNY

I stared at the man in the Kittyhawk club for a very long time. I had never seen him before. He was a rugged fellow. His face was weathered by the wind and the sun, and his eyes were as sharp as tacks. He wore blue jeans, a sleeveless shirt and a pair of sturdy construction boots. He held a bottle of beer in one fist and his smile was fast and wide. The stranger looked like a cattle man from a mid-western ranch although he was not American. I couldn't place his accent. He was talking to one of the local boys about motorcycle engines. They laughed like brothers. He looked like a man who could wrestle a horse to the ground and then ride the beast to Mars. I would have to be careful of this man.

It was August. It was impossibly hot up in the mountains. Tommy and Gina didn't believe in air conditioning. Instead two ceiling fans turned the turgid air above the bar. Honey seemed to have melted into her own skin. She was even more listless than usual. She sat next to me on a bar stool and fiddled with a raggedy strand of dark hair. Her eyes were dull. The ghostly white dress clung to her little body like a shroud. She wore nothing under the dress and didn't seem to care.

I couldn't imagine the mountains without Honey. She had done well to fall in with Tommy and Gina. God alone knew what Honey would have done without the Kittyhawk. She might have become a painter or a pop star, a writer or a warrior. She might have had a husband and kids, two dogs and a sedan. Looking at her now, however, none of that seemed likely. She would probably have run with the bad boys and the villains, the pirates and the scarecrows. She would probably be dead. I was pretty sure that Tommy and Gina had somehow saved her life. Honey belonged up here in the woods with the starlings and the shadows.

Gina handed her a glass of water and smiled at me.

"Seen Tommy?" she said.

I shook my head.

"He's out the back having a smoke," said Gina. "Big dumb fuck. I told him to quit for his health. He promised to stop but he still sneaks out and thinks I don't know. We're not kids. I've known that man for a million years. Of course I know when he's having a cigarette."

I smiled, picked up my beer and headed outside. The afternoon sunlight exploded in my face. I paused for a second to let the jagged pins of white light behind my eyes subside. It was hotter than bedlam. The air was as dry as chalk. I felt the sweat prickle on my arms.

I found Tommy crouching beneath the wreckage of the helicopter. He didn't see me approach and jumped when I called his name.

"Fuck, man!" he exclaimed. "Don't creep up on an old man."

He stubbed out his cigarette.

"Gina doesn't know, OK?"

I laughed.

"Gina knows, Tommy. She just told me I could find you out here having a smoke."

"Damn!" said Tommy and grinned. "That woman's good."

We sat together in the shade of the helicopter. He looked good in his frayed khaki shorts and faded Rolling Stones t-shirt. His body was trim and tanned. He seemed full of good humour. It turned out that Tommy's life had recently taken a surprising twist.

A long time ago, he explained, he and Gina had made a cheap porn flick called *Mondo Fanny*. In their previous lives as outlaw pornographers they had made many such movies on a budget of beans. They sold these movies directly to a grateful public from the boot of their car as they travelled across America. It was a long time ago.

"Long before the internet," said Tommy. "Long before all this technology that the kids today take for granted. If you wanted to jerk off to a movie then you had to make a goddamn effort! It wasn't like you could just click a link with one hand and whack off with the other. Pornography took dedication, man. Back in the day you had to fucking *apply* yourself!"

I laughed and rolled Tommy a cigarette as he continued with his story.

"But the gods of pornography move in mysterious ways," he said. "That movie was a turkey. At the time we were traveling with a motorcycle gang for protection and we filmed the movie in a log cabin that the bikers owned just outside Portland. To be real honest with you, I can't remember much about the movie. There were a lot of drugs around at the time. But I remember it was a good weekend and we had one hell of a party."

He took a long drag on his cigarette and exhaled with a smile.

"So, anyway, the movie gets made and we send the thing up to Canada as usual. We pick up the end result from a warehouse a few weeks later and begin to ship it out to the good folk who admired our work. God-fearing people one and all. I still salute the goddamn freaks to this day! Gina and me thought no more about this movie until just the other week."

I looked at Tommy.

"*Mondo Fanny*? That is the worst title for a porn movie I have ever heard."

"Yep," said Tommy. "Completely fucking lame, right? But get this. A few days ago I get an email from some kid in Tucson, Arizona.

Says he's in the movie industry and blah-blah-blah. I'm, like, sure kid, whatever. He says he wants to talk and can he phone me. So I give him my cell phone number here and sure enough he calls. He sounds a little shell-shocked on the phone, like he's talking to some big hero or something. Like he's dialled his mom and got Superman instead. He's all nervous and polite and 'gosh' and 'gee'."

Tommy paused.

"Then this kid offers me a million dollars."

I was stunned.

"For *Mondo Fanny*?"

"Nope," said Tommy. "One million dollars to advise this kid and his business partners on a movie they want to make about how we made *Mondo Fanny*. There's also a book deal which is a separate thing. I get to tell my story and this kid gets to make a movie about my movie. He says he's ready to go into production just as soon as I sign some papers. His people in Hollywood are sending them over. Can you believe that shit?"

I let his words sink in until I could see nothing ahead but a brick wall.

"No," I said slowly. "I absolutely cannot believe that shit."

Tommy slapped my back and stood up.

"Another beer might make it easier," he drawled. "Hell, might as well make it a crate!"

"Tommy," I said.

"What?"

"Put your cigarette out."

He looked at the butt in his hand and grinned. We walked back together towards the bar. Tommy turned to me.

"You sure Gina knows?"

I nodded.

"Damn!" he said.

That afternoon passed in a blur of emotions. I was happy for Tommy and Gina but I had a bad feeling in the pit of my stomach. I no longer felt as if I was standing alone on solid ground. The seismic plates of the earth had imperceptibly shifted.

"What are they going to call the movie?" I asked. Tommy arched an eyebrow. I stared at his face and then at Gina.

"Oh, you are fucking kidding me?"

Tommy roared with laughter.

"Nope," he said. "*Mondo Fanny* is finally going to hang large on billboards across the good old United States of America! We're going to hang that motherfucker in outer space!"

"Tommy," said Gina with a kindly smile. "Shut the fuck up."

As part of the deal, Tommy explained, he and Gina would have to move to California to be close to the production set. I frowned.

"For how long?"

"Well," said Tommy, "that all depends on this kid and his people. It's a whole new ball game. I know that me and Gina can make a movie in one afternoon but this is going to take a little longer. Six months. Maybe a year."

My head was spinning with the beer and the heat. I was shocked.

"What are you going to do with the Kittyhawk?"

Tommy handed me yet another bottle.

"Have you met Dieter?"

I shook my head. Tommy waved at the stranger on the other side of the bar. The stranger looked up and smiled. He strolled towards us with a casual authority. He grinned at Tommy and glanced at me.

"Dieter," said Tommy, "meet Cal. He's a good friend."

The stranger held out his hand.

"Good to meet you, Cal," he said. "Dieter Delbeck. Call me Deet. Don't call me Diet. I will kill you."

I gripped his hand and stared at his expressionless face. There was a moment's uneasy silence. Then Dieter Delbeck slapped me on the back and everybody started laughing.

"Joking," said the big man. "Just joking. Not all South Africans are pricks. Some of us enjoy a sense of humour."

I smiled and let go of his hand.

"Right."

"Deet's going to be minding the store whilst we're in LA," said Tommy. "He's a rude, obnoxious, no-bit, shovel-headed South African but he's all we could find at short notice."

Later that evening the temperature dropped by a couple of degrees. I helped Tommy and Dieter move a few tables and chairs out into the back yard. We set them up near the helicopter. Gina prepared a healthy feast of grilled chicken and Greek salad. Everybody helped themselves from the bar.

It was a pleasant evening. The air was heavy with perfume and the sky was thick with stars. But there was dark news on the horizon.

Dieter Delbeck held court at the table. Tommy was happy to defer to the big South African. Deet was funny and charming and easy to like. I asked him how he came to be on Kolasios.

"Fucked if I should really know, Cal" he said. "I work for a construction company. They pay me god's own salary to travel from here to there scouting for suitable land. The company wants cheap land to develop. Greece is in the shitter. So here I am."

It all sounded so simple. Dieter Delbeck was going to buy land on Kolasios. He was going to roll in the bulldozers and dig up the land for a company that wanted to build a luxurious mountain retreat.

"Where?" I said.

Dieter shrugged.

"Up here somewhere. Not too sure exactly. There's a lot of land around here and no one seems to know exactly who owns it. I need to find a farmer and wave some dollars in the old fellow's face. Best land registry in the world, Cal. Fast fucking cash! No man on earth can resist cold cash."

I was angry. I couldn't just sit back and let Dieter *fucking* Delbeck run amok up here in the mountains without my permission. Goddamnit! I needed his plans. I needed to check his maps. I needed to clarify his exact intentions. I needed to talk him out of the whole fucking project. Shit! He couldn't just be allowed to dig up the earth. The forests had held their secrets for too long.

Times were changing. I could feel it in the air pressure. The future of the island lay in the hands of men like Dieter Delbeck. They were strong and bold and saw opportunities where no one else thought to look. The old army of lazy Greek rogues would soon be side-lined and mothballed. The jealous old fools who had reaped the rewards in recent years could never dream of what was to come. It was a new era. A slick, sure-footed era of vicious fortune designed to eviscerate the old ways. The self-important generals and the preening baby-kings in the local villages would soon be reduced to trading donkeys for millstones. Men like Dieter Delbeck would sweep through the island like piranhas and locusts. The energy of Kolasios would be diluted and drained until only the white heat remained.

I smiled at Dieter. He handed me a beer.

"Good luck," I said.

"No luck involved," he replied smoothly. "Just progress."

I stood up and punched a few songs into the jukebox. The sound of Patti Smith's hushed, siren swagger filled the space.

'Jesus died for somebody's sins...but not mine'

The island had already changed. It would never be the same again. It was too late to avoid the inevitable. In just a few months my state of mind had shifted. There was a tension where once was calm. At night I imagined the planets colliding and the crows circling overhead. I would wake up in a sweat. I saw the world as a mutant wasteland of crushed and molten bones. We lived amongst the jagged rocks and scrabbled in the earth like feral rats for trinkets and scraps. The sea had become a boiling, blood-red cauldron. The sky had been ripped from the universe and only a black wound remained.

I was scared.

Quite a few ex-pats were talking about leaving the island. Those who had work were fighting for their wages. Those who had retired saw their pensions dwindling by the month. The herd was gradually moving back to familiar pastures. The Greek adventure had soured for most of them. Unencumbered by much brain and even less skill, the slow-witted and charmless were keen to escape. Mervyn and Moira were heading back to the Welsh valleys at the end of the season. Their house was still unfinished. The property developer was in prison. Mervyn told me proudly that he had landed a job on hospital radio.

"They like a bit of chat on hospital radio," he said. "They're invalids, see, and they need something to get them through the day. I don't play to the cancer crowd, mind. No point. They're all going to die."

"Right," I said.

One of the twisted blonde witches who ran Kolasios Crystal Weddings was heading back to some dreary patch of land just outside Portsmouth.

"I can't wait," she said. "I've had enough. Seven years is enough, don't you think? I'm going back to my brand new Peugeot 107 and the big superstore up on the by-pass. You know what I miss about England? Lamb! I cannot wait for a decent leg of lamb. Not the scraggy old meat they sell you here. Back home you can get proper lamb. And mint sauce. Back home you can eat like a civilised human being."

"Won't you miss the weddings at all?" I asked.

"God, no," she snorted. "Whiney little girls with their infantile dreams and hen-pecked grooms who couldn't tie their own shoe laces if their lives depended on it. That's not to mention the hellish in-laws and the fussy little children and the moaning, bleating, screaming new-borns that I always wanted to drown in a bath of their own spit. No, love, I'm getting out whilst I still have my sense of decency and romance!"

Even Mikki was heading back. She had never really recovered from the absence of Jesus in her life. Since the fire there had been no word from the authorities. She had wrapped herself up in self-help books and handed in her notice at the boutique hotel. The manager told her not to bother working out the season. Instead he opened the hotel safe and handed her some cash.

"What is your name?" he snapped. "I do not remember."

Mikki burst into tears and stayed with us for a few days. We drove her to the airport and watched her slip through passport control carrying her life's belongings in one ruck-sack. She never looked back. No one ever looked back at those who had chosen to stay. It was just too sad.

The big South African found me standing next to the jukebox. I had been a million miles away in my own head. I had been careless. It never paid to dream.

"Listen," he said, "I have a proposition for you."

He steered me towards a table in the corner of the Kittyhawk.

"Tommy tells me you're a straight-ahead kind of bloke," he began. "You certainly don't seem like the rest of the piss-heads up here."

I smiled and lit a cigarette.

"Thanks," I said.

"I need a guide," Dieter continued jovially. "I need someone who knows the island and can show me around. Kind of like a Sherpa, I guess, but without the luggage. Or the turban. Someone who can see the bigger picture. Someone with a brain. I'm looking for land up here in the mountains and I need someone to steer me in the right direction. I'll make sure it's worth your while. Very worth your while."

I told him I'd think about it. It was a lie. I already knew the answer.

"Sure," he said. "Take your time. You know where to find me."

He stood up and went back outside. For a while I watched Honey dancing barefoot with herself behind the bar. I smiled. I didn't want to disturb her.

I said goodbye to Tommy and Gina. Tommy insisted we drink one final shot of tequila together.

"To *Mondo Fanny!*" he said. We all groaned loudly and cheered.

Tommy shook my hand and Gina held me tight. Just for a second we were closer than we'd ever been. It was just the three of us there alone in the yard. I wished them a safe journey to California.

I never saw them again.

23

THE END

The army was on the move. It was unusual to see the heavy iron convoys on the road before the end of the season. It wasn't good for business and the island was enjoying something of an autumn gold rush. We passed the grim procession of tanks and camouflaged artillery as the low-loaders crawled south towards the remote firing ranges at the bottom of the island. Kat waved at the young combat soldiers sitting inside the old German jeeps. They stared back at us with no emotion. Kat sighed and let her hand ride the breeze.

We were heading to the Klef in Pilafkos to help Nikos remember his old grandmother who had recently died peacefully in her sleep at the age of a hundred and one. She had always been a friendly old crone. We used to see her stringing beans in the shade behind the kitchen with her feet in a bowl of water. We never heard her utter one single word but she would always smile and wave at passers-by. She had lived and died in one of the apartments above the Klef. It was a strange place. The walls were littered with ancient photographs. Religious artefacts filled every corner. It was a dark apartment and it didn't smell too good.

Nikos hadn't sounded particularly upset when he'd phoned yesterday. He wanted Kat to be the DJ at the wake.

"Tell her to wear something sexy," he'd said. "And to play big Rock music!"

I asked him whether he thought that might not be appropriate.

"Why not?" Nikos had shouted. "My grandmother is not deaf. My grandmother is dead. She cannot hear!"

I told Kat what Nikos had said. She promptly threatened to burn down the Klef.

"What am I supposed to wear?" she spat. "A bikini? A wet t-shirt? A see-through fucking space suit? Tell him to play his own big rock music!"

"He's paying us both in food and drink."

"I'll do it," said Kat. "But I'm wearing jeans."

The party was already underway by the time we arrived. I parked the car in the shade and paused beside the yellow plastic elephant. Someone had scrawled *R.I.P Fat Boy* down the length of its goofy trunk. I patted the elephant's hollow head and walked inside.

The Klef was busy. Busier than it had been for most of the season. Nikos was shaking cocktails behind the bar. He was sweating profusely and dancing around like a broken fly. His cousins were already drunk. They were sprawled on their bar stools laughing and yelling loudly at nothing in particular. Older relatives stood at a distance and eyed everyone suspiciously like owls under the moon. I recognised a few ex-pats amongst the guests. The usual cast of carrion crows and thieving graveside whores who'd turn up to anything so long as it involved a free beer and a burnt sausage. I didn't feel so bad. At least technically one of us was working. As if on cue a white line of feedback cut through the Klef. Kat grinned at me from behind her computer screen and gave Nikos the finger.

The barbecue, it turned out, was late.

"Harry's drunk," explained Nikos. "I'm waiting for my mother to finish serving the cakes."

I stared at Nikos' old mother as she hobbled through the crowd balancing plates of home-baked *baklava*. She looked tired and sad. I offered to pull Harry together and help with the barbecue. Nikos nodded and handed me a beer.

"Can you tell Kat to play *The End* by the Doors?" he said. "It is my favourite song."

"No," I replied and walked out of the bar.

Harry wasn't the old boy's real name. His real name was Aristotle but he had shortened it to Aris a long time ago and now everybody just called him Harry. I found him sitting under a lemon tree in the beer garden. He looked like a raddled old prune. He was swaying like a bowling pin and held a clear plastic bottle in one hand. I could smell the moonshine from a distance.

Harry was always drunk. He was small and stooped and spent his days shambling from bar to bar until he could stand no more. Then he would go fishing. It never mattered to Harry what time he set out in his little wooden boat. He never cared for the logic of it all. He would just stumble down to the beach, untie his boat and drag it into the water. Then he would wade through the waves and heave himself aboard. Harry would chug out to sea in the little boat and return a few hours later with his haul. He exchanged the fish for *souma* and cigarettes in the village square. Sometimes he caught quite a lot of fish. Other times he caught nothing at all. On the days that Harry caught nothing he would organise an impromptu lottery and grandly announce that the winner would receive a bottle of *souma* and two packets of cigarettes. Unsurprisingly Harry always won his own lottery and no one dared complain.

Harry slept in his clothes. He wore the same stinking shirt and stained trousers held up with string for months on end. He once told me that the sea was his bathroom and the bar stool was his bed. He was an old man completely untroubled by the complications of the modern world. He had never owned a watch. He had never owned a radio or a car or even a mirror or a toothbrush. Harry never even bought his own boat. He'd won it in a card game during the war.

"How's life, Harry?" I said. "You having a drink?"

Harry frowned and stared at me with hopeless eyes. I sat down beside him and swigged my beer. It was never a good idea to startle Harry. The *souma* made him unpredictable. It was always best to approach Harry directly from the front rather than tack sideways or creep up behind him. Harry was like a lunatic or a crab. He didn't like surprises. He could get jumpy and sometimes even violent if the mood took him the wrong way. It was always best to treat Harry like a child.

"Fuck off!" said Harry. I laughed.

We sat in silence under the lemon tree for a while. Even though it was nearly October the sun was still warm and the skies were clear. I could hear Nikos and his cousins shrieking and cheering like hysterical school girls at the bar. A few of the older relatives and ex-pats had moved outside to escape the noise. It seemed a little tactless. Nikos had always claimed, however, that the Klef was a true party bar no matter what the occasion. Even the death of his old *yia-yia* could not quash the ego that drove the rabid little man.

I helped Harry fill up the huge metal half-drum with coal and kindling. We lit the sprockle-wood and sprayed Harry's *souma* over the whole thing. Pretty soon the smoke had cleared and the coals were glowing red. Harry was mesmerized by the flames. He stared into the drum as if hypnotised by the heat. When he began to sway unsteadily I led him back to the lemon tree and sat him down. Just for a second I thought he might cry. Instead he began to shuffle his feet in time to Metallica.

I fanned the flames with an old dustpan. Nikos' uncle wandered over and nodded approvingly. It was the old way. I had seen restaurants using hair dryers and electric fans to achieve the same result. Somehow it always seemed a little brutish and unfair to approach a simple fire with a hair dryer. Flames needed oxygen to thrive. They didn't need bubble-perms.

Nikos' mother limped up with a plate of lemons and began to slowly clean the crusted metal grate. I sighed and gently prized the griddle from her gnarled hands. She smiled and handed me the lemons. Nikos' uncle took her arm and led her back to the bar. I rubbed the lemons briskly over the grate. The heat from the fire was getting uncomfortable. I handed the dustpan to Harry and helped myself to another beer from the fridge at the end of the bar.

Nikos looked agitated.

"Why will Kat not play *The End* by the Doors?" he said. "It is a very important song for me and my cousins. She has refused."

I popped the cap from my beer and stared at Nikos.

"It's the worst song that has ever been written," I said. "It's dull, pretentious and lasts for about seven days. It would kill any party stone dead. No one likes *The End*, Nikos, because it is a truly awful song. It does not have one redeeming feature. It is a useless song. I don't blame Kat for refusing to play it."

Nikos was affronted.

"I don't care. Tell her to play it. It is my party."

"It's Kat's computer," I said.

Kat was a little drunk. She had helped herself to a bottle of wine and was making steady progress.

"It's medicinal," she laughed. "It makes it easier to listen to this shit!"

She pointed at the computer screen to where she had selected the forthcoming tracks.

"I don't even know who Blackfoot are," she said. "Who are Blackfoot? Where do they come from? Do they wear hats? I bet they wear big hats. Shit!"

"Nikos wants you to play *The End*."

"Nikos can try and fuck me in both ears because that's not going to happen either," she said angrily. "No one plays *The End*. Ever. It's the law."

I glanced at Nikos. He was lining up shots of tequila on the bar for his cousins. Maybe I'd tell him later. Let him down gently.

"By the way," said Kat, pouring herself another glass of wine. "Why is Harry trying to set himself on fire?"

I spun around to see Harry dancing around the barbecue in a cloud of sparks. He was laughing and shouting at the fire with the dustpan raised above his head like some kind of trophy. I groaned and walked back out of the bar towards the monumental blaze. Nikos' uncle appeared with a pot of water and together we damped down the flames. Harry was still giggling and yelling like a mad man. I sat him down again under the lemon tree and told him not to move. By the time the coals were white hot Harry was subdued and morose.

"Where is the food?" I asked. "Did you bring any food to put on the fire?"

"No," said Harry.

I pointed at the giant cool box standing beside the lemon tree.

"What's in the cool box, Harry?"

Harry turned his head slowly and stared at the cool box as if for the first time.

"Fish."

"Fish is good," I said. "That means we can put the fish on the fire and everyone can eat fish."

Harry shook his head and suddenly grabbed my wrist.

"No!" he shouted. I jumped back.

He tried to stand up but his legs began to buckle. He jabbed a finger towards the bar and took a deep breath.

"That fucking *malaka*," he bellowed, "owes me a bottle of *souma!*"

His face was red with rage. I glanced towards the bar.

"Nikos? He owes you *souma* for the fish?"

"Yes," said Harry.

I stared at the wretched old man for a second.

"For fuck's sake...!"

I fetched a bottle of the rancid hooch from the fridge and began to arrange the fish on the grate. Harry had been busy. There were maybe fifty or sixty silver fish in the cool box. Their dead eyes were clear and fresh. I dug them out of the ice with my hands and brushed them down with oil before tossing them onto the fire. The older relatives walked over to help and it wasn't long before we had an efficient system in place. Harry sat under the lemon tree and nursed his bottle of *souma* like a furious baby.

Nikos' mother had dragged a long trestle table into the middle of the beer garden. The table groaned under the weight of the salads and cheeses and cold meats that she had prepared. Every now and then I would carry plates of fish over to the table when they were ready. Nikos and his cousins were the first to help themselves, followed by the older relatives and then the ex-pats. It was quite a feast.

A few tourists had joined the party on their way back from the beach. As the sun began to set everybody raised a glass to Nikos' grandmother. Everyone, that is, except Nikos and his three cousins who were engrossed in a Greek-league grudge match playing out on the large, flat-screen TV hanging over the bar. Nikos' uncle stood up to make the toast. It was a sombre moment. A single tear fell from his sister's eye. She quickly wiped it away with a paper napkin.

As the family began to clear away the empty plates, I joined Harry under the lemon tree.

"Nice fish, Harry," I said. "It must have taken you a while to catch that many?"

Harry seemed to have passed the point of utter inebriation. He sounded relatively lucid and sober.

"It was easy," he said. "Boom!"

I stared at Harry's twinkling eyes as he swigged his hooch.

"Boom!" he repeated and tapped his barnacled nose.

I looked around nervously.

"You stole the fish?"

Harry belched and slapped his thigh.

"No, no, no," he whispered. "I blew them out of the fucking sea with dynamite. Boom!"

I was amazed. I'd heard dark tales of the mysterious blast-fishing trips in the middle of the night. Some people even claimed to have heard the muffled explosions rolling around the moonlit bays and coves. It was never discussed in public for fear of reprisals and the stories became no more than sinister folklore. It was impossible to believe that an old soak like Harry could be involved. Handling dynamite required a steady hand and at least one focused eye. Harry never seemed to possess either.

But that evening he sat under the lemon tree and calmly told me how he made beer-bottle bombs using stolen agricultural fertilizer and syphoned fuel. It sounded so simple.

"So if I gave you an empty beer bottle," I said, "you could make it into a bomb?"

"Yes," said Harry. "But it would cost you a full bottle of beer, a bottle of *souma* and a packet of cigarettes. It is illegal, you know? I do not work these things for free."

"So it would be a beer for a bomb then?"

Harry nodded slowly.

"And a bottle of *souma*. And a packet of cigarettes. American cigarettes. Do not bring me Greek cigarettes."

I laughed.

"Can you make a bomb out of anything?"

Harry looked at me as if I was simple.

"No," he said. "I cannot make a bomb out of a banana. That is a stupid thing to ask."

"What about a pipe bomb?" I said. Harry thought about this for a minute and then nodded slowly.

"Yes," he replied, "but you must be very careful. They can be very unstable."

I stood up and patted the little old man on his shoulder. His brief moment of sobriety was obviously fading fast. His eyes had clouded over and his head began to droop.

"Thanks, Harry," I said. "I'll let you know."

I didn't realise it at the time but Harry had unwittingly started a chain of events that would ultimately cause death and destruction on an unimaginable scale. It might sound fanciful reading this now, but I blame Harry. I blame Harry for everything.

A huge cheer went up from the bar. I heard the sound of breaking glass and crockery. Nikos was standing on top of the bar waving his fists in the air. His three cousins were hugging and dancing and screaming in each other's faces. Nikos tripped and fell off the bar laughing. He stood up, grabbed a bottle of vodka and poured most of it over his head. Then he filled up shot glasses on the counter and every time the goal was replayed on the television screen the four of them tipped the alcohol down their throats.

"This is my life!" Nikos shouted at the top of his voice. "Fuck you all!"

The older relatives outside shook their heads in dismay and ignored the commotion. The ex-pats laughed and the tourists looked a little alarmed. Everyone looked distinctly uneasy, however, when one of the cousins left the bar and returned with a shotgun.

It was an old hunting gun that had once belonged to Nikos' father. Nikos snatched the shotgun from his cousin, walked out into the garden and blew a hole in the sky. The crack of gunfire echoed around Pilafkos. Nikos' cousins were cheering and swearing and laughing and trying to wrestle control of the shotgun. Nikos fired again. Then again.

Eventually Nikos' uncle got to his feet. He carefully put his glass of wine on the table, walked very slowly over to his nephew and slapped him hard in the face. Nikos stumbled backwards in shock and surprise. His uncle grabbed the shotgun and without a word placed it against the kitchen wall before returning to the table and resuming his conversation as if nothing had happened. Chastised and humiliated, Nikos retreated to the bar where he sat scowling at his uncle and cursing his cousins.

It was getting late. Most of the older relatives had left. Nikos' mother had retired to her bed. I thanked Nikos' uncle. He smiled. After a while it was just the tourists and ex-pats left. I found myself trapped at a table with Charmless Mike and Lacey McDuggan. Mike was a seaside comedian and quiz master at the all-inclusive hotel resort nearby. Lacey was his ageing blonde assistant with a mean face and a scratch-card soul.

"You can't tell proper jokes anymore," said Charmless Mike. "You used to have your classic comedians. Eric Morecombe. Ronnie Corbett. Chubby Brown. Davidson. Dawson. Manning. Now it's all smart-arsed student types taking the piss. Proper jokes are over."

He shook his head into his pint.

"Proper jokes were racist?" I ventured.

Lacey's lemon face contorted with disgust.

"Nothing wrong with being offensive," she sneered. "Some people deserve to be upset."

"I used to tell this joke about a black fellow, a paki and a lesbian," said Mike. "Bob Monkhouse wrote the original joke and I just changed it around a little. Now, you can't tell me that Bob Monkhouse was a racist? He was the housewife's favourite, for god's sake! Kiddies and old women loved that man. But no, no, no, old Mike here can't tell a joke like that anymore. I don't know where it will all end."

I wasn't really listening. I didn't want to talk to them and I didn't want to stab them both in the leg. Instead I went to the bathroom and stared at myself in the mirror. I looked old. It didn't really bother me. Age was something you just grew into. I liked my eyes. They were still blue. Blue eyes were still considered to be lucky in some parts of the world. My blue eyes were no more a window to my soul than anything else. I stared at myself for a very long time but my eyes gave nothing away.

I splashed water over my face. I was aware of someone shouting outside. The music had stopped. Someone tapped on the bathroom door. It was Charmless Mike. He looked concerned.

"I think Kat's a bit pissed," he said.

I followed him into the bar. I surveyed the scene in front of me and sighed.

Kat was standing in the middle of the bar cradling the shotgun in both hands. It was levelled on her hip and pointed at Nikos and his three cousins who were cowering in one corner. Nikos' hands were raised as if in surrender. His cousins looked rooted to the spot in terror.

"Kat," I said gently. "Can you put the gun down?"

She looked up at me and grinned.

"Tell that motherfucker that I will not play *The* fucking *End* by the Doors!"

I glanced at Nikos.

"I really don't think she's going to play the song, Nikos."

Nikos looked at me with panic in his eyes.

"OK, OK," he stuttered. "It's not a problem."

I turned back to Kat.

"See? It's not a problem. Will you put the gun down now?"

Kat didn't move. She stared straight at Nikos and his cousins for a while. There was silence in the bar. Charmless Mike took a step towards Kat. I held out my hand to stop him. Time stood still.

Then Kat just put the gun down on the floor and walked out of the Klef without a word.

Mike breathed a sigh of relief and looked at me.

"Guess the party's over then?"

I finished my beer and turned to leave.

"It's over," I said. "Go home."

24

SPA

It was a fine October afternoon. The sky above the forest was blue and infinite. Dappled sunshine filtered through the trees and cast a golden warmth across the clearing. The air was heavy with the scent of pine and wild flowers. Some people believed the incense was a sign that the spirits were trying to attract your attention. I smiled. The spirits up there in the clearing might want to join the union and form an orderly queue.

I sat on an old tree stump and stared at Dieter Delbeck. He wasn't such a big man after all. I had swung the spade at the back of his head and he'd toppled like a tin soldier. I had dragged him into the clearing by his boots and buried him up to his neck in the earth. He was still unconscious. His square head was caked in dust and a tiny trickle of blood had dried under one nostril. I idly tossed a pine cone at his face but I missed. I didn't care. Dieter Delbeck wasn't going anywhere.

Up until about an hour ago it had been an almost pleasant day. Dieter and I had arranged to meet that morning at a derelict cafe on a deserted stretch of coast road. The abandoned cafe was little more than a shack held together by lizards and old soda adverts. The cardboard hoardings flapped in the wind and the whole tattered cabin seemed to moan. Dieter collected me in his battle-green Land Rover which had seen better days and together we rattled up into the mountains.

The South African was on a mission. He had spent the past few weeks driving around the island looking for land on which his company could build their latest venture. The future of luxury resort spas, he explained, lay not by the sea but as far away from it as possible.

"A beach is a beach is a beach," Dieter said. "Beaches are for morons. A beach is just a stretch of sand and rock to remind the moron that he is on holiday. Give a simple man a beach and he will be docile and happy for a fortnight. The average man is easily pleased. An ice cream. A cocktail. A sunset. A beach. Fuck them! I am not interested in the average man. The average man is useless. We are a little more ambitious."

He lit a cigarette and handed me the packet.

"I think I have found a spot," he continued. "It's going to take a lot of work and a lot of money but it is perfect. I'd like your opinion, Cal"

We clattered through the pretty mountain villages which lay idle and sleepy in the autumn sunshine. Old men sat outside cafes drinking coffee and stared at the Land Rover as we passed with blank, expressionless faces. There was hardly any traffic on the road as we continued to climb. It was nearly the end of the season. The island needed to rest and breathe for a while. She needed to fill her lungs and expel the fumes which had clogged her arteries for months. The island was as tough as a mustang but she could not race forever.

After maybe an hour Dieter pulled over to buy a bottle of water from a kiosk just outside Epikyndos. He switched off the diesel engine and the mountain silence flooded through the open window. We got out and stretched our legs. The young woman inside the kiosk watched us silently. The village itself was little more than a jumble of tiny houses and one internet cafe which served as a meeting place and the only link to the outside world. It was deserted. An old tractor lay rusting in the field behind the kiosk. There was very little beyond Epikyndos except acres of deep, dark forest and imposing granite rock.

"What do you think?" said Dieter. "Pretty fine, huh?"

He swigged from the bottle of water and passed it to me. I stared at the sleeping village and the empty road ahead.

"You're going to buy Epikyndos?"

Dieter roared with laughter.

"No, you fucking idiot, man," he said. "I'm going to buy that fucking monastery!"

He pointed up to the derelict sanatorium which stood on a remote plateau high above the village. It had been built by the Italians during the Occupation and had since been left to rot with its secrets and ghosts intact.

"It's not a monastery," I said. "It's an old sanatorium. It was built to incarcerate the mentally ill during the war. It's not a good place, Dieter. It's really not a good place."

Dieter shrugged and climbed back into the Land Rover.

"It'll be a damn fine place when I've finished with it," he said. "Get in. I want to check out the nut house."

The steep road leading up to the plateau was little more than a dirt track. Branches from the overhanging trees brushed against the Land Rover and broken rubble crunched beneath the tyres. I gripped the dashboard as the old jeep bounced and rocked into the shadows of the ruined sanatorium.

Dieter parked in the middle of what had probably once been an ornate square and killed the engine. Dead trees now framed the strangled gardens which lay buried beneath an ocean of weeds and creepers. Rows of iron benches still sat bolted into the concrete around the square's perimeter. A drinking fountain lay smashed on the stones where it had fallen many years ago.

The dilapidated sanatorium dominated one side of the square. The stone columns and sweeping arches still remained but its facade had been hammered by the elements and war machines alike. The peeling paintwork around the entrance was riddled with bullet holes. Broken shutters swung from empty windows in the breeze. I could see nothing through the windows except for the dark heart of the cavernous asylum.

Dieter set off towards the cloisters on the far side of the square. The fanciful beige brick buildings had been built originally to house the medical staff and soldiers who had taken such a keen interest in their unfortunate patients. The bombed-out shells were broken and twisted but glimpses of their previous life could still be found. Marble floor tiles snapped and splintered underfoot. A picture frame – blackened by smoke and warped out of shape – lay in the rubble at the foot of a crumbling staircase. Bakelite switches hung from their wall sockets on ancient copper wire. Even the intricate mosaic patterns in the bath house had survived.

We picked our way carefully through the building. Dieter seemed obsessed. He investigated every nook and cranny like an excited child. He kept up a running commentary as he stalked through the wreckage.

"Water feature there. Aquarium. Lillies floating on the surface. Koi carp. Keep it peaceful. Tranquil sounds. Let in the light. Lots of light. A sun deck here...."

He paused in the middle of a large desolate room and stared up at the sky through the latticework of scorched timber beams. He held out both arms and grinned at me.

"An observatory! Right here! A window into space!"

I lit a cigarette and walked out into the sunshine. I didn't want to be here at all. I didn't want Dieter to be here. We were heading towards uncomfortable territory.

The South African emerged from the cloisters and slapped me on the back.

"Listen, man," he said. "Let me show you something. Let me try and show you what I see."

He strode across the square towards the sanatorium. I followed at a distance. We paused at the entrance and stared inside. The reception area had been destroyed by bullets and mortar bombs. Only the concrete staircase leading to the dormitories on the upper level remained intact. A long, dark corridor stretched out into the belly of the building. After maybe five meters the daylight faded to no more than shadow. Broken pipes hung from the ceiling. The floor was obscured by piles of rubble. There were several doors along the corridor. The doors were heavy and rusted. Each had an observation window fitted into the iron frame. The doors, I knew, hid the secrets of the sanatorium's cells and makeshift operating theatres.

Dieter stepped over the threshold. I stubbed out my cigarette and followed. He stopped in the middle of the reception hall and I hoped he would go no further.

"Welcome to the Sunny Heights Health Spa and Executive Retreat!" he said with a smile. "Please follow me."

We picked our way through the rubble and bomb craters towards the sombre corridor. It was cold in the sanatorium. I glanced over my shoulder at the bright sunshine outside. The wind had picked up. Dead leaves swirled through the square.

A huge crash broke the silence. I whirled around to see Dieter standing in front of the first iron door.

"Bastard!" he said.

He lifted one boot and aimed again at the centre of the door. This time the door shifted maybe one inch and Dieter barged it open with his shoulder.

"Fish spa!" he said triumphantly.

I peered inside the grim chamber and looked around at the peeling grey walls. There was nothing inside except a low concrete bench and a small broken window. I noticed an old tin mug lying in one corner of the room.

Dieter glanced at me and laughed.

"Lick of paint," he said. "That's all it needs. And soft lighting. Scatter rugs. Pictures of palm trees. That sort of thing."

He edged out of the room and moved down the corridor. He paused outside another iron door. It was slightly ajar. He rested his shoulder against the door and pushed. The hinges creaked and the lip of the door scraped across the concrete floor like broken nails on a chalk board.

"Head massage!" he said and stepped inside.

The room was bigger than the first. It looked like it had been smashed to pieces with a pick axe. The floor was littered with broken tiles and brick dust. An enamel sink lay shattered next to a length of rusted chain. Taps and pipes had been ripped out of the bare stone walls and flung to one side. It was as if someone had systematically attacked the room in a rage.

"Incense and pastels," said Dieter. "A calm place. A place to relax."

It was now so dark in the corridor that I could barely see Dieter at all. I followed the sound of his voice as he spun his yarn.

"This place could be huge, man," he said. "I'm telling you. You might see rubble and trash but I can see the future of this goddamn island right here. Right here in this old monastery."

"Sanatorium," I said.

Dieter chuckled in the shadows.

"Whatever, man."

We had reached the end of the corridor. Only one door remained. It was shut and would not budge.

Dieter disappeared into the gloom. I watched his silhouette as he walked slowly back towards the light at the end of the corridor. He returned after a few minutes with a metal crowbar. He forced the crowbar into the small gap between the door and the wall. He grinned at me.

"Where there's a will..."

I heard the lock snap and Dieter pushed open the door.

"Deep-sea sleep pods!" he said and turned to face the last room. He paused and I heard him snatch his breath.

"Jesus Christ, man" he said quietly. "What the fuck happened in here?"

The cell in which the bridesmaid had spent her last few hours was bathed in sickly daylight from a single window. The walls and floor were spattered with her blood which had dried and turned as black as ink. A single feather lay in a congealed pool of dark flesh and muscle. Dieter was silent.

"Obviously someone died in here," I said. "I'm going outside."

I sat down on one of the old benches in the square and lit a cigarette. I was angry. It was a fucking stupid plan to come here. It was a plan that now left me no option. It was already underway and it was unstoppable.

I heard the sound of a door slamming inside the sanatorium. Moments later Dieter walked out into the sunshine. He rubbed his hands on his jeans and sat down next to me on the bench. I handed him the packet of cigarettes and waited for him to light up.

"Listen," I said. "What do you hear?"

The South African frowned and gazed up at the sky.

"Nothing."

I flicked my ash on the ground.

"Exactly," I said. "Nothing. No birdsong. No bees. No cicadas. Just nothing. Not even the local wildlife wants to visit this place. It's a cold property. People died here, Dieter. People were tortured and killed in this place and most people believe that it should be left alone as a mark of respect."

Dieter stood up and walked slowly to the edge of the plateau. He sat on a low stone wall and stared out across the village below and the acres of patchwork farmland that stretched away towards the hazy blue sea on the horizon. I joined him on the wall and we sat in silence for a while.

"The birds will be back," he said eventually. "The birds will always come back."

I sighed and offered to buy him a beer in the village. Dieter nodded brusquely and stood up. Which is exactly how the big South African came to be buried up to his neck in the ground.

He was still unconscious. I sat on the tree trunk and listened to the breeze. The South African's eyes were closed and his breathing was slow. His square head looked faintly ridiculous. He was no longer a man. He was just a Head. He could have been seven feet tall or he could have been a dwarf in a bucket. I picked up another pine cone and lobbed it lazily towards the Head. The pine cone fell short. I was about to try again when the South African's eyes suddenly opened.

He groaned and tried to turn his head. He stared at me in bewilderment. I shrugged. The South African began to struggle. Then he began to rant and rave. I couldn't really blame him. It must have been uncomfortable for such a hearty, able-bodied man to feel so restricted.

I stood up and walked towards the Head which by now had taken on a murderous expression. I knelt down in front of it and lit a cigarette. I took a drag and then placed the cigarette gently between the Head's parched lips.

"Don't try to struggle," I said. "It will only make it more difficult to breathe."

The South African spat out the cigarette and glared at me.

"What the *fuck* is this about, boy?" he growled.

I stood up and walked back towards the tree trunk. I sat down and crossed my legs.

"Well," I said, "I guess it's about your plans for the Sunny Heights Spa. I really can't let you move forward on that one."

"You can fuck off," replied the Head.

I smiled.

"I can't let you just dig up the plateau. It would be most awkward. You see, I personally knew the last person to die in that sanatorium."

The Head frowned and seemed to relax a little.

"So this is personal?" the South African said. "Shit, Cal, that's no problem. Why didn't you say so? There's no need for all this drama. We can find a solution. Just get me out of the ground and we'll have a beer together. Come to some sort of arrangement."

I picked up a stone and stared at the Head.

"No point," I said. "It's not a personal issue. The last person to die in that sanatorium was a young English woman. She had come over to the island to be a bridesmaid at her friend's wedding. They had an argument and fell out over a boy."

The Head looked puzzled.

"How did she end up in the sanatorium?"

I tossed the stone from one hand to another.

"I put her there," I said. "She was unconscious at the time. I locked her in the last cell that you saw with a wild goose. A goose can be a vicious beast if it feels threatened or trapped. The bridesmaid lasted for about twelve hours, I think. Maybe more. It was quite a mess. Then I cut her body into pieces and buried the bridesmaid here in this clearing somewhere. I can't remember exactly where."

The Head was silent for a moment and then arched one eyebrow.

"I don't believe you."

"Suit yourself," I said and raised one arm. I paused for a second and then hurled the stone at the Head. The stone hit the South African's jaw with a crack and ricocheted across the clearing. The Head blinked with shock and pain.

"Jesus fucking Christ!"

I sat back down on the tree trunk and picked up another stone.

"All this was quite a while ago," I continued. "The bridesmaid's parents were distraught. They're still searching for her but..." I shrugged, "...the authorities in Greece are rather slow. It's a national trait. *Siga siga*. Slowly slowly."

The South African began to grunt and struggle manfully to free himself from the hole. The veins on his neck began to throb. Beads of sweat formed on his brow. His efforts, however, were futile. I waited patiently for him to calm down.

"You see," I said, "if I let you bulldoze the plateau and the sanatorium in order to build the Sunny Heights Spa then pretty soon you'd want to expand. You're the kind of man who cannot sit still. You have to keep moving. I admire your ambition to a certain degree, I really do, but that ambition is why you're stuck in a hole with a bruised jaw. That is why you're going to die in that hole. Because if I let you expand your empire then one day you'd find this clearing and then you'd find the dead people that live here and then I'd go to jail. I cannot let that happen. I have a wife, you know?"

The South African tried to shake the sweat from his eyes but it was a hopeless task. I raised my arm again and launched another stone at the Head. This time the stone fell short but it bounced up and hit the South African on the bridge of his nose. There was a loud snap as the bone splintered. The South African roared like an animal. Blood began to flow down his face and drip from his chin.

I picked up another stone and took careful aim. I hit the Head in the temple and knocked the South African unconscious. I sat on the tree trunk and smoked a cigarette. After a few minutes the Head regained its composure. It was not in a good mood.

"So what are you going to do?" the South African snarled. "Kill me? If you kill me here then my company will send out teams to scour this island and they will be pissed off. They will find you, arrest you and shoot you without a trial. You have no fucking idea who you're dealing with."

The Head was covered with blood and dust. One eye had swollen to the point where it was no more than an angry slit. I picked up the largest stone I could carry and walked towards the Head. The South African began to thrash in the ground. I stood over the Head as he spat out a broken tooth along with gobs of red phlegm.

"I suppose that's the point," I said. "It really doesn't matter."

I raised the rock above my head and brought it down with all my strength. There was a sickening thud as the skull collapsed and the cervical vertebrae shattered under the force of the blow. The bloody Head twitched and then lay still in the ground.

I took a deep breath and stared at the silent clearing for the very last time. I rather liked the place. It was peaceful. But this was not the time to feel sentimental. I walked back to the Land Rover and unclipped the spare petrol can from the rear door. I unscrewed the cap and began to splash the fuel around the clearing. When the can was empty I placed it on the ground next to the South African's broken head. I fished in my pocket for my Zippo lighter and flicked the flint. It caught at the first attempt. I held it in my hand for a second. No regrets, I thought. No regrets. I dropped the lighter on the ground and turned to leave.

There was the faintest pop and crackle as the fire curled around the smallest leaves and twigs. White smoke began to rise into the air. I could already feel the heat. The noise grew louder as the ravenous flames took a hold of the clearing. I heard a muted rush as the flames sucked the oxygen out of the air and I turned around just in time to see the clearing explode into a fireball. I staggered backwards and gasped for breath. The flames had already reached the tall pine trees on the far side of the clearing. I watched the grand old branches buckle and dip down to greet the elegant inferno. The leaves caught fire and set sail into the sky on a shower of sparks.

It was already out of control. I ran back to the Land Rover and gunned the engine. I could see the fires in my mirrors. By the time I reached the coast road they had taken a hold of the horizon. I parked the Land Rover beside the derelict cafe and watched the thick black smoke as it curled across the setting sun. I climbed into my own car and headed back to town. On the way I passed the fire trucks racing towards the mountains with their sirens screaming. I resisted the urge to turn back. It was over now.

25

EXIT

The fire raged for three days and nights. The October winds picked up the flames and together they raced across the mountains with a ferocious force. It was an unequal contest. Every fire truck on the island was deployed but they simply could not deliver sufficient water to make much headway. Someone declared a state of emergency. The army postponed the training exercises on the south of the island and sent their soldiers into battle with bulldozers and water cannons. The French and Italian navies sent sea planes to flood the fire from the air. The little Cessna aircraft would land on the sea, fill up their tanks with water and head fearlessly into the clouds of grey smoke to jettison their loads into the path of the fire. At night you could see the eerie glow on the horizon and hear the sea planes as they buzzed the mountains. The pilots worked around the clock. They slept in shifts so that the planes could remain in the air until eventually the flames began to slowly abate.

It was a dangerous time. Pockets of fire ignored the call to surrender and continued to fight like wildcats. A single venomous spark could easily re-ignite the inferno and the wind was a vicious adversary. The fires were stealthy and spiteful but the will to fight was gradually sapped. It was only a matter of time and sure enough the malevolent force was finally tamed and brutally extinguished. The little sea planes circled the mountain one last time. The island was declared safe. But there was a terrible price to pay.

Eighty thousand hectares of forest had been destroyed. All that remained was a ghostly lunar landscape of silver ash and charred black stumps. It was a barren and hostile environment. The land was cracked and skeletal. The scorched earth was littered with the baked carcasses of the animals which had been incinerated as they tried to escape. It would take years to regenerate.

Ten people died in the fires. I couldn't really count the South African because technically he was dead before the fire had even started. Three soldiers were killed by smoke inhaled through their faulty respirators. A fireman was crushed when the handbrake failed on his truck. Two Canadian tourists were trapped by the flames after they had driven up into the mountains to take souvenir photographs for the folks back home in Vancouver. The final happy snap as their rental car exploded in the forest would probably never grace the family album.

Tommy and Gina never made it to LA. They died in the fire alongside Honey and the old drunken priest. Tommy had decided to stay and fight the approaching inferno but the Kittyhawk was soon overwhelmed. There had been nowhere to run. I felt numb and disturbed at the news. It was an unacceptable body count. The fire had been a mistake. It had been my only mistake.

"What are you going to do?" said Kat.

I stared at her sad, beautiful face and shook my head.

"I don't know."

That afternoon we had had driven down the West coast to a little taverna on the beach. The old man who ran the place told us that he had been preparing to close for the winter when the fires broke out. He and his wife had agreed to stay open for a few more days and it had been a wise decision. Many tourists came to his taverna to enjoy a meal at sunset and to watch the fires on the horizon.

"Business has been good," he said. "Next year I will frame many photographs and hang them on the wall. Maybe I will be famous!"

The taverna was deserted. Kat and I sat down at a table in the corner by the window. We ordered a bottle of wine. I hadn't eaten for days but I couldn't face any food. I lit a cigarette and stared out of the window.

"Maybe I should make a phone call," I said after a while. "We have the money for a good lawyer."

Kat smiled.

"I think we're going to need more than a lawyer. Maybe you should phone God instead."

I glanced up as a police car pulled off the main road and parked outside the taverna. It was the only car I had seen since we had arrived. The officer behind the wheel got out and straightened his uniform. He was a big man with a trim moustache. He wore a pistol in a black holster on his hip. His partner remained in the car and sat staring through the windscreen with a stony expression. I told myself that there was nothing unusual about any of this. It was just a regular patrol and the guys were bored. I was tired and jumping to conclusions.

The policeman pushed open the door and glanced briefly in our direction. I heard him order two iced coffees from the old man. He sat down to wait at a table near the counter. I felt him watching us intently.

He wasn't a local officer. Everybody on the island knew the local boys because everybody was somehow related. The local police would always stop and chat to cafe owners and customers during their breaks. Everybody knew each other's business and the police were no exception. Having a relative in the force could be greatly beneficial. Family disputes were seldom settled in a court of law. They were settled over coffee and Sunday lunch.

I looked out of the window at the patrol car. It was a white Opel with mainland plates. I knew the island police drove an exclusive fleet of ageing Citroen Xsaras. These two cops were a long way from the beaten track. I figured they were probably on the island to help with the mountain of paperwork generated by the fires. It was a logical explanation.

The officer in the car had not moved a muscle. He sat rigidly in his seat watching the world through impenetrable green sunglasses. I heard his colleague stand up and pay for the drinks without a word. A gust of wind blew through the taverna as he pushed open the door.

I helped myself to another glass of wine.

"When I was a kid," I said, "I always wanted to be a policeman. Strange, isn't it? I wanted to be a proper London bobby, plodding the streets in my big boots and helping old ladies across the street. There wasn't any real crime back then. None that I knew about at that age anyway. I was only four years old. Coppers just strolled around drinking cups of tea and patting urchins on the head. Sometimes they helped to rescue a kitten from a tree or return a stolen bicycle to the postman. I thought it would be a very exciting job. But then I saw my first red fire engine and I wanted to be a fireman instead. They had bigger helmets and got to slide down poles. Somehow they seemed much more heroic."

I rolled a cigarette and sipped my wine.

"What made you change your mind?" asked Kat.

I thought about this in silence for a minute or two.

"When I was six," I said, "my parents bought me a plastic trumpet. It was gold with red valves. I can't remember whether I ever produced a single note. I used to stand on the arm of the settee in the front room and pretend I was performing at the Albert Hall. It was all in my head. I thought that all I had to do was somehow just stand on a stage and the audience would swoon. I didn't realise that I might have to learn how to play it properly or anything. It never occurred to me. But I guess the world is a simple place when you're only six years old."

I gazed out of the window at the patrol car. The two officers sat inside and sipped their iced coffee through long straws. I noticed the mirror on the passenger door was angled towards the taverna. It might have been pure coincidence but I felt sure they were watching our table.

"You don't have to make a phone call," said Kat. "I have a bad feeling."

She leaned across the table.

"What's to stop us leaving the island right now? Tonight? We could just pack up and start again somewhere else. We could get out of Europe altogether. Fuck Europe! It's not the same as it used to be. It's just a big jigsaw that never fits together. We could go to Panama. Bolivia. Cuba. Your cousin Samantha's in Havana."

"Sam's under house arrest in Cuba," I pointed out. "There's a difference."

Kat had a point. It would be very easy to just walk out of the taverna, climb into our car and head straight to the airport. We had enough money to survive for a while. Maybe that was the smart thing to do. Just walk away. But it was never going to be that simple.

"I can't" I said. "I can't just leave Tommy and Gina like this. It was my fault. I should make it right."

"Fine," said Kat irritably. "Make the call. I still have a bad feeling."

I stood up and went outside. It was a fine afternoon. The two policemen pretended not to stare as I pulled out my phone and searched for a number. I looked at Kat through the window. Her red hair caught the sun. She was tired. None of this had been her fault. Kat was innocent. She was all I had left in the world and I was about to screw that up too. And for what?

I hesitated. There was no point to any of it. It was just a stupid game. I had no honour and I had no motive. If I had any honour then I could always invent a motive. I could fake a conscience. I could plead insanity. I could even tie myself in a knot and jump out of a building. It was a sickness. You see? Right there! A little motive creeping around the corner. It was a sickness, your honour. I had a fever. Enough motive to maybe strike a deal. But if I was honest I just felt empty. I had felt empty for a very long time. I needed to rest.

I punched the number into the phone. Captain Manni Trelliosos sounded surprised to hear my voice.

"Are you OK?" he said in his deep growl.

"Yes and no," I replied. "We have to talk."

It was a long conversation and I began to worry about my battery. Captain Manni seemed reluctant to let me go. He was playing for time. I could hear it in his voice. Captain Manni asked me to wait. I noticed one of the policemen in the patrol car pick up the radio handset on the dashboard. I began to feel uncomfortable as I paced in slow circles. So I negotiated twenty four hours for myself and hung up. As I put the phone back in my pocket the police driver started the engine and the patrol car moved off slowly towards the coast road. I walked across the car park and watched it disappear into the distance. I looked up at the sky and checked my watch. I did not want to be late.

I pushed open the door and sat down. Kat poured me a glass of wine and nudged it across the table. The old man had turned on the radio. The sound of duelling *bouzoukia* filled the taverna.

"We have twenty four hours," I said.

Kat shrugged.

"That's nice."

I sipped my wine.

"Don't worry. Everything will be fine. He wants you to be there as well."

Kat raised an eyebrow.

"For the paperwork," I said. "He was quite adamant. You have to sign a bunch of documents. It's Greece."

Kat stared out of the window. She didn't say a word for maybe five minutes. I gently touched the back of her hand. She turned back to face me and smiled.

"Twenty four hours then," she said. "We'll never see another like it."

We raised our glasses and drank to the future.

26

The smoke from Harry's bombs had cleared and the Klef was a mess. I looked around at the wreckage. Tables and chairs had been blasted into the beer garden. Water from a broken pipe spread across a frosted carpet of shattered glass. The yellow plastic elephant had been knocked from its plinth and now stood at a drunken angle. Bits of Nikos lay scattered around the bar. There wasn't much left to identify. I noticed a bloody chunk of meat hanging from the TV screen. Liverpool were still celebrating a goal.

Kat lay dead at my feet. Her red hair rested in a pool of dark blood. Her eyes were closed. There was a small hole in her forehead as if she'd been hit by a nail. The hole was clean. Neat. The back of her head had simply gone.

I looked up and saw Captain Manni in the distance. He was surrounded by armed police and combat soldiers. He gesticulated wildly in my direction. I couldn't hear a thing. I stared at the big man helplessly. One of the policemen handed Manni a megaphone. He raised it to his mouth. I still couldn't hear anything. There was no sound in my head. My ears were still ringing with the sound of the explosion. I felt a little queasy.

Captain Manni began to slowly walk towards the Klef. The police and soldiers followed with their guns drawn. The two marksmen on the roof opposite had not moved. Their rifles still pointed at my face. I raised my hands above my head.

Suddenly my hearing returned with a pop. It was a relief. As the concussion subsided I heard the Captain's amplified voice through the tinny megaphone.

".....GUN!"

It didn't make a lot of sense. I looked around. There was no gun. The Captain paused by the drunken elephant and raised the megaphone once again.

"CAL! DO YOU HAVE A GUN?"

I winced. The megaphone was unnecessarily loud and crippled by feedback. I shook my head.

"No!"

He lowered the megaphone and took a step forward.

"Did Kat have a gun?"

I looked down at the body of my wife.

"No," I replied. "She had a pair of sunglasses."

The Captain seemed to relax. He handed the megaphone to one of the soldiers and waved at the troops to lower their weapons. All but the snipers on the roof complied. I breathed a sigh of relief and lowered my hands.

Captain Manni picked his way carefully towards me across the beer garden. Broken glass crunched underfoot. He gingerly side-stepped what looked to me like a severed arm lying in the rubble. Maybe. It could have been a chair leg. My vision was a little blurred. I opened my mouth but Manni raised one hand.

"Wait," he said.

A policeman appeared at my side. He was young and looked nervous. His navy blue uniform didn't really fit too well. He cleared his throat.

"Where are you? What is your name? How many fingers am I holding up now?"

I peered at his hand.

"Three."

The policeman nodded and turned to Manni.

"Close enough," he said. "He's fine."

The young policeman turned and walked back towards his colleagues. Manni surveyed what was left of the Klef. He sighed and pulled a packet of cigarettes from his breast pocket.

"This is a big fucking mess," he said and offered me a cigarette. My hands were shaking uncontrollably. He smiled and lit one for me before handing it over. I inhaled gratefully. He looked down at Kat's body.

"I'm sorry about your wife," Manni said. "They were only supposed to shoot her in the leg. Too fucking keen, these boys. Too much sun."

I nodded. It was a reasonable explanation. My wife had just been shot in the head because it was hot! That was all. Too much sun. If the weather had been slightly cooler then Kat would still be alive. Obviously.

I stared at Manni. He didn't seem to be about to volunteer any more information. We smoked our cigarettes in silence for a while.

"Why were they trying to shoot her in the leg?" I asked eventually.

Manni dropped his cigarette on the ground and stubbed it out with his boot.

"It's been a long day," he said. "Will you come with me? We have some paperwork."

He threw back his head and roared with laughter.

"Of course we have paperwork! This is fucking Greece!"

I followed the big man out of the beer garden and past the yellow elephant towards an empty patrol car. I noticed the rooftop snipers had disappeared. The armed police were standing in groups. They moved aside to let us through. The soldiers were already climbing back into their trucks.

As we reached the patrol car Manni fumbled behind his back and produced a pair of handcuffs.

"It's just procedure," he said. "You've had a shock. It's only a precaution until we reach the station."

He clipped the cuffs over my wrists and opened the patrol car's door. I stepped inside and tried to make myself comfortable on the back seat. The handcuffs dug into my wrists. I found that if I kept my hands perfectly still then it wasn't so bad. Manni instructed one of the policemen standing nearby to drive me back to Kavindos.

It was almost dark. The car moved off up Bakery Hill and headed north along the winding coast road. I gazed out of the window at the silver moonlight already shimmering on the surface of the black waters below. It was a beautiful sight. So many postcards. Moonlight over Kavindos bay. Simple white houses framed by colourful bougainvillea and frangipani. Wooden fishing boats bobbing happily on an emerald sea. Old women dressed in black selling oranges by the side of the road under a clear blue sky. Ancient temples and monuments bathed in the golden light of another perfect sunset.

Balmy evenings spent in tranquil tavernas with a bottle of wine and a sketchbook. You bought the sketchbook in a local shop selling sandals and sun cream. You liked to sit at your table and draw the characters who chatted and smiled without a care in the world. Everybody was so happy and friendly. The perfect holiday. Maybe one day you could sell your art? It had always been a passion. You weren't getting any younger. You didn't want to end up like the old boys in the pubs who lived with all the ghosts of past regrets. Maybe it was time to take the plunge before it was too late. Maybe you should move here. Set up as an artist. Sell your pictures on the beach. How bad could it get?

It was the air that had first drawn Kat and I to Kolasios like so many before us. The air and the warmth. We had left behind somewhere cold, grey, twisted and frail. It seemed like a long time ago. It was really only five years since we had arrived by ferry boat. I didn't know whether we'd managed to live the dream and I didn't really care. Many more people would surely follow. In one way or another we were all just immigrants.

The Chief of Police was waiting for me in the little police station. It was an ornate building on the outskirts of the village. It had been built originally by a successful merchant who had made his fortune trading spices and supplies from the Middle East. There was a little courtyard with a red-flowering Love tree and a water well. Pots of fragrant shrubs decorated the perimeter.

The Chief unlocked the handcuffs and offered me a coffee. I rubbed my wrists and nodded. He was an articulate, dapper little man with a mane of thick hair and a striking moustache. He was wearing beige jeans with a copper-coloured shirt and sandals. An Indian charm hung from his neck on a leather chain. He looked more like a successful Italian artist than a policeman. I watched him pour the coffee from a jug sitting on a small stove in one corner of the main office. A telephone rang on the front desk. The policeman looked up from the two mugs, glanced at the phone and shrugged.

"It is late," he said and winked at me. "They'll call back in the morning. Milk? Sugar?"

The station house was quiet. The only other person present was the police officer who had driven me from Pilafkos. He sat outside in the courtyard smoking a cigarette and talking into a mobile phone. It was late. The village was silent.

The Chief coughed politely and handed me a mug of coffee. He motioned for me to follow him into a small white room. The room was furnished with just one desk and two hard chairs. I could feel a light breeze blowing through a small window set high up in the wall. The Chief switched on the desk light and tutted before adjusting the angle so that the glare was softer and more diffused. A stack of manila files sat on the desk along with an ashtray and a clipboard.

"Make yourself at home," said the Chief. "Of course you can smoke if you wish."

I reached for my cigarettes and sipped the strong coffee as the little man placed a pair of silver reading glasses on the bridge of his nose. He opened the first manila file and flicked through the loose pages with his neatly manicured fingers. After a few minutes he closed the file and placed it on the desk. He removed his spectacles and looked up at me with a concerned expression.

"I would like to apologise for the death of your wife," he said. His voice was gentle and calm.

"It was a mistake. Naturally we will assist with any arrangements you should care to make for her funeral. I am not proud of this matter. It was unfortunate and unnecessary."

He reached across the desk for his mug of coffee and took a delicate sip. He looked back at me and stroked his flamboyant moustache.

"Is there anything you would like to ask?" he said.

I stared at the Chief of Police. He held my gaze with his soulful eyes.

"Is there anything...anything I'd like to ask?" I repeated in disbelief.

The little man nodded sympathetically and glanced down at the manila file on the desk.

"Of course," he said. "You are upset. Please allow me to show you something."

He reached for the file and opened the cover. Then he took out a black and white photograph, carefully turned it around in his hands and slid it across the desk. I stared at the photograph for a very long time. It didn't make much sense. I could feel the police chief staring at the top of my head. I gazed at the body of the dead woman in the photograph. She was bloated and bedraggled. Her skin looked as if it had been rubbed raw with sandpaper. An identity plate had been placed at the feet of the body. I peered closely at the name. I frowned. It was almost impossible to associate the rotten, blackened corpse in the picture with the memory of Isabella May.

I looked up at the Chief of Police.

"I don't understand," I said.

The policeman sighed and slipped the photograph back into the manila file.

"We found the body of this woman in a cave not far from here," said the policeman quietly. "She had been left to drown. She could not escape because her spine had been broken in several places by a heavy implement. The sea began to rise and she was trapped in the cave."

He shrugged.

"That is not a good way for anyone to die. We believe your wife was responsible for the murder."

I stared incredulously at the Chief. I was amazed.

"Kat?" I said eventually. "Why would she do such a thing? How can you be so sure?"

The police chief sipped his coffee and patted the manila file in front of him.

"Science," he said. "We found traces of fibres and DNA. The body was discovered by a shepherd. I don't know why a shepherd would be in the cave but that is not the point. I suppose he was trying to smuggle contraband. Maybe he had stolen his neighbour's goat. It happens. Anyway, he was kind enough to alert the police here in Kavindos. We do not have a murder squad on the island and so we had to contact the mainland. They sent a team to investigate. Your wife was careless. Even though the body was badly decomposed the investigators managed to find traces of DNA. Fingernails. Scratches. That sort of thing. The evidence was fairly conclusive."

He paused and reached for a cigarette. He smiled at me.

"Your wife had, how shall we say, fairly *distinctive* hair. It wasn't natural. She used an expensive dye. It wasn't so hard to identify."

My mind was spinning. I tried to look as puzzled as possible. It was a fine balance. I distracted myself with a cigarette.

"Unfortunately," the chief of police continued, "this victim was not alone."

He reached into the same manila file and produced another two photographs. He placed the first on the desk in front of me. I leant a little closer and recognised the body of Jesus on a cross. The limbs were badly bruised and broken. His blond curls hung matted and mildewed across his head. His neck lay twisted at an obscene angle.

The chief of police exhaled a thin cloud of smoke.

"I'm afraid we found traces of your wife's DNA both on the boat which caught fire as well as on the victim's body. The Norwegian boy was still alive when he was nailed to the cross. There was water in his lungs when he washed up on the Turkish coast. There were signs of a struggle on the boat. Also signs of intimacy."

I blinked. Kat and Jesus? Jesus! No, wait, Anders fucking Christ! I was glad the little prick was dead. I would have killed him myself.

The third photograph was of a large woman lying face down in a bath tub. It was an undignified corpse. I tried not to laugh. It was difficult to see exactly where the rolls of sallow flesh ended and the mountain of pimply buttocks began. I recognised the back of Grace's head.

I looked up at the police chief.

"Grace drowned in the bath," I said. "It was suicide. She was having an affair with a local artist. She was very fat and very unhappy."

The police chief shook his head slowly.

"I'm afraid she was poisoned before she drowned. As I have already said, your wife was careless. I am sorry."

He carefully gathered up the photographs and placed them back into the file. He placed the file back on top of the stack on the desk.

"There could be more," he continued. "These files represent people who have recently disappeared on this island. Reports have been filed by friends and family. They are desperate to know answers. It is quite a list. Some lived here on the island like you and your wife. Others were simply working here for the summer."

He picked up the clipboard and adjusted his silver spectacles.

"A young woman visiting the island for her friend's wedding...a disabled gentleman...a holiday company representative...all have been reported missing. A family of tourists. Gone. A Belgian aristocrat. Gone. Who knows? I just don't know what we will find but it seems likely that your wife might have been involved in all of these mysteries."

He placed the clipboard gently back on the desk.

"We shall see," he said. "More coffee?"

He stood up and opened the door. I heard voices outside in the station house. General chatter. The smell of pizza. Coffee. Cigarette smoke. I leant back in my chair and stared up at the window. I felt the cool breeze on my face and listened to the songs of the night birds. I smiled.

The Chief of Police returned after a few minutes with two more cups of coffee. He placed them on the desk and sat down.

"It would be very helpful to us if you could answer some questions."

I nodded.

"Your wife left no direct family," he said. "We have been in touch with the German authorities and it seems that she left no records at all. She was adopted at a very young age. Her foster parents died some years ago in a fire. Her natural parents cannot be traced."

He rested his chin on the tips of his fingers.

"This makes our task very difficult."

He smiled.

"Perhaps you could be so kind as to shed some light? Anything at all might be useful. Take your time. Have a cigarette."

It was a long night. Dawn was breaking outside as the police chief and I emerged from the little white room. I yawned. The police chief patted me on the back and handed me an envelope.

"Your passport and papers," he said. "Please get some rest. We will be in touch."

He held open the front door and I walked out into the courtyard. I paused for a moment. The ancient Acropolis stood over the village silhouetted against a velvet, purple universe. The sky looked like glass. I took a deep breath and inhaled the heady scent of lavender and frangipani. I reached for my cigarettes.

A voice behind me made me jump.

"Everything OK, Cal?" said Captain Manni Trelliosos.

I turned to see the big man sitting on a wall beside the Love tree.

"It's been a long night."

He nodded.

"It's going to be a long winter too," he said.

I walked over and sat down beside him on the wall. Captain Manni gazed up at the tree and then looked at me.

"Do you know the story of the Love tree?" he asked. I glanced at the policeman and shook my head.

"It's an old story," he said slowly. "The Love tree is also known as the Judas tree. It is an unusual tree. Legend would have us believe that it was named after the tree on which Judas hanged himself after betraying Jesus. Every season the flowers turn from white to red. This is supposed to represent Judas' blood and shame in the eyes of God. I find that very interesting."

I stared at the Captain's inscrutable face in the shadows of dawn. I put the cigarette to my lips and searched for my lighter.

"Here," said Captain Manni. "Allow me."

He reached into his breast pocket and produced an old petrol lighter. The brass casing was scorched and blackened by fire. It looked familiar. The Captain flipped the top of the Zippo and cupped his hands around the flame.

"American," he said. "The best."

He blew out the flame, closed the lid and put the lighter back in his pocket.

He stood up.

"You should go now." he said and stared down at me for a second. Then he turned and strolled slowly back towards the station house.

I stubbed my cigarette out in the earth around the Love tree and walked out of the station house into the empty cobbled streets. The village was still asleep. I hiked uphill towards the main road and flagged down a car heading south towards Pilafkos. The old man behind the wheel had a kindly face. He smiled and held out his hand.

"My name is Savvas," he said. "Welcome to Greece."

Printed in Great Britain
by Amazon

51893542R00144